GOOD MURDER

Good Murder is the first in the series of crime-caper novels set in 1940s Australia that feature William Power; it is followed by *A Thing of Blood* and *Amongst the Dead*. Robert Gott is also the author of *The Holiday Murders* and its sequel, *The Port Fairy Murders*.

For my parents, Maurene and Kevin Gott,
who raised a family in love with words,
and for Ed and Sheila Rooney,
who provided generous access to their
phenomenal memories.

GOOD MURDER

ROBERT GOTT

SCRIBE
Melbourne • London

Scribe Publications
18–20 Edward St, Brunswick, Victoria 3056, Australia
2 John St, Clerkenwell, London, WC1N 2ES, United Kingdom

First published by Scribe 2004
This edition published 2015
Text and illustrations copyright © Robert Gott 2004

Edited by Margot Rosenbloom
Typeset in 10.5/15 pt Janson by the publisher

Printed and bound in Australia by Griffin Press

The paper this book is printed on is certified against
the Forest Stewardship Council® Standards.
Griffin Press holds FSC chain of custody certification
SGS-COC-005088. FSC promotes environmentally
responsible, socially beneficial and economically viable
management of the world's forests.

National Library of Australia Cataloguing-in-Publication data

Gott, Robert. / Good Murder: a William Power mystery.

9781925321081 (paperback)
9781922072122 (e-book)

1. Murder–Fiction. I. Title.

A823.4

scribepublications.com.au
scribepublications.co.uk

This is entirely a work of fiction. All of the characters are products of the author's imagination, and they bear no relation to anyone, living or dead. Only the streets they walk down are real.

CAST OF CHARACTERS

THE POWER PLAYERS

Adrian Baden
Tibald Canty
Bill Henty
Annie Hudson
William Power
Arthur Rank
Kevin Skakel
Walter Sunder

THE DRUMMOND FAMILY

Mrs Drummond
Fred Drummond
Joe Drummond
Polly Drummond

THE POLICE

Detective Sergeant Conroy
Senior Constable Harvey
Sergeant Peter Topaz
Constable Valentine

SIGNIFICANT OTHERS

Mal Flint
Augustus (Augie) Kelly
Patrick Lutteral
Shirley Moynahan
Charlotte Witherburn
Harry Witherburn

CONTENTS

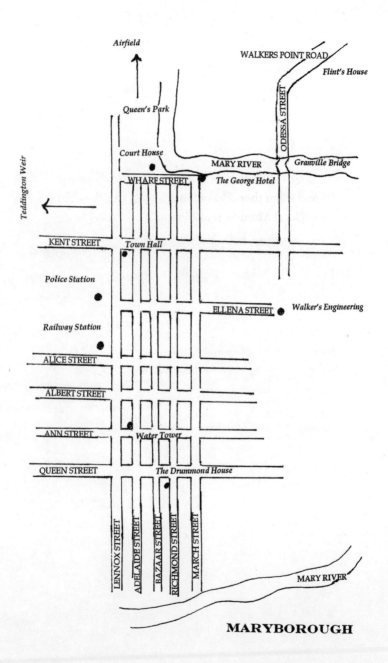

MARYBOROUGH

Look round about the wicked streets of Rome
And when thou find'st a man that's like thyself,
Good Murder, stab him; he's a murderer.

Titus Andronicus. Act V, Scene 2.

PART ONE

Chapter One

MAKING AN ENTRANCE

THE WATER TOWER IN MARYBOROUGH sat on the corner of Adelaide and Anne Streets. It held one million gallons of water and, for two weeks in August 1942, it also held the body of a 24-year-old woman named Polly Drummond. Afterwards it was impossible not to be appalled by the realisation that each time we drank a cup of tea we were imbibing Polly Drummond, and that each time we took a bath we were splashing ourselves with Polly Drummond. As she slowly dissolved up there, bloating and exuding the corrupt gases and liquids of the dead, we in the town strained her through our teeth, gargled her, washed our hair with her, and imbedded her in the very clothes we wore.

I was among the gawkers who gathered at the bottom of the tower when word was passed around that her body had been found. My interest was not entirely voyeuristic. I was, after all, the main suspect in her murder.

She had been discovered by two city council workers who had climbed the 52 feet to the top of the tower to fix a faulty indicator. They knew immediately who it was floating face down in that reservoir. The *Maryborough Chronicle* had been publishing almost daily accounts of the search for the missing woman. In a small town like Maryborough, everyone knew Polly Drummond, and everyone had a theory about what had happened to her. Many of those theories featured me.

Getting Polly out of the tower and down to the ground was no easy task. I can understand the reluctance of those helping to simply sling the body across the shoulder and climb down. Eventually, using a block and tackle, Polly's body was clumsily lowered to terra firma. This took more than two hours, and by this time most onlookers had given up and gone home. I hung well back, in the grounds of the Christian Brothers school opposite. There was no one from Polly's family to accompany the body to the morgue. Her brother, who I knew slightly, had himself died two days previously, and her mother was barking mad. I did not believe my presence would arouse anything more than further suspicion. Under cover of the gathering darkness I walked back to the hotel where my company and I were staying.

There was a war on, don't forget, and I was doing my bit. That's why we were up there, in Maryborough. The William Power Players were boosting morale all over rural Queensland by bringing Shakespeare to the barbarians. We had played Gympie before coming to Maryborough. It had not gone well, to be perfectly honest. We had underestimated their readiness for a daring tilt at *Troilus and Cressida*. It was an artistic triumph for those with eyes to see and a heart to feel, but Gympie was a bit light on in those departments. It didn't help that the crowd had been agitated by the news that there had been heavy losses in the Solomon Islands and that the Germans were advancing rapidly on Stalingrad. The progress of the war often had a detrimental effect upon how our performances were received. Only a handful of people turned up for the second night's performance. Gympie is a small pond, and I had overestimated the population of pond life that might wish to drag itself out of the slime for one evening. We decided to move on to Maryborough and mount a challenging new take on *Titus Andronicus*.

The 'we' I mention was my troupe, my company, the Power Players. There were eight of us: my leading lady Annie Hudson (not a great talent, but very easy on the eye); Kevin Skakel (clubfoot, unfit for active duty); Bill Henty (blind in one eye, unfit for active duty); Arthur Rank (one arm, and one testicle as a matter of fact, unfit for active duty); Walter Sunder (65 years old, unfit for active duty); Adrian Baden (queer, unfit for active duty); and Tibald Canty (morbidly obese, unfit for active duty). I happened to be slightly flat footed, although not in any obvious way. In fact, I didn't even know it until I enlisted and had the medical. I wouldn't have been accepted anyway. Entertainers, particularly first-class ones, were considered a reserved profession. What we offered was more than a bag of flesh to stop a bullet.

Despite Annie Hudson's frequent suggestion that, in view of its personnel, playing a scene with the Power Players was like working in a field hospital, we were a professional outfit. Everybody had been connected in some way with the business before the war. Theatre was in our blood, no matter how small or large our parts had been. Tibald Canty, to choose just one of the troupe — the largest one, as it happens — had had quite a successful career in radio, although his real love was the kitchen, and he had trained under some of the best chefs in Europe. Unfortunately he couldn't appear as his character when it was mooted to put his radio show on the stage. Listeners thought he was a 25-year-old dentist, lean and smouldering, with coal-black hair and crisp blue eyes. The sight of a 40-year-old obese man with thinning, dirty yellow hair was considered too disillusioning, even in the early days of the war. He was replaced on stage, and afterwards his replacement slipped into his radio part, too. That freed him up to join my company.

In 1942, I was in my prime. I was a serious actor. Whether I was a great actor is for others to judge. I have learned, though, to take the judgements of others with a grain of salt. I have presence. I can hold the stage. I can drag an audience to its feet with the lift of an eyebrow. I have elegant eyebrows, shaped by nature, not by tweezers. I looked like Tyrone Power (no relation) only finer, not so swarthy, higher-browed, bluer-eyed.

When the Power Players arrived in Maryborough, the war was going badly. American soldiers were everywhere down south and causing trouble. A man named Leonski had been charged with the brownout murders in Melbourne. He'd strangled three women and was going to hang. We all talked about it, and I thought the time was right to do a Grand Guignol piece of our own devising about the wickedness of human nature. The mass murderer would be a Eurasian with impeccable credentials. He wouldn't be unmasked until the final scene when we learned that his mother was Japanese and his father was German. No-one in the troupe thought it was a very good idea. Annie Hudson, who I thought might jump at the chance to play three different victims in the one piece, said it was a particularly lousy idea. I suspected she realised that it was outside her range.

The Power Players travelled everywhere by truck. We had been allocated fifteen thousand miles annually for travel, and we had to be careful not to exceed them. With theatrical runs that were much shorter than expected we found ourselves on the move a great deal, and it's surprising how quickly we ate up those miles. Strictly speaking, it was Annie's truck. She'd paid for it with the money she'd made from her advertisements, and she'd made quite a few. They were print advertisements, mostly, and drew on her resemblance to Greer Garson — a rather low-rent version of Greer Garson, but she certainly resembled her. She'd also done a couple of radio spots. You only had to ask her and she'd tell you all about it. In 1942 she peered out at you from every magazine and newspaper you picked up. She was Connie, the bad-breath girl in the Colgate advertisement. There she was, looking all wide-eyed and lonely in the first frame and saying, 'I'd like to go places and do things.' That would be OK, she is advised, 'but first check up on your breath'. All it takes to turn poor Connie into a social success is a quick brush with Colgate Dental Cream. I'm in that ad, too, in the last frame where Connie is pictured smiling at two tuxedoed admirers, apparently breathing in the mint-masked effluvium from Connie's mouth. I'm the one with his back to the camera. The moron who managed to get his face shown pleasured the photographer orally. There are some things I won't do. It's a matter of class.

That's where I met Annie, on the bad-breath girl photo shoot. I was setting up the Power Players in Melbourne at the time, and I offered her a place, promising her all the leading lady parts. When she said that she would buy a truck, the deal was sealed. Later, though, her pointed reminders as to who owned the vehicle made me think that I had paid a high price indeed for transport. She claimed that the only reason people came to see us at all was to see her. She was the bad-breath girl and the Tampax girl ('All dressed up and then *couldn't* go! …') and people knew a star when they saw one. I kept quiet when she was doing one of her star turns. As actor/manager

I had a responsibility to the whole troupe, and part of that responsibility involved not losing the truck. We were regularly reminded, half-jokingly, that it was *her* truck and that she might just drive away in it.

The truck sat three in the front, or two if the passenger was Tibald, who weighed twenty stone at the time. The rest of the troupe rode in the back with the costumes, the props, and bits of all-purpose scenery. We wove stage magic with a minimum of scenery. It was all about the voice; my voice, mainly. Annie was at her best when looking distressed in grainy newspaper ads about her bad breath or untimely menstrual flow. There was no music in her voice. None at all. The truth is that the success or otherwise of her stage career was entirely dependent upon the reliability of her truck and the availability of petrol.

It was a cool August morning when we lurched down Ferry Street in Maryborough for the first time. My initial impression of this almost-coastal town was that it was unnervingly flat. The eye ran up and down its wide streets unimpeded by dip or hillock. There had been no attempt made to soften the brutal simplicity of these thoroughfares with trees of any kind. For a person used to the huddled houses of inner Melbourne (albeit the house I grew up in was rather grand), Maryborough's homes seemed unnecessarily generous in size, although this was partly an illusion created by the stilts on which many of them sat. The imagination of the inhabitants did not extend to their gardens. The enormous Queenslanders perched above either a riot of grasses and vines, with the odd ragged and shapeless paw paw or mango, or a blasted heath of sour and ugly earth.

We'd chosen Maryborough because we'd heard that the war had had a remarkable effect upon it. The influx of airmen and soldiers, and the shifting of industry to a war footing, had shaken it out of the drowsy torpor that anaesthetised the inland towns we had visited and failed to arouse. The awful truth — something best avoided in the normal course of events, or at any rate left undisturbed by poking at it—was that the Power Players were ideally suited to performing in small, remote places, where our limitations might pass unnoticed, camouflaged by the greater limitations of our audiences. I had ambitions or, in this context, dreams, that my own talent might provide somebody in one of those godforsaken towns with the transformative experience of art.

I was optimistic about Maryborough, prospering as it was in response to the need to build ships to keep Hirohito at bay. And build ships they did. Walkers Engineering was the pumping heart that kept Maryborough going. If ever proof was needed that war could quicken the economic pulse of a community, Walkers was it. Twelve hundred men beavered away in there, turning out Corvettes for the navy. They travelled to and from work in a great shoal of bicycles that flowed up Kent Street each morning at seven o'clock and ebbed back down Kent Street each afternoon at four. To be unemployed in Maryborough, a man would have to be dead and buried. Surely, here *Titus Andronicus* would release its power to mesmerise and appal.

My troupe drew curious gazes on that first morning. There were few cars about, and the only truck we saw was a military vehicle. We turned into Kent Street and began looking for a suitable hotel. The Royal Hotel would have been ideal, but it was far too grand for our budget. It had obviously been built at a time when the town was flush with money from timber and gold. There were well-dressed women drinking in the lounge, looking prosperous and metropolitan, and doubtless the wives of officers put up there for the duration.

We found a place we could afford close to the river but close, too, to the centre of town. The George Hotel, on the corner of

March and Wharf Streets, had three storeys that seemed to have a tentative grasp on the site. They leaned nervously away from the Mary River as if not wishing to attract its attention. The Mary River runs at speed through the town, its waters muddied by the churning drag of energetic tides. It floods with a viciousness that is almost personal. People were still talking about the flood of '37 and declaring that the town was about due for another drowning. They got their drowning all right, but it wasn't quite what they were expecting.

The proprietor of the George was a sinewy, pale-skinned man with hair the colour of copper wire and eyes of a most peculiar, insipid, yellow-flecked green. He welcomed us with open, hairy arms. Customers who stayed and paid were obviously unusual in his hotel. I wondered if the insistent wash of the Mary River, audible through the open door of the bar, had anything to do with it. There were a few men in the bar, and they looked us up and down before returning indifferently to their beer. The proprietor, who declared that his name was Augie Kelly, ran the place more or less on his own.

'The food's not great,' he said. 'I do the best I can, but there's not a big demand and there's not much in the way of decent stuff available.' As he said this he looked at Tibald, wondering, I suppose, if he was expected to provide enough food to maintain his weight. 'I'm not a good cook either,' he added. 'I had a good cook, but he joined the AIF.' Turning those unsettling eyes in my direction he explained further, moving his large hands about apologetically. 'You may not know, but the government is going to bring in austerity measures that will affect public eating houses. Three courses only, and no hors'd'oeuvres.'

I did not imagine that three courses of anything had been served in this hotel for a very long time.

'It's twenty shillings a week, each,' he said.

'That,' I said icily, 'seems rather high, especially in the absence of hors d'oeuvres.'

'If you can do better anywhere else, be my guest,' he said, folding those hairy arms aggressively.

Tibald interrupted him.

'My good man,' he declaimed in his deepest Falstaffian voice, 'show me your kitchen.'

Augie was taken aback. 'Why?' His eyelids twitched suspiciously as if he thought Tibald was already on the hunt for any available food.

'If the space is agreeable and if the equipment is even a few steps up from primitive, I will cook for your establishment in consideration of a reduction in our tariff.'

'Now why would I do that? How do I know that you can even cook?'

Tibald raised an eyebrow. 'Do I look hungry?' he asked.

'Mr Tibald Canty is not only a fine actor,' I interposed, 'he is also a chef whose skills would intimidate Escoffier himself.' I took the liberty of putting my arm around Augie Kelly's bony shoulder and giving it a little squeeze. 'I can guarantee that in no time at all the word will spread that you are serving great food at the George. This will become the only place to eat in town, and that will mean a substantial increase in your profits. There must be people, even in a town like this, who like food. Imagine your dining room filled with people licking their lips and buying your booze.'

'I don't have much stuff in there,' he said uncertainly, but there was no hostility in the look he gave me. I knew we had him. If there's one thing I've learned from staying in hotels, it's that every hotel proprietor dreams of greatness. Most of them settle for squalor because after a while even that becomes a standard requiring effort.

'All right,' he said. 'Let's see what you can do, but I'm not guaranteeing anything.'

The speed with which he acquiesced was unsurprising. He could not afford to turn my troupe away. Even if we stayed for only a week, it would mean more money than he had earned in a long while.

He allocated rooms on the third floor for the men, but gave Annie Hudson a room on the second floor. It was, he said, the best room in the hotel. Not for the first time, I admired the effortless, almost unconscious, ease with which Annie subdued men.

'If business improves, you can stay for eighteen shillings a week.'

'Fifteen', I said quickly, 'and it goes down further if business really improves.'

'Show me the kitchen,' Tibald said, before Augie Kelly could object.

I followed them both down a narrow corridor. The others in the company peeled off to explore their rooms and to lie low. No one ever wanted to join me on my first excursion into a new town in search of a place to perform, which is what I would be doing after the tariff had been settled.

The kitchen was dark, filthy, and malodorous. Flies buzzed, drawn by the seductive promise of rancid fat. I thought Tibald would change his mind on the spot and express his disgust in tariff-raising eloquence. I didn't want him to do this because I had already assimilated the financial relief his cooking would provide. We would all pitch in, at least until *Titus* was up and running. I was looking forward to telling Annie that she would have to drag out her French maid's costume yet again and wait on tables. At least we would eat well. To my astonishment he didn't recoil in horror from the grim spectacle of a room that seemed to be held together by forces no stronger than congealed lard and darkness. Instead he uttered a little whoop of joy.

'It's an Aga,' he said, in a tone normally reserved for the highest expression of stage joy. 'I can't believe it. Here, in the middle of this cholera zone you call a kitchen, you have an Aga.'

'You mean the stove?' Augie said, puzzled.

Tibald looked at him with such exaggerated pity and contempt that his expression could have been seen from even the cheapest seats in the house.

'Be in the dining room at 8.00 pm,' he said imperiously, 'and if you have any friends, bring them. Now, I need the name of your purveyors. I will purchase the food for this evening's meal and I will charge it to this establishment.'

Tibald drew a red handkerchief from his pocket and wiped his mouth. It created the unfortunate impression of slobbering at the mere thought of food.

Augie said nothing.

'I presume you have preferred providores.'

'I don't even know what that is,' Augie said, 'but frankly it sounds expensive, and this new law means that we can't charge more than five shillings for any meal — not that there's a single person in this town who'd pay that much for a meal anyway. Where do you think you are? Paris?'

'Oh no,' said Tibald. 'I don't think I am in Paris, at least no part of it that's above ground. If you give me the name of a butcher and a dry goods merchant, that will be a start.'

'You can go to Geraghty's for flour and stuff, and Lusk's for meat, but you can't charge anything. I don't have an account, and even if I did I don't think I'd be sending you off to spend my money on spec.'

'All right, Mr Kelly,' I said. 'I quite see your point. We will pay for this evening's meal as a demonstration of our good faith. If it is unsatisfactory we will pay you for one night's accommodation and be on our way. You have nothing to lose and a reputation to gain. May I suggest that you shave before dinner.'

I bustled Tibald out of the kitchen and towards the truck.

'I hope,' I said with studied calm, 'that you can live up to your notices, because if this meal is a failure, we're ruined.'

'Who's going to replace me in *Titus* if I'm cooking every night?'

'Nobody,' I said. 'I'll just cut the part out. Nobody here will notice.'

I suspect Tibald was secretly glad to be out of *Titus*. My interpretation was a little too athletic for him to feel comfortable in his role. The somersaults I had wanted him to do were proving arduous and he was definitely disgruntled about wearing a leather posing pouch and nothing else.

I dropped Tibald in Adelaide Street with ten pounds to spend. This was more than most people earned in a week. It was a fortune for us, but I knew that it would pay off. I then began to reconnoitre for a suitable hall. Maryborough is sensibly, if dully, laid out, its streets running logically in a treeless grid. A town without the aesthetic imagination to plant trees along its wide, sun-blasted streets might not be ready to embrace the poetic jungle of the Bard, I thought. As I drove I began to have grave doubts about our chances of a successful run in Maryborough. Each citizen who stared at the truck as it passed seemed to me to be a wretched dullard. The general witlessness threatened our very existence. Where were the public servants posted here to support the military, and hungry for the thea- tre they no doubt took for granted in Brisbane, or Sydney, or

Melbourne? I had had such high hopes for Maryborough. I had imagined it as a sort of Antipodean Stratford. Instead, as I explored its streets, it was revealing itself to be little more than a flat town, an inconvenient distance from the ocean, watered by a river that moved through it with the slippery ease of a tapeworm. There was at least pleasure to be had from the sublime thrill of martyrdom in the service of art. But this was a private joy I could share with no one.

Maryborough didn't seem to me to be a town whose residents were expecting the Japanese at any moment. There was not an air of poised readiness. A few people had built decent shelters in their backyards, although from what I could discern most had desultorily dug a deep trench, propped some corrugated iron on top and, I supposed, watched it fill with water. If a bomb ever fell in Maryborough its citizens were in greater danger of drowning in their back yards than of being blown up.

There wasn't anything promising in the way of a hall in the centre of town. The Town Hall, oddly identified by the inscription 'City Hall' over the columns at its entrance, was far too imposing for our requirements. I didn't imagine that we could fill it once, let alone for a season, however brief. So I drove down Kent Street away from the Town Hall, not knowing where I was headed but feeling my way confidently. It was not possible to get lost in a town of this size. I turned left into Ferry Street, and within a few blocks had crossed the Lamington Bridge into a settlement called Tinana. It was a sort of suburb of Maryborough and, apart from its sawmill and a slightly dilapidated hall, it seemed practically uninhabited. Off-Broadway is one thing; off-Maryborough is quite another. I turned the Bedford around and headed back into town, keeping to Ferry Street. The only traffic was bicycles, and there were plenty of those. They were obviously how most people got around in this town. Near the corner of Ferry and Walker Streets I found what I was looking for. A squat, wooden hall, its paint peeling badly, announced over its door, 'Roller skating here.' Presumably this was a weekend feature because it was firmly shut. There were no blackouts on the windows, so it could not have been used at night. We carried our own blackouts as we were well used to preparing halls to receive us. I would return on Saturday and negotiate a price with the owner of this charmless space. We had transformed grimmer structures into Globes with the honeyed cadences of Avon's swan. This mean little hall would become our wooden O.

I returned to Adelaide Street to find Tibald standing outside Lusk Brothers Meats surrounded by parcels. Blood was oozing from several of them, and flies were gathering. We loaded his goods into the truck, and he seemed very pleased with himself. Tibald was an alchemist. He could turn pig shit into strawberry jam.

'We need to go to Geraghty's in Lennox Street', he wheezed. 'They deliver, so all I have to do is point.'

This was just as well. The exertion required to lug his parcels from Lusk's had taken the wind out of him.

'What have you got back there?' I asked.

'Never mind,' he said. 'It didn't cost much. It's mostly bones for stock and a few bits and pieces. Fortunately today isn't one of the beefless days.'

Friday had been declared, by government decree, one of two beefless days each week. We would win this war, apparently, by eating vegetables.

I didn't inquire any further about Tibald's purchases. It doesn't do to know what part of the beast Tibald uses. By the time he has finished with it, it has become sublime. I don't want to know that the delicious morsel I am about to put in my mouth is a sheep's testicle.

'Mr Lusk is coming to dinner tonight,' he said. 'I have promised him tongue.'

'Your private life is your own affair,' I said.

'Perhaps you'd be happier in vaudeville after all,' he countered. 'Mr Lusk knows meat, and he'll appreciate my skills. Perhaps he'll send his customers to the George.'

'You're talking like it was The Ritz.'

'I've eaten at The Ritz, in 1934, and I am a much better chef than whoever insulted my palate that night.'

I was about to turn the key in the ignition when the piercing rise and fall of an air raid siren made me jump. Surely this was a malfunction or a drill. Why would the Japanese want to drop bombs here? Did their Intelligence really extend to knowing that Walkers Engineering was turning out battleships? The reactions of people in the street indicated that this wasn't a drill. They seemed startled, and then wardens began appearing from shop doors, and a policeman arrived and marshalled people towards the shelters.

'We'll have to leave everything,' I said.

Tibald was not leaving his meat.

'You go.' He clambered fatly into the back of the truck.

'Don't be ridiculous. What if a bomb lands on the truck? Surely you don't want to die surrounded by offal.'

'We're all just offal, you know. Bones and offal. I'm not leaving this for some crooked warden to help himself.'

I wasn't going to argue with him and instead followed the lead of the few people still on the street. We ended up in the shelter outside the Town Hall. I barely had time to look about me and confirm my worst suspicions about Maryborough's citizens when the 'all clear' blasted forth. I think there was a general air of disappointment that no bombs had fallen. The strongest impression I received of these people, our potential audience, was an undifferentiated adenoidal utterance, unsullied by elocution, that passed for conversation. The language of Shakespeare would be as foreign to them as Swahili. My spirits sank.

I drove up Lennox Street to Geraghty's, and waited in the truck while Tibald placed his order. I was drubbing my fingers on the steering wheel and singing an air from '*Iolanthe*' to myself when I became aware of a figure lurking near the rear of the truck. I caught sight of him briefly in the side mirror, and after a few moments he reappeared on the passenger side, having first lifted the flap of canvas at the back. I thought this was a bit rich. Perhaps Tibald had been right to be worried about his meat. This clown mustn't have realised that I was in the car. I opened my door and stepped down, intending to confront the thief. I walked around the engine to meet him but he had ducked around the other side. He moved so quickly that he came up behind me and startled me mightily by clamping his hand on my shoulder. I actually jumped and let out what I blush to admit sounded more like a girlish squeal than a banshee call to arms. This doesn't create a firm impression in the mind of an attacker that here is someone to be reckoned with. On the contrary it suggests that his next move should be to say 'Boo!' very loudly and the truck would be his.

'Haven't seen you in town before,' he said. He spoke so remarkably slowly, stretching every vowel as if it were taffy, that I had time to turn around before he had reached the word 'town'. I was relieved to find myself face to face with a policeman. He was about my height, just under six feet, and was dressed in crisp khaki. His digger's hat was pushed up so that his face was fully visible. There were sweat stains under his armpits, and a faint waft of body odour wrestled with the Lifebuoy soap he had used to battle it. He was about my age, I guessed — thirty, perhaps slightly younger. His fair skin had seen a lot of sun, and it had been tanned against its natural inclination to pallor. He had brown hair, cut close to the scalp, and eyebrows that were thick but not unruly. They gave the impression that they ought to have been joined, although they were not. He needed a shave, even though it wasn't yet two o'clock and doubtless he had shaved that morning. His eyes were blue and had a limpid quality that made me think that they might water easily. I took all this in rapidly. I see faces and try to assign them to roles. What would this walloper be suited to? Horatio, maybe. I wondered why he was not in the army.

'The Power Players,' he said, nodding at the name on the side of the truck and doubling the number of syllables. 'Actors, are you?'

'I'm William Power,' I said, and held out my hand. He shook it. 'I can see why you're a policeman.'

'Sergeant Topaz.' He smiled at my jibe, but there was a hint of indulgence in it that I didn't like. I don't mind giving offence, but I do mind being indulged. He pointed his thumb at the truck. 'Use a lot of fuel, does she?'

'No more than we're allocated.' Was I sufficiently haughty, or did I sound defensive?

'I didn't mean anything by it, Will. Just interested. You here for a show?'

'*Titus Andronicus*,' I said, expecting him to look bewildered.

'Awful bloody play,' he replied. 'Right up there with *Cymbeline*. I suppose you get to splash a bit of blood around. That must be fun.'

'It has hidden depths,' I said, bristling unreasonably, I was aware, at his criticism of the play I had chosen. I would not presume to find fault with the way he issued a summons or arrested a thug, after all. His gimcrack education may have been sufficient to teach him a thing or two about Shakespeare, but

I did not believe for a second that he had any insights to offer. 'Perhaps you will change your mind when you hear the poetry read properly.' The sounds of the voices in the air-raid shelter came back to me. 'I don't suppose you've ever actually seen it performed?'

'No, no I haven't. I read them, that's all. All the plays. Sonnets, too. Where's it on?' His enthusiasm mollified my annoyance somewhat.

'I don't know yet. We've only been in town for a few hours. I've seen a hall, in Ferry Street I think it is. A skating place.'

'That'd be Wright's place. Not exactly Drury Lane.'

'This isn't exactly London.'

'No,' he said. 'No.' Somehow he managed to cram that second 'no' with a sentence's worth of dubiousness about our talent.

'I'll have a word to Wrighty, see if we can fix you up with the hall. I wouldn't mind seeing what you can do. Most of the entertainers who come through use the Town Hall, though. Where are you staying?'

Before I could answer his question, Tibald answered it for me.

'We're staying at the George Hotel, Sergeant, and we would be very grateful if you could put in a word.' He had galumphed out of Geraghty's without my noticing. Topaz took in Tibald's bulk, and I thought I detected at the corner of his mouth something like disgust that rationing and shortages had done nothing to curb this man's obviously epic appetite. When he spoke, however, it sounded to me like the exaggerated politeness of a man who thinks he has been caught in unguarded rudeness.

'Good afternoon, sir,' Topaz said.

He and Tibald moved away from the truck and engaged in

a conversation that included an exchange of furrowed brows, laughter, and a vigorous handshake. The ability to create such sudden intimacy was one I lacked and envied. People generally found my reserve off-putting, and read it as haughtiness or arrogance. This unfortunately meant that I almost always got off on the wrong foot with people. I got back into the truck and leant on the horn. Tibald clambered up into the passenger seat.

'You were pretty chummy,' I said, as I ground through the Bedford's gears.

'He's a nice chap as it happens, and he's coming to dinner at the George tonight. At least there'll be two influential locals there. You should be bloody happy about that.'

'I'm not sure that I like him. He's …'

'He's what? Unimpressed by William Power?'

I immediately saw the justice in Tibald's brutal remark, and laughed.

'Well, that's a good enough reason not to like someone, don't you think? Where to now?'

'The fish depot. It's directly opposite the hotel.'

The dining room of the George Hotel saw a return to the days of fine dining last night. In an atmosphere softly lit by candles and hurricane lamps the Hotel's new chef Mr Tibald Canty, originally of Melbourne, demonstrated to an appreciative group what was possible under the soon to be introduced austerity measures for public houses. He presented three courses, a fish soup, a flavoursome selection of meats in delicious sauces and a dessert of berries. Attending the dinner were Mr Lusk,

Police Sergeant Peter Topaz, and councillor Tom Doohan and his wife Marjorie, who was wearing a frock of ivory suede taffeta with rosettes of ruching on the bodice. Mrs Doohan said that it was nice to dress up in these times. Also attending the dinner was Miss Polly Drummond. She was accompanied by LAC James Smelt. Miss Drummond chose a frock of white Swiss organdi. Members of the touring theatrical company, the Power Players, filled out the guest list. Miss Annie Hudson, who will be known to readers as the girl in the Colgate advertisement, currently touring with the Power Players, wore a bouffant gown of ivory ninon mounted on moire and stiffened net. The bodice was frilled with valence lace which was also introduced discreetly at the hem line. The proprietor of the George Hotel, Mr Augie Kelly, said that he was pleased to offer Maryborough fine food at an affordable price. Mr Canty's austerity menu is available each evening and can be enjoyed for less than four shillings a head.

Annie put the *Maryborough Chronicle* down.

'I told you it would be a good idea to invite that society matron at the paper.'

'I spent half an hour talking to her,' I said, 'and she didn't bother to mention me. She promised that she'd put something in about *Titus*. Maybe I should have worn a taffeta frock.'

'Maybe you should have felt her up. You know, for the good of the show.'

'It's funny. The last thing you say is only the most revolting thing you've ever said until the next thing you say. Have you noticed that?'

Adrian Baden came into the dining room where this conversation was taking place. Of all the actors in the company he was the most talented. He was about 25, with the pared body of a distance runner. He was a queer, but he was not the mincing, pantomime type. I knew about his propensities because he had been genuinely taken aback when I had not encouraged his advances. He had assumed that I was a chum. When I asked him why he would think this he had simply shrugged and said that I gave off fairy vibrations.

'Besides,' he had said, 'I asked Annie and she said that you were definitely queer.'

I had assured him I was not, and that I had kept my relationship with Annie deliberately professional in preference to chaotically personal. My failure to sleep with her did not make me queer, although I could see how such an explanation might be a salve to a bruised ego. I'd had no idea that Annie had taken my carefully maintained distance so personally. However I didn't mind the fact that Adrian was bent. He was reliable and was the only one, apart from me, who could speak the verse. What he did with his body below his vocal chords was entirely his affair.

Adrian sat down at our table. Annie looked at him and said for the thousandth time, 'All the best men are queer. How are you, darling?'

'The facilities are adequate,' he said, 'and we are very close to a wharf. And where there's a wharf, after dark there's a man who wants to be fucked.'

It was at precisely this moment that Augie Kelly came in. If he heard Adrian's gross remark he chose to ignore it.

'Last night was a great success,' he said. 'If Tibald can get people in here, we can do each other a favour and give the bloody Royal Hotel a run for its money.'

I could see that he had Tour d'Argent delusions. He was wearing a freshly pressed shirt, and his copper hair had been carefully slicked and parted. Overnight he had decided to play the part of the sophisticated hotelier.

'Your flies are undone,' I said, and they were. He buttoned them up without blushing and with an unseemly lack of haste. I presume he thought Annie might enjoy watching his fingers fiddle so close to his genitals. He was wasting his time. Annie mostly had good taste in men, and he was definitely not her type.

Over the ensuing weeks, Augie Kelly found a far more compelling reason for keeping us on at a reduced rate than the success of Tibald's cooking. He fell in love.

The first of Tibald's dinners had indeed been a success. The candles were a brilliant touch. They softened the decayed and drab appointments in the George's dining room. The single poppy focussed the eye and distracted it from looking up at the mould that had gathered in the corners of the ceiling. That had been Adrian's idea. There had been a pleasant buzz in the room, helped by Augie's providing a halfway decent bottle of Madeira. I spoke briefly to Peter Topaz, but the fact that I felt that he had the upper hand meant that I was awkward and dull, or it seemed that way to me. As soon as he saw Annie he made a bee-line for her, and it was perfectly obvious that she hadn't the least inclination to repel his advances.

The night of this dinner was the first time I met Polly Drummond. She was there with the soldier boy named Smelt. He had bad skin and a few bristles above his top lip that were trying very hard to approximate a moustache. At one point I saw him place his hand on her knee and move it up to her thigh. She didn't discourage him, but threw her head back and blew smoke from her cigarette into the air. I assumed they were on intimate terms. At first glance she appeared rather ordinary, almost what the French call *jolie-laide* — sort of halfway between being pretty and being plain. It depended on how the light fell across her features. She didn't look more than twenty (I found out later that she was twenty-four), with dark hair cut into a bob.

It didn't really suit her, but I imagine she'd picked the look out of a magazine, and some clumsy Maryborough hairdresser had attempted to make her resemble the picture.

In the days after the dinner I discovered that Polly Drummond smelled of honey and that her mother was barking mad. I also learnt that her younger brother, Alfred, was frighteningly unstable. He had joined the RAAF and was training as a wireless air gunner. I thought asking him to do two things at once was ambitious. There was an older brother but he had headed for the Gulf in '39 and hadn't been heard from since.

My first impression of Polly was that she laughed too easily and too loudly. She was not unaware, if I may indulge in that litotes, of her effect on men. She moved with a casual and sinuous grace that hinted at the sensual possibilities her acquaintance might offer. I was not attracted to her initially. I thought she made rather a fool of herself by asking Annie Hudson for her autograph. Annie, of course, took full advantage of the opportunity, and found a copy of that day's *Chronicle* and attached her signature to her advertisement for Tampax. She handed it to Polly with the condescension of a Garbo or a Crawford. She could have signed the Colgate advertisement, but that would have meant explaining that the chap in the last frame, with the back of his head to the camera, was me. Naturally, Polly would have wanted my autograph as well, and Annie wasn't having any of that. Hogging the limelight was one of Annie's less endearing qualities. Fortunately, the opportunities to indulge it were infrequent, and we did not come to blows over it.

I saw Polly Drummond late in the afternoon on the day following the dinner. I was sitting in the dining room tinkering with the script. Arthur Rank was with me. He was a shy man who had lost his arm and a testicle in a harvester accident in outback

New South Wales. He had been barely sixteen then, and in the intervening twenty years had learned to use his single arm with astonishing dexterity. He could roll a cigarette more rapidly and skilfully than any man I have known. I don't think many people knew about his other injury.

One night, not long after he had joined the Players, he drank too much rum and told me tearfully what had happened the morning of the accident. He took off his shirt to reveal the ghastly damage done to his flesh. The left-hand side of his torso, from the blunt stump of his amputation to the belt of his trousers, looked as if it had been flayed and the pieces put back willy nilly. The thick hair on his chest grew normally on the right side then stopped abruptly where it met the quilted, discoloured expanse of grafted and ruined skin. Without a word, and with tears streaming down his face, he unbelted his trousers and lowered them to show what else the harvester had taken from him. His thigh was heavily scarred, as was one side of his groin. He lifted his penis, which had escaped injury, to expose fully the place where one half of his scrotum had been torn from his body. We never spoke of it afterwards. He was a lousy actor, but I didn't care. He was the only one in the company in whom I could confide. I suppose I believed that the badly injured live in a sort of permanent state of grace.

The hotel was quiet. There were a few men in the bar, and I could hear Tibald bashing about in the kitchen as he prepared that night's meal. Augie was expecting good patronage after the newspaper article. He'd been strutting and preening all morning and trying to engage me in conversation. A couple of RAAF officers had come in earlier and booked tables for themselves and their girlfriends, and there would also be a few walk-ins, no doubt. Arthur noticed Polly first. She was leaning in the doorway.

'I'm not disturbing you, am I?'

I thought she was doing a bad imitation of some movie star she'd seen at the pictures. She was smoking and striking an attitude that was unnaturally cinematic, as if she was aware of how the curve of her silhouette looked from where we were sitting. She pushed herself away from the door-frame and came over.

'I think I left my lipstick here last night.'

Her voice was slightly nasal, with vowels hammered flat by the pounding heat of her many Maryborough summers. She took in Arthur's empty sleeve, and did not flinch or stare or give the faintest acknowledgement that there was anything unusual about him. I liked her for that. In fact, she put out her hand and said, 'Polly Drummond.' Arthur stood up, took her hand, and gave his name.

'Do you sing?' she asked.

'Badly.'

'It's just that I saw a man in Sorlei's show who looked just like you and he had a beautiful voice.'

Sorlei's was a revue company that haunted us. Wherever we went, there they were. They were big and successful, and rural Queensland loved them. They always played the town halls and never to empty houses. They were lowbrow, of course.

'When were they in town?' I asked.

'A few weeks ago. They were terrific. They had this comic who made me laugh so hard I thought I'd pee. Excuse my French. And like I said there was a man who sang and he looked like Arthur, but he juggled too, so …'

'So it couldn't have been me,' said Arthur. Polly's smile grew into a laugh, and Arthur laughed, too. I had never seen him so at ease with a stranger.

'I've come from work. I work in Manahan's, over in Adelaide Street. Did you find my lipstick?'

'Someone would have said if it had turned up,' I said.

'Oh.' She did a good impression of disappointment, but I didn't believe for a minute that that was why she was here.

'It'll be dark soon,' she said. 'Could one of you walk me home? It's not far, just up in Richmond Street.'

'I'll walk with you,' I said.

'You come, too,' she said to Arthur.

I felt a twinge of pique when she said this. It took me by surprise, that twinge. Why should I be jealous of the attention this shop girl paid to Arthur? And yet I was.

Outside the hotel the air was warm and felt more like the summer ahead than the winter and autumn behind. It was four o'clock. The factory whistle at Walkers Engineering went off just as we began walking up Wharf Street towards the Bank of New South Wales. By the time we reached the corner of Richmond and Kent Streets we were caught in the extraordinary daily spectacle of the twelve hundred Walkers workers hurtling down Kent Street on their bicycles. There were no cars on the road at all. It was clogged with cyclists. Several of them called to Polly, and she waved at them and laughed. One of them drew away from the pack and skidded to a halt beside us.

'Tell Fred I'll see 'im at the dance next Satdee,' he said. 'And tell 'im to bring the moolah he owes me.'

'Tell him yourself,' Polly said.

'Just tell'im that's all,' he said, and rode off. He did not acknowledge our presence.

'He's a creep,' Polly said.

'Who is he?' I asked.

'He's nobody, and I mean nobody.'

We had to wait several minutes before we could cross Kent Street. It was impossible to do so until the mass of bicycles had cleared. They were like wildebeests on the Serengeti. We walked up Richmond Street until we crossed Queen Street. Not much was said. The meeting with the cyclist had upset Polly and she had fallen quiet.

'We're here,' she said suddenly, and turned in at a gate. I had not expected her to live in a large house, and this was a very large house indeed. A broad staircase rose to a verandah surrounded by wrought-iron railings. In the space between the railings and the roof, rectangles of lattice kept the sun out. The central part of the house rose above the roofed verandah and gave the impression of some grandeur. The front door was carved elaborately, and was balanced on either side by windows that extended almost from floor to ceiling. Like most of the houses in Maryborough it was raised on stilts, but these were obscured by more lattice artfully placed all around the base. There was fretwork wherever a verandah post met the roof. What made the house stand out from its neighbours, though, was the lushness of its garden. The front yard of Polly's house boasted a stand of tall, thin palms on either side of the front staircase and at each of the corners of the house. Smaller palms and ferns clustered at the bottom of the mature palms. The effect was pleasing, and in summer must have created an illusion of coolness.

'Nice house,' said Arthur simply.

'Too nice for a girl who works in a department store you mean,' she said.

Arthur was caught off guard. This wasn't what he had meant. He didn't think like that. It was what I thought, though, so I was glad he had said it. Polly rescued him from his embarrassment. She smiled at him and said that she was just kidding.

'My grandfather made a pile out of timber. He built this. He had servants and all. My dad was hopeless and lost all the money. Don't look too close. You'll see that it's falling down. There's no money to repair anything.'

The front door opened and a woman in her sixties emerged. She was small, and stood at the top of the steps with her hands on her hips.

'That's not papists with you, is it?' she screeched. 'I won't have papists in the house!'

Polly didn't reply. She looked at me and said that the circus was due to arrive tomorrow, and that I should take her to the railway station to watch it come in. Before I had a chance to comprehend this, she said that she would be ready at midday.

She ran up the stairs, past her mother, and into the house.

'Go on,' Mrs Drummond screamed at us. 'Get away from my gate! No papists here! No papists!'

She looked about her as if she were searching for something to throw at us. We headed back to the centre of town.

'She's crazy,' was all Arthur said. 'Don't get mixed up with that family.'

I thought he was talking about Polly's mother, but I wonder now if he wasn't talking about Polly herself. Somehow I felt mixed up with the Drummonds already. Polly had spoken to me as if we had been going out for some time. It was as if we were picking up from where we had left off. I was pathetically flattered by this, and I should have known better. If I'd said 'no' at this point, the hideousness of what happened soon afterwards would not have turned my life from relative order to terrifying chaos.

Chapter Two

IN THE WRONG PLACE

THE SECOND NIGHT OF TIBALD'S COOKING was as smashing as the first, although the entire menu was fish and crustaceans. It was a Friday night — a beefless day. There wasn't a full house, by any means, but the word would spread and the crowds would come.

The next day I arrived at the Drummond house at midday exactly. I'm a stickler for punctuality, it being the courtesy of kings. I mounted the steps, crossed the verandah, and knocked on the door. It was opened by Mrs Drummond.

'What do you want?' she asked. 'We don't want papists here.'

'I'm here,' I said patiently, aware that I was speaking to a mad person, 'to see your daughter, Polly.'

'She doesn't want papists here either.'

'I assure you, Mrs Drummond, I am not a papist.'

'Don't believe you. You look like a papist. You can tell them by their eyes, and you've got popish eyes.'

Polly emerged from the gloom behind her mother and spoke sharply to her.

'Leave off, mum. Go inside.'

Mrs Drummond spat at my feet. The glistening globule of drool landed on the floor. I was taken aback.

'Popery!' she snarled, and retreated.

Arthur was right. This was a mistake, but when Polly slipped her arm through mine and I caught the waft of honey that came from her hair and skin, I rationalised that all I was doing was walking her to the station to see a circus come to town. What harm could flow from that?

We weren't the only ones who wanted to see the train carrying the circus roll into Maryborough. There were bicycles everywhere, all headed towards the railway station in Lennox Street. We reached it just as the Sole Bros. Circus and Zoo arrived. The place was swarming with children, but there seemed to be an equal number of adults as well. What was the big deal? When we pushed our way onto the platform I saw what the attraction was, or rather I smelled it first. The circus had loaded its motley assortment of wild beasts onto the train. The tigers paced in their cages, and the pungent reek of their urine billowed over the crowd. There were two lions, four camels, a zebra, a black bear, and an elephant that didn't look happy about its accommodation. Its chains clanked as it strained against its mean, cramped cage. There were several horses that would need to be spruced up before they took to the ring. The journey had been punishing for all the animals. People stared and pointed and squealed with laughter when the elephant drooped its trunk over its barrier and snatched a sandwich from a child who had come too close. The child bawled, terrified, but his mother rapped him on the head with her knuckle, and said it was his own silly fault and that she'd told him not to leave her side.

The circus people left their carriages and started the complicated business of unloading the animals. This would take some time. The good citizens of Maryborough stared at the circus folk with the same fascination they had lavished on the beasts. Here was a species that generated both curiosity and suspicion. All I saw was a group of absolutely filthy men and their equally squalid women. They looked like they shared the same straw as their exhibits and paid no attention at all to the crowd. There was one man — he was obviously the ringmaster, as indicated by his battered top hat — who put a crate on the ground and stood on it.

'Ladies and gentleman,' he said, in a voice that fell far short of Barnum and Bailey extravagance. 'The unloading will take some time, but we will be parading the animals through the town to the showgrounds in two hours' time. Tell your friends, and watch the spectacle pass by.'

People drifted away. I would have liked to stay to see how they managed to persuade the elephant down from its cage, but Polly wasn't the slightest bit interested in the mundane workings of the circus. She was there to enjoy the thrill that proximity to a tiger excited. I suspect the frisson produced by proximity to circus people was a drawcard, too. Gypsy lovers with burning eyes were thin on the ground in Maryborough. One of the rouseabouts brushed past us, and the overwhelming impression left by him was not of wild sex but of excrement. Whether it was his own or the elephant's would be mere speculation.

Polly didn't want to go home, and from my short acquaintance with her mother I can't say that I blamed her. We had a milkshake in King's in Adelaide Street. I felt silly sitting there, slurping lime-flavoured milk like a teenager. Polly wanted to know about the acting profession. It was thrilling, she said (she really did use the word 'thrilling'), to be talking to an actual actor. What was it like? Had I ever met Clark Gable? What was Claudette Colbert really like? And James Stewart? Was Cary Grant really that handsome in real life? Were the rumours about him and Randolph Scott true? She couldn't wait to get home and put all this in her diary.

'I put everything in my diary,' she said.

I had to admit that I had never met any of these people. She was surprised and a bit peeved, as if I had brought her to King's under false pretences, even though it was she who had brought me. It was as if she thought the enterprise of acting dissolved geography and disrupted the laws of time and space to the extent that a conversation with Cary Grant in Hollywood in the morning might logically precede a milkshake with her in a café in Maryborough in the afternoon.

'You look like someone in the movies,' she said.

'Boris Karloff?' I raised an eyebrow to indicate the absurdity of the comparison.

'No,' she said, but not before giving it serious consideration. 'But someone.'

'Tyrone Power,' I said and did not raise an eyebrow but brought them together to assist her in the identification. She mustn't have heard me because, instead of answering, she said, 'Let's go to the pictures tonight.'

I should have declined.

Polly didn't want me to walk her home. She said she was visiting someone first.

'It wouldn't be that Smelt fellow, I suppose,' I said, unable to disguise the pointless, irrational, and ridiculous jealousy in my voice. As if that spotted oaf represented any kind of competition, however far he had managed to get with Polly. His bumbling country advances, and his doubtless rapid, brutal coupling, learned from observation of horses and dogs, were no match for a man with the poetry of Shakespeare at his disposal.

'Jimmy?' she said with reassuring dismissiveness. 'Why would I be calling on him?'

I didn't press her further.

When I returned to the George, I found Sergeant Peter Topaz at the bar, talking animatedly with Bill Henty. Henty was the only member of my troupe I didn't trust. As an actor he was serviceable, useful because he was willing to slip into a dress if the part required it. This was something Adrian was reluctant to do, which surprised me. I had made the mistake of expressing this surprise soon after his arrival in the company.

'I'm queer, not mentally ill,' he said. Perhaps he wasn't aware of the great tradition of cross-dressing in the theatre. I didn't discuss it further with him, but gave those roles to Bill Henty instead. Henty was blind in one eye. When you looked at him, it was clear that there was something peculiar about him. It took a moment to register that one eye was green and the other was brown. The green eye was blind, and he never explained how this came to be so. It didn't affect him in any noticeable way, and he even drove the truck occasionally. He was no good to the army though. You need two eyes to shoot straight apparently. He was twenty-eight, with thinning, reddish blond hair and an unhealthy obsession with his body. He exercised excessively, seeming to spend every moment away from rehearsals doing press ups and sit ups, and he skipped with the ferocity of a prize fighter. We rubbed each other the wrong way.

'You won't run away from anything by running on the spot,' I told him once.

'You're running to fat,' was all he'd replied. This, I hasten to add, was not true. I knew the value of *mens sana in corpore sano*, but I didn't confuse it with obsessiveness verging on insanity.

'Is that right?' I heard Topaz say as I entered the bar.

'Too right,' was Henty's reply. I presumed they had been talking about me because Henty looked at me with just a flicker of sheepishness, as if he'd been caught out.

'Don't believe everything you hear, Sergeant', I said.

'I was just telling Sergeant Topaz here what a fine actor you are,' Henty said as he rose from his stool. His smug satisfaction at his quick-wittedness filled me with annoyance. He left before I could counter it.

'Sergeant Topaz,' I said, feigning indifference to Henty's witticism. 'What can I do for you, or is this the pub where you drink while you're on duty?'

'Will,' he said with studied patience, 'a little pomposity goes a very long way.' Topaz ran his fingers across his close-cropped scalp and scratched at his chest between the buttons of his shirt. 'I've done you a favour, and I'd like a favour in return.'

'Oh yes,' I said. Sergeant Topaz had a gift for catching me on the back foot. I was suspicious of him. Why would a local plod in a small town be interested in doling out favours to an acting troupe? I couldn't guess at his motivation, unless of course it involved Annie Hudson. That would make perfect sense. Perhaps Topaz fantasised about stepping out with the girl who could provide him with a guarantee of both oral and genital hygiene.

'I said I'd look into the hall rental for you, and I try to keep my word. I spoke to Wrighty, and he's keen. In fact, he's not going to charge you a cracker, just tickets to opening night for him and the missus, and one meal a week here. I suggested that, said you'd feel bad unless you could offer him something. I hope I wasn't speaking out of turn.'

With discounted accommodation and nothing to pay on the hall, we might break even on this part of the tour.

'Thank you, Sergeant,' I said, and I was happy with the way I uttered it. I think I managed to express gratitude with the hint of an apology for any earlier rudeness.

'Call me Peter,' he said, and held out his hand.

'Peter.' I shook it. 'When can we have a look inside the hall?'

'Monday. Two o'clock. Wrighty'll be there to give you a key so that you can let yourselves in whenever it's convenient. It's no good on weekends, of course. Skating.'

Topaz thwacked his hat against his thigh and began to head for the door.

'There is one other thing,' he said, and turned back towards me. 'There's a little favour you can do for me. I've been asked to emcee the Comfort Fund dance next Saturday night. I hate that sort of thing, standing up in front of people. I thought maybe you could do it instead. It'd be a good way to get people to know you're here.'

'What's involved?' I asked, but I had already decided that I would accept even if it involved taking my clothes off and hanging from the rafters.

'You know, jollying people along. It's being advertised as a dance and jollification, so you'd be in charge of the jollification bit. There'll be two orchestras, the Ambassadors and the Brown Out. Tell a few jokes between sets, let people know when supper is ready, that sort of thing. There might be a raffle, so you'll run that, too. Try to keep everybody happy so that the air force blokes don't start any fights.'

'All right,' I said. 'I'll do it.'

The relief on his face was touching. It is astonishing that the thought of public speaking can unman even the burliest of thief-takers.

'Say hello to Miss Hudson for me, will you,' he said before stepping into the street.

I met Polly at the Embassy Theatre. I'd wanted to pick her up and walk with her, but she'd refused the offer, saying that it wasn't far and that she was used to walking places on her own at night. I was standing in the street outside the theatre peering into the darkness in the direction from which I expected her to come. There were people everywhere, but there were no lights, and the Maryborough night was deep. She saw me before I saw her. A man standing beside me lit a cigarette, and the flare from his match illuminated my face briefly. She tucked her arm through mine and said, 'Don't you just love the movies?'

I wanted to say that my love of the movies didn't really extend to the two pictures showing that night. I was about to endure *Cowboy Serenade*, a Gene Autry abomination, and something called *I Killed That Man*, starring the oily Ricardo Cortez.

The films were appalling, but Polly was enthralled. I wasn't expecting any intimate explorations under the cover of darkness, but if I had been I would have been disappointed. Polly was engrossed in what was happening on screen. At interval someone called Happy Jack Clark attempted to entertain the full house with tired music-hall jokes. In Maryborough, the movies meant a big night out, and in keeping with the grandeur of the occasion live entertainment and a raffle were *de rigueur*. This kind of evening seemed to be what most people in this town understood by theatre. The pool of available local talent was neither wide nor deep, as evidenced by Happy Jack Clark's performance. I thought, as he plodded through his exhausted repertoire, that if I ever ended up doing that for a living, I would appreciate it if somebody shot me. After a few endless minutes he introduced the manager of the theatre, a man named Hennessy. Polly whispered to me, 'He's not married to the woman he lives with.'

'How shocking,' I said, simply because I thought that this was the reaction Polly was looking for. Hennessy was greeted with hoots and cheers, and bizarrely began throwing packets of biscuits into the audience. People leapt from their seats and squealed with delight when they grabbed one, no doubt crushing the contents into crumbs in the process. He then drew the winning ticket for that night's raffle, and a severe-looking woman stepped up on stage to claim her prize.

'Rigged!' some wag yelled, and there was general laughter in approval.

Hennessy took centre stage, and an air of expectancy gripped the first few rows. They were mainly children, and I could see them straining forward. Hennessy reached into his pocket and withdrew a fistful of coins. He scattered them at the foot of the stage, but almost before they had hit the ground the lights went down. There was a mad, hysterical scramble as boys scrabbled about in search of precious threepences and pennies. There was, too, the promise of at least one one-shilling piece. The screen flashed into life outlining the backs of boys still hunting on the floor, and the credits for *I Killed That Man* rolled. Ricardo Cortez was top-billed. The movie was garbage. Polly loved it.

Polly let me walk her home when the films were finished. It was late, and with clouds blocking the moon the streets were impenetrably dark and slightly menacing. By the time we'd turned into Richmond Street we were the only pedestrians on the footpath. A few bicycles slid by, but not a single car.

'You look a bit like Ricardo Cortez,' she said. I disguised

the fact that I found this offensive — Cortez looked like a low-rent gigolo — by saying that I felt a bit guilty about leaving the rest of the company to help out with that night's dinner at the George.

'You're the boss,' she said, and yawned. 'We're here.'

We went in at the gate and she suddenly kissed me, tentatively at first and more deeply when she met with no resistance. I drew her tightly to me and let my hand stray across her breast. She pulled away.

'I thought you were a gentleman,' she said, in a poor imitation of Scarlet O'Hara. To show that she hadn't really minded, she came back to my arms and drew my mouth down to hers again. I didn't disrupt the moment by taking further liberties. I would leave that to her. Just as her hand was finding its way inside my shirt, a match sparked into flame on the steps behind us. There was a breeze, and the match flickered uncertainly before the tobacco caught. I was startled, and drew back from Polly's embrace. The man on the steps sniffed, and I felt Polly's hand, still resting on my chest, tense.

'Who's this one?' he asked, and sniffed again.

'None of your business,' Polly said sourly.

She took my hand and pulled me towards the steps. The man didn't move from his position halfway up, and we had to squeeze past him. On the verandah, Polly said to me, 'Come inside and have a cup of tea.'

I was aware that this was an act of defiance directed at the figure on the steps, rather than the expression of a desire to get to know me better. I accepted nonetheless. I'd liked the touch of her hand on my bare skin.

We headed down a dark corridor with rooms on either side towards a dim, yellow light. A single lamp nudged shadows feebly out of corners. Under it, in an armchair worn with sitting, Polly's mother sprawled. She was asleep. There was too much furniture in the room, and all of it had seen better days. Polly put her fingers to her lips and indicated that we should pass through into the kitchen. We'd taken a few steps when the front door slammed and Mrs Drummond's eyes popped open. Before she had a chance to utter a sound, the man entered the room, bringing with him the smell of tobacco and beer. He was dressed in the uniform of the RAAF.

'Fred Drummond,' he said, smiling now, and pushed his hand towards me. I took it automatically.

'William Power.'

He leaned towards my ear and whispered, 'Have you fucked her yet?'

I was stunned by the casual obscenity, and unnerved by the impertinence.

'What kind of a question is that?'

'My kind,' he said, and laughed.

Polly had heard what he'd whispered, but her only reaction was to look at him as if she might spit on him.

'I'll put the kettle on,' she said, and passed into the kitchen, abandoning me to her brother and her mother. Fortunately, Mrs Drummond had dropped back into a deep sleep.

'What did you say your name was?' Fred asked, and there was something aggressive in his tone, as if he was blaming me for having a name he couldn't remember.

'Will,' I said, reluctant this time to offer him more.

'Sit down,' he said, only it sounded like 'Siddown'. He wasn't going to lavish the energy required to sound the 'T' on me.

I sat in an uncomfortable chair with arms that were greasy and with an antimacassar that was stained with hair oil. Fred sat opposite me. He leaned forward with his elbows on his knees and with his hands dangling between his legs. He had big hands. Ugly hands. I watched them twitch, and then moved my attention to his face. He was grinning at me stupidly. He looked about twenty-one, and was clean-shaven and well-groomed. His features were regular, and he might have been handsome except that the muscles in his face were slack. This made him look half-witted.

'You're in the RAAF,' I said.

He looked at his sleeve in mock surprise. 'Christ. I must be.'

I ploughed on, reluctantly.

'What branch?'

'Wireless air gunner,' he said, reasonably. The rapid shifts in mood and tone were disturbing. 'Just learnin'.'

His hands gripped an imaginary machine-gun and he directed his fire at me.

'Ack, ack, ack, ack, ack, ack, ack,' he chattered and shook with the gun's imagined recoil. Mrs Drummond snorted in her sleep, oblivious to the noise around her. Fred turned his weapon towards his mother.

'Ack, ack, ack, ack, ack,' he chattered again.

Polly came in, carrying a teapot and two cups.

'Where's mine?' he asked belligerently.

'Drop dead, Fred,' said Polly. I suddenly began to feel sick. I wasn't shocked by Polly's words but by the hatred in her voice. I felt claustrophobic, as if I had been drawn into a shrinking box where the air hummed with malice. I wanted to get out of there and never return. When Fred leapt suddenly to his feet my blood fizzed in a kind of panic. It seemed possible that terrible violence might erupt here, among the clutter and small-town banalities of ugly knick-knacks and badly composed family photographs. The air was electric. Nothing in fact happened at that point. Fred simply went into the kitchen and got himself a teacup.

'Ignore him,' Polly said when he was out of the room. 'He's not the full quid.'

I didn't recognise this Polly. Her face was distorted with the anger and revulsion this house aroused. I could taste her saliva in my mouth, and it was poison.

When Fred returned he took his seat and held out his cup, expecting Polly to pour tea into it. Polly stood, took the teapot by its handle and walked towards him. She tipped it as if to fill his cup, but at the last moment swung her arm back and, with the momentum gained, brought the teapot down hard on the side of his head. Its lid flew off, and tea sprayed over Fred and onto the furniture. There was a frozen moment when no one could assimilate what had happened. Fred's hands flew to his face, and then he roared his rage and threw himself at Polly. They crashed to the floor, the thud of Polly's head as it hit the floorboards competing with the clatter of toppling china figurines. Mrs Drummond woke and screamed incoherently, not looking at the scene before her, but lost somewhere between waking and sleeping, staring open-mouthed into the middle distance.

'They're here! They're here! The papists have come!' she screamed.

Fred's hands were closed around Polly's throat, and she was gurgling and kicking. I launched myself onto Fred's back and dragged him off. He didn't put up much resistance but sat with his legs splayed, feeling the side of his head. I think he was crying. Polly lay still for a few seconds but, like a thing possessed, she let out a yowl and attacked Fred with renewed ferocity. Her hand found his genitals and she squeezed so that he doubled over and made an unholy sound that was a mixture of pain and nausea. I attempted to wrench Polly's grip away. With her free hand she raked her nails across my neck. I felt the warmth of flowing blood immediately. I staggered to my feet and backed out of the room.

The last I saw of Polly Drummond was the flip flop of her bob as her head moved back and forth in rhythm to the tightening of her hold on her brother's testicles. The scene before me in that dim, yellow light was like something out of Dante. Mrs Drummond screamed, Fred moaned, and Polly grunted with the effort. I hurried down the corridor and into Richmond Street. A light rain was falling. The cool drops stung my neck where Polly's fingernails had ripped my flesh.

It was later that evening that Polly Drummond was murdered.

Chapter Three

AT THE WRONG TIME

ANNIE HUDSON HAD READ in *Modern Screen* that Joan Crawford never left the house without full make-up. She had, Miss Crawford said, a responsibility to her fans to look like a movie star at all times. Annie, hilariously, felt a similar responsibility, which is why, when we went to Wright's Hall on Monday for the first time, she was wearing the kind of make-up you would apply if you were expecting a Klieg light to be turned on you. I can't be sure, but I think Adrian had applied a hint of mascara as well. I don't think Mr Wright had had much to do with theatre people, and we were a little overwhelming. The whole company came with me to the hall, except for Tibald, who was organising the kitchen to his satisfaction. After the first few successful dinners, and a growing profile in the town, he had begun to assert his right to be temperamental.

'I can't work without a proper *mise en place*,' he snapped

when I suggested that he come with us to Wright's. 'And I can't organise my *mise* unless I'm left alone!'

It was obvious that Augie's Tour d'Argent delusions were contagious.

The interior of the hall was bland and exhausted. Its windows were filthy — not that that mattered as they would be covered by our blacks. The floor was uneven, and badly rutted and dented with skate damage. There was a small room off to the side at the back. This would serve as our dressing-room and our off-stage space. We would erect a small stage and work without curtains in the authentic, Shakespearean way. I would instruct the company to refer to the audience as 'groundlings', to help them get in the mood. You would be surprised how details like that can affect performance and commitment. The hall wasn't ideal and the acoustics were dreadful, but the price was right. I took the key from Mr Wright and shook his hand. He was to come that night to the George to seal the deal with Tibald's three-course, war-time austerity miracle. When he had gone I turned to my company and said, 'Our real work can now begin.'

'Your neck's bleeding', said Annie, and her revulsion was a little overdone, considering that the ooze was the merest trickle.

Our first rehearsal went badly. I had hoped that, as professionals, they would have learned their lines. Adrian was word perfect, but he was the only one. Walter Sunder, whose age (he was sixty-five) was his only real asset, barely had a third of his part off. He was almost impossible to direct. He could never be heard from beyond the third row. Still, we needed someone to do the elderly parts, and with only minimal make-up available all he had to do was appear shirtless to provide an audience with a convincing demonstration that all flesh was indeed grass. In his case, rather dry and withered grass.

Kevin Skakel wasn't much better. In fact, he was worse.

When I pressed him to prove his claim that he had his part down, he took umbrage and limped to the back of the hall, his club foot hitting the boards just that bit harder than his good one. If he'd been able to act he'd have made a decent Richard the Third.

Annie, to give her credit, knew most of her lines, although in the brief run-through I did with her she was as animated as a table-ready flounder. I attempted to explain, yet again, my vision of the play to the company, and to convey roughly how I saw it being blocked out in this space. The men weren't happy about the leather posing pouches I wanted them to wear. I thought the pouches were both dramatic and sensible. They certainly cut down on costuming costs.

'I'm not serving somebody in the hotel one night and parading practically naked in front of them the next,' said Bill Henty.

'And putting them off their food for life,' said Annie.

I stepped in to stop the argument descending into a slanging match, aware that there was no love lost between Bill and Annie. They were forever sniping at each other. I think perhaps Annie may have turned him down at some stage. I don't inquire too closely into the private lives of the members of my company.

After a few futile and frustrating hours at the hall we returned to the George to prepare for dinner. We had adopted a routine by now. Each person knew his job, and nobody seemed to mind too much doing it. I think waiting on tables was preferred to acting. With each day the George was becoming a bit more spruced up. Augie Kelly's delusions of grandeur had prompted him to try to turn the dining room into some sort of palm-court fantasy. He had the walls and ceiling patched and painted, even though this meant people ate their dinners with the smell of paint and turpentine stripping their nasal passages. He had put large potted palms in strategic places, and made sure that there were flowers on every table. I had to admit, the room looked elegant. The inappropriately heavy drapes he had hung hid the ugly black-outs from the diners. In a matter of only a few days, the George had established itself as a place to take a girl for a decent meal. Word spread through the services, and most of our customers were air force or, occasionally, army — officers of course, showing a local girl a good time and hoping for something in return.

When we returned from the hall I retreated to my room and went over the script. I needed to drop four characters to make it work. Fatigued by rewriting Shakespeare, I decided to take a bath before going down to help out with the serving. There was no one in the bathroom when I entered, although someone had taken a bath recently. It had probably been Kevin Skakel, who shed extravagant amounts of hair whenever he bathed, and never cleaned up after himself. Sluicing out the tub was essential to avoid contact with the disgusting detritus of the Skakel moult. There was no hot water, but the water that came out of the tap was comfortably tepid. I slipped in, adjusted to the initial shock, and closed my eyes. I must have fallen asleep. How else would it have been possible for someone to enter the bathroom without my knowing it? That, however, is what happened.

I opened my eyes suddenly and, sitting on the edge of the bath, was Sergeant Peter Topaz staring at me. I was comprehensively discombobulated, sat up violently, and spilled water over the edge. Topaz stood quickly, but not quickly enough to prevent his trousers being doused. There was nothing else to do but to play this calmly, as if waking to the sight of a policeman perched on the edge of one's bath was a perfectly ordinary experience. I slid back down into my previous, comfortable position.

'I don't suppose it occurred to you to knock,' I said, trying not to sound peevish.

'I did knock. There was no answer, so I thought I'd better check that you were all right.'

'I'm touched. You get a lot of drownings in baths in this town, do you? What are you doing up here? I don't think I know you well enough to meet socially under these conditions.'

'I was looking for you. I was told you might be in here, taking a bath.'

'So you thought you'd come and watch.'

Topaz walked over to the door that he had left half-open and closed it, quietly. He returned to the bath and once again stared down at me. I confess I felt at a considerable disadvantage.

'That's a nasty scratch on your neck,' he said. 'You have to watch those things up here. They get infected.'

My hand flew automatically and guiltily to the wound inflicted by Polly's nails.

'I did it in my sleep, last night.' I closed my fingers over when I said this so that he couldn't see that the nails were blunted by careful filing. I look after my hands. They are expressive. I didn't tell him the truth because it was none of his business and because I hadn't yet considered properly how I felt about the incidents of the previous evening. At the time, while walking home, I had told myself that I could not possibly see her again; that there was madness there. In the light of day, however, my resolve had weakened. There was something exciting about her. Perhaps I would see her again, after all, but stay well away from her house and its inhabitants.

Topaz seemed to be examining my body almost forensically. His eyes travelled up and down it in unembarrassed assessment. It made me uncomfortable and self-conscious, and my decision to remain calm mutated into umbrage.

'What the hell is this about?' I snapped, and there was real rancour in my voice this time.

'Have you seen Polly Drummond today or yesterday?' he asked, his eyes settling on the scratches on my neck.

'What? No. Why would I have seen her?'

'So you do know Polly Drummond?'

'She was at dinner. The night you came. Yes, I know her.'

I didn't like the way this was going.

'You saw her after that, though. After that dinner, I mean.'

There was no point lying. I had no reason to lie. I saw her. So what?

'She came here the other day. Friday. Asked me to walk her home. Arthur came, too. We went to see the circus arrive, and the movies.'

'All three of you. You, Arthur, and Polly.'

'Are you investigating something, or are you genuinely interested in my social life?'

'Her brother's worried about her.'

'Hah!' I said contemptuously. 'Her brother is insane.'

With that, I stood up, wrapped a towel around my waist, and clambered out of the bath. Topaz made no move to leave.

'You were with Polly on Saturday night.'

It was a statement, not a question. I wasn't about to deny anything.

'If you are insinuating that I spent the night with her, I most certainly did not. We went to the movies, saw two wretched films which she inexplicably enjoyed, I walked her home, and that's it. I stayed for a bit until Polly and Fred started arguing, and then I left.'

Topaz stood between me and the door, not aggressively, but deliberately, with his arms folded. I pulled the plug in the bath and began to move past him. He turned slightly to allow me through but, just as I touched the door handle, he said coolly, 'She's missing.'

'What do you mean, "missing"?'

'Her bed wasn't slept in on Saturday night and she didn't come home on Sunday. She's not home yet and she didn't turn up at work this morning.'

'Oh, for heaven's sake, she's a big girl. She probably got fed up with the arguing — the whole family's crackers, you know — and went to a friend's house.'

'Nope,' he said.

I opened the door and walked into the corridor. Topaz followed.

'Her brother says she left the house about ten minutes after you did. Catch up with you, did she?'

'If she had caught up with me, Sergeant, that wouldn't be any of your business, but as it happens, she didn't.' It seemed inappropriate to call him 'Peter', given the professional tone he was adopting.

'Her brother is worried, that's all. I said I'd ask around. So if you do know where she is, even though it's none of my business, I'd like to be able to pass on that she's all right. So, can I tell him she's all right?'

I had reached the door of my room by this stage.

'You can tell him what you like, but I have no idea where she is. I didn't see her after I left the house. Now, unless you want to look under my bed, can I please get dressed? I have to help with downstairs.'

'Make sure you put disinfectant on those scratches. They look nasty.'

His solicitude was actually a threat. He hadn't believed a word I had said.

'One last thing,' he said. I sighed noisily.

'Yes, Sergeant.' I stressed his title to indicate that I felt he had put distance between us.

He lowered his head so that I could see its crown, and patted it with one hand.

'Tell me honestly — do you think I'm losing my hair?'

I believe the American expression 'out of left field' just about covers this question. Without missing a beat, not wishing to give him the satisfaction of thinking that he had taken me by surprise yet again, I examined the top of his head and said, 'Actually, yes. I think you're thinning on top there.' It was a lie, but it wouldn't hurt to give him something to worry about.

The next two days of rehearsals were draining. *Titus* was starting to take shape but it was going to be a struggle to sell it to a town used to dancing bears and second-rate vaudevillians. Bill Henty snidely suggested that Annie should appear with one breast exposed. At least people would show up. I think she was flattered by the notion that just one of her breasts would be sufficiently magnetic to ensure full houses.

'Which one do you think?' she asked. 'Left or right?'

'It doesn't bother me,' said Henty. 'I've only got one good eye anyway.'

It was when we had returned to the George on Wednesday that Annie plonked the *Chronicle* down in front of me. There it was, confirmation that Polly Drummond was now officially missing and that foul play was suspected.

SEARCH FOR MISSING GIRL

The search for Maryborough girl, Miss Polly Drummond, entered its third day yesterday. Last seen at home on Saturday night, police are without any real clues as to her whereabouts. Any information which would assist in the investigation would be welcome. The search will continue.

'So where have you put her?' asked Annie salaciously.

'What are you talking about?'

'Oh, come on, Will. We all know you were keen on her.'

I bridled at this impertinence.

'I took her to the movies. I knew her for precisely two days. I was not keen on her.'

'All right.' She made a gesture to indicate that she thought I was lying. 'Far be it from me to pry.'

Everyone in the company, except for Arthur, made some snide remark about my having gone to the pictures with a missing girl. The reason I didn't think it was cute, or funny, was that I had a growing suspicion that Fred Drummond had had something to do with his sister's disappearance. For the next few days I opened the paper with a sense of dread. There was a small notice every day, asking for help in finding Polly and letting people know that she was still missing. By the fifth day it had become clear that she was probably dead. The police began searching the river banks and local dams. I was expecting a visit from Peter Topaz, but he didn't come. Perhaps he, too, suspected Fred Drummond, and was directing his questions to him.

The Saturday night of the Comfort Fund dance was lit by a brilliant moon. The Town Hall filled quickly, and soon a pall of cigarette smoke hung in the air. I took the stage and faced the people of Maryborough for the first time.

'Ladies and gentlemen', I announced into the inadequate

microphone. Although it made my voice sound a little flat, there was nothing I could do about it, and so I ploughed on. I introduced myself suavely, gave the Power Players a plug, and thanked the organising committee of the dance as well as the ladies who had given of their time to decorate the hall so beautifully. Well, I was hardly going to tell the truth and declare the paper streamers and arches of bougainvillea tired and tacky. The Brown-Out orchestra struck up a jaunty swing tune, and the dance floor became crowded with couples. There were a lot of uniforms there, almost all of them airforce.

I scanned the crowd from the side of the stage, trying to get a feel for the citizens of this town. Under the subdued lighting inside the hall, they scrubbed up pretty well. The women were well dressed, probably hoping to score a description in the next day's paper. There was little evidence of clothes that conformed closely to the government's austerity dress code. Several men were wearing double-breasted suits, and several others were wearing waistcoats beneath their jackets. Both of these were considered wasteful of cloth and labour, but perhaps they were ancient items taken from the back of the wardrobe and seen only at dances and funerals. The mayor was wearing the drab Dedman suit, the preferred official style, setting an example. I saw two men who I recognised from the bar of the George, as well as some of the people who had eaten in Tibald's dining room. Adrian was there, hoping to pick up some soldier boy, no doubt, and no doubt he would succeed; and Bill Henty was there, too, wearing tails which fitted him snugly, and he knew it. Annie Hudson hadn't yet arrived, but she was coming. 'And not alone,' she had said pointedly.

The orchestra played three tunes before I announced the terms of the raffle and the existence of a door prize. Some lucky person would take home a hamper that contained starch and blue, sunflower seeds, condensed milk, camp pie, and Clement's corn flour, 'And let's put our hands together and thank Hetherington's for their generous donation'. My gracious recognition of the supplier didn't arouse much interest. There was polite, desultory applause, and it was clear that I would have to work hard to get the crowds' attention as the night wore on. The orchestra started again, and the swell of voices was overwhelmed by the music. I left the stage and walked along the side wall, behind the tables at which wall-flowers and non-dancers sat, towards the rear of the hall. The air had become thick with cigarette smoke, and I wanted some fresh air.

I picked my way through the incoming throng of well-scrubbed young men and cheaply perfumed young women. I saw Topaz before he saw me, and I saw that the glamorous creature on his arm was Annie Hudson, all dolled up and accepting the looks she was getting like the gracious star she thought she was. Topaz was wearing a decent suit, borrowed probably, and he was grinning like the cat that ate the canary. Annie, in fact, looked like a canary, in a yellow dress that made no attempt to hide what lay beneath. They made their way over to me.

'I'm going outside,' I shouted against the din. Topaz just nodded, but I felt his eyes on the back of my head as I reached the door and left the hall. On the lawn outside, lightning bugs of inhaled cigarettes flickered here and there. The moon was strong, and white teeth glowed amid the laughter and the shouts of recognition as friends met.

I felt a hand fall heavily on my shoulder. The fingers curled into a painful clutch, which I ducked out of, and I turned to see who had had the temerity to grab at me. It was Fred Drummond. He was in uniform and he was drunk — bloody-minded drunk. Breath hissed from behind his teeth, his rage so raw it was beyond language. He stood there, like a Neanderthal, arms hanging by his side, air rushing up from his lungs. There were people all around us, some of them noticing that a confrontation might be about to begin. I did not want to end up wrestling Fred Drummond before a live audience. Quite apart from anything else, I was fairly confident of his ability to turn my face into a piece of raw beef. He grabbed my shirt-front, and I heard buttons pop.

'Where is she?' he said, and before I could even take in what he was saying he screamed the question again.

'Where is she!!!???'

I was aware that the chattering and laughter around us had stopped.

'Get your hands off me!' I said, with a fierceness borrowed from my repertoire of stage emotions. I felt anything but fierce. Fred Drummond was a quivering, unpredictable mass of sinew and psychosis, and the moonlight glancing off the whites of his eyes made him appear truly demented. He let go of my shirt and, as I foolishly attempted to tuck it back into my trousers, he landed a punch with full force to my right eye. My head snapped round and pulled my body after it so that I sprawled on the ground, landing heavily on my left shoulder. All sound had been sucked out of the world except for a small gasp which may have come from a person near me, or from my own mouth. I turned, numb with shock, and saw Fred Drummond standing at my feet, both fists clenched and his lips drawn back ferally over his teeth.

Suddenly a figure moved in front of Drummond, and another figure moved close behind him. I couldn't see clearly, but it seemed as if the man behind Drummond wrapped his arms around him. The man with his back to me delivered two sharp, ferocious punches to Drummond's belly, and he doubled over, released now from the grip that had pinned his arms to his sides. The man who had punched him looked down at me before moving off into the night. I recognised him as the cyclist who had given Polly a message about money that Fred owed him. Fred was gasping, supporting himself with one hand on the ground and clutching his stomach with the other. I almost felt sorry for him, until he vomited — most of it splashing onto my right trouser leg and seeping into my shoe. The last few bars of 'In the Mood' leaked from the hall, followed by muted applause. This was my cue, and I knew that after the next number I was expected to run the raffle and tell a few jokes. This was, after all, advertised as a 'jollification', a state I felt some distance from at that moment.

I was helped to my feet by an airman who thought I 'should stay off the grog, mate.' I didn't bother to correct him, anxious as I was to put some distance between me and the temporarily discommoded Fred Drummond. I squelched my way towards the door. The show must go on, and there's no show without Punch, or in this case, Punched. I ran that raffle as though nothing had happened, feeling all the while my eye swelling and a creek of blood dribbling down my face. Naturally, my appearance excited comment, and the whispers and giggles echoed weirdly in my ears until suddenly they seemed to come from very far away. My nostrils were assaulted by the foul odour of the contents of Fred Drummond's stomach. The warm metallic taste of blood filled my mouth. All eyes were upon me, and someone was pointing at me. Her mouth was moving, but I could not make out what she was saying. The only sound that reached my ears was the sound of my own breathing, and it was noisily expressive of panic. I had experienced this sensation before, and I knew that it was a prelude to passing out.

I tried to make it into the wings, but the steps I took led me to the edge of the stage where I swayed precariously for a moment before falling forward into darkness. It's quite a drop from the stage to the floor of the auditorium in the Maryborough Town Hall. I was unconscious when I hit the boards, so I neither heard nor felt the nauseating crack of my arm breaking. I floated in and out of consciousness, my body having been presented with a few very good reasons for going into shock. A montage of faces peered at me. Someone may have said, 'Give him air.' Someone certainly said, 'He stinks of sick.' It sounded like Annie Hudson. A stretcher was produced from somewhere, and I closed my eyes and willed myself back into the anaesthetised safety of unconsciousness.

I woke in a hospital bed. Peter Topaz was standing at the end of it.

'Why is it that whenever I open my eyes, you're there staring at me?'

'It must be love.'

I propped myself up, groggily, and discovered that my left arm was encased in plaster.

'Great dance,' said Topaz. 'Absolutely first-class entertainment. When I asked you to emcee, though, I don't recall suggesting that you do it three sheets to the wind.'

'Hey, I was *not* drunk. I passed out, that's all, and it was just a delayed reaction to being punched in the eye by that lunatic Drummond. I hope he's locked up.'

'We did have reports of a drunken brawl between the two of you.'

'He was drunk. I was sober. He was screaming something at me about his sister.'

Topaz pulled a notebook from his crisply ironed top pocket and flicked through it.

'"Where is she?"' he read. 'Are those the words he used?'

'You have been busy, haven't you? Yes. Those are the words he used. Only a lot louder and a lot more deranged.'

'And?' He scratched at his chest through his shirt.

'And what?'

'And where is she?'

'Is that a serious question?'

'I'm not suggesting that you have her stashed away in some cosy little love nest. I'm afraid it's worse than that. I'm pretty sure she's been murdered.'

He was watching my reaction very closely, although the swollen state of my face would have made interpreting any little flicker difficult. As it was, I had no interest in disguising my reaction. I was frankly horrified, not just at the notion that Polly Drummond had been murdered, but that Peter Topaz might actually believe that I had had something to do with it.

'Are you accusing me of murder?' I said. My voice was shaking, and not just with indignation, but also fear. I felt helpless to defend myself.

'I'm just making inquiries. You were one of the last people to see her alive.'

'You don't know yet that she isn't still alive.'

'That's true,' he said, and smiled at me. 'I'm sorry if I've upset you. It's probably the last thing you need right now. That eye looks pretty bad. Fred must have landed a solid one.'

It was only when Topaz drew attention to my eyes that I realised that I had been looking at him through only one of them. The injured one had closed over.

A robust woman with red, chapped hands and large, impressive breasts came into the room, and in a business-like manner took my unplastered wrist and timed my pulse. She was the matron of this establishment.

'You've been in the wars,' she said. 'I don't know why people drink, really I don't.'
'I was not drinking,' I said testily.

'Of course not. You come in here covered in your own sick, and you've obviously been in a drunken fight, but you weren't drinking. Really, Mr Power. I didn't come down in the last shower.'

'No,' I countered. 'I imagine there have been many showers since you first came down in one.'

'You can go home today,' she said haughtily. 'Your clothes are in a bag at the end of the bed. They haven't been cleaned.'

'It's all right,' said Peter Topaz. 'I took the liberty of getting you a clean change of clothes. Arthur — is that his name? — went into your room and collected them for me. He was going to come along, to see how you were, but I said there was no need, I'd have you back at the George before lunchtime.'

'Why are you being so kind to me?'

'Well, Will, it's like this: I think that you murdered Polly Drummond, and I want to keep an eye on you.'

The smile that spread across his face when he said this was not the smile of a man who wished it to be known that he was only joking. It was a smile which eloquently expressed the certainty that he had found his man and that all he had to do now was wait for the evidence against me to mount up.

'I think,' I said, 'that I'm going to be sick.'

'Of course,' he said, and I threw up all over the bed sheets.

If I had been expecting a sympathetic welcome back at the George, I would have been disappointed. The whole company was gathered in the kitchen, helping prepare for the following night's dinner. The George did not serve dinner on a Sunday night. Vegetables were being chopped into tiny dice, and bones were being roasted for stock. Tibald said that I looked like shit, and that he hoped my unfortunate introduction to the people of Maryborough wouldn't put them off coming to his dining room. Adrian snidely muttered something about the inadvisability of getting mixed up with rough trade. Bill Henty said that if I'd been fitter I might have been able to look after myself better. I said that I was going up to my room and that I didn't want to be disturbed. Peter Topaz, who was hanging around to consolidate his attachment to Annie, no doubt, said that he hoped I felt better soon. I gave him what I calculated to be a withering look, but it is difficult to be withering with only one eye at one's disposal.

'Sergeant Topaz thinks that I murdered Polly Drummond,' I announced. I had hoped that this statement would arouse a chorus of outrage and disapproval, and that Topaz would be embarrassed and obliged to defend his absurd accusation before a hostile audience. Instead, my words were met with silence. It was not the silence of the recently appalled, but the silence of those who have just had a suspicion satisfactorily confirmed. Annie Hudson was the first to speak.

'And did you?'

I could easily have wrung her neck at that point and been sent down for life a happy man. I hadn't expected Annie to turn on me.

'Thanks very much,' I said. 'Thanks for your loyalty and support.'

'There's no need to get all hot and bothered,' said Adrian. 'It's a natural question.'

'Well, pardon me, Adrian, if I seem a little upset to discover that my own company thinks that I might actually be capable of killing someone.'

Tibald took a noisy sip from a spoon dipped into a steaming pot on the Aga.

'Given the right set of circumstances,' he said, 'we are all capable of murder. This is delicious.'

'Relax,' said Annie. 'I don't think any of us believe you've got the balls to commit a murder.'

'You have an offensive remark for every situation,' I said, and left the room. I was furious with all of them. Only Arthur unequivocally and inoffensively came to my defence. He said that it was perfectly obvious to anyone with half a brain that I did not have the killer instinct. His loyalty was reassuring, and reaffirmed that, of all the members of my troupe, he was the one on whom I could most depend. The cast on my arm felt heavy, and a dull ache began to insinuate itself into my consciousness. I ran a bath but didn't enjoy it. The effort required to keep the cast dry made me sit uncomfortably. I decided that the next day I would have to confront Fred Drummond. The vehemence of his attack on me made me think that perhaps he was as innocent of wrongdoing as I was. If I could reason with him when he was sober, perhaps we could piece together Polly's movements that night. Perhaps, too, I could convince him that I had nothing to do with his sister's disappearance. I was anxious to avoid any further public confrontations with him, and I was sure that unless I got him on side he was capable of inflicting far more damage than a swollen, discoloured eye.

The next day I borrowed Augie's bicycle. It was awkward manipulating it with one arm in a sling, but I managed quite well. I rode down Lennox Street towards the airfield, where I assumed Fred Drummond would be training. Trying his house first was out of the question. I wanted to meet him in a place where he would be reluctant to attack me on sight. If he wasn't at the airfield I would wait until he turned up.

When I arrived at the aerodrome I was told that I would not be able to enter the wireless air-gunner training area without authorisation. I was not willing to give up, not after having ridden this distance perilously balanced on an ancient bicycle. I pushed it around the perimeter fence until I reached a place from which I could observe the buildings that constituted the training facility. After only a few minutes a man in a RAAF uniform came across to where I was standing, wanting to know what business I had there. I introduced myself.

'Oh, yes,' he said. 'I was there the other night when you came a cropper. Too much turps, eh?'

'No,' I answered patiently. 'I was sober.'

'Oh, I see. Just feeling unwell.'

'I'm after Fred Drummond,' I said, allowing him his limp facetiousness. 'I believe he trains here.'

'He does,' he said. 'He's up at the moment.'

'Up?'

'Flying.'

'Is he any good?' I was making conversation. Fred Drummond's machine-gun skills were of no real interest to me.

'Dunno,' said the airman. 'Seems OK. Had no complaints.'

'You don't think he's, well, a bit touchy?'

'Don't really know 'im, mate. He keeps to himself pretty much. We get a lot of blokes through here. He doesn't stand out. That'll be him now.'

The rough chug of the Wackett's engine grew louder as it came into view. It flew in low across the river and wobbled towards the runway. From where I was standing behind the fence I could see Fred clearly as the Wackett passed overhead.

In an action that must have been contrary to the regulations, he turned what I thought was the gun in our direction. I threw myself to the ground, painfully jarring my plastered arm. I expected a spray of bullets. When none came I raised my eyes and saw the airman shaking his head in disbelief.

'Jesus, mate, you'll break the other one if you're not careful.'

'He turned those guns on us. I thought he was going to shoot.'

The airman laughed.

'Bullshit,' he said. 'There are no guns in a Wackett. He must have been mucking about. Maybe you're just not used to them coming in so low. Got a fright.'

The aircraft landed and came to a stop. I stood up and dusted my trousers with my good hand. I felt foolish. Fred Drummond was nuts — I was sure of that — but even he wasn't crazy enough to strafe civilians.

'I'll tell 'im you want to see 'im,' the airman said, and walked towards the stationary Wackett. Two figures had emerged from its cockpit and were conferring. The airman joined them and pointed in my direction. They were too far away from me to hear what they were saying. I imagine he was telling them the hilarious story of my diving to the ground to avoid being machine-gunned by an imaginary weapon. Fred detached himself from the conversation and headed in my direction. I would be lying if I said I wasn't nervous. I didn't present a very intimidating figure with my broken arm, my swollen eye, and my bicycle. I was glad that there was a fence between us.

Fred Drummond's eyes were fixed on mine as he approached. There was something about his eyes that was creepy. They had a dull sheen to them, and there was no warmth there. They were like the unforgiving eyes of a shark or a leopard. When he got to within a few feet of the fence he stopped, laughed like a child, and pointed at my eye.

'Ouch,' he said. 'I don't remember breaking your arm, though.'

'You didn't. Well, not directly.'

'Yeah. I heard you fell off the stage. That must've been funny. Wish I'd seen it.'

'I guess you were too busy being beaten up yourself.'

'Those arseholes. They'll keep. I've got big plans for them.'

He shifted gear rapidly, moving from infantile glee to itchy anger with no stops in between.

Up to this point, I thought the conversation had been going quite well, considering that one of us was unhinged. I thought I would try to shock him into a sort of clarity by confronting head on what was between us.

'Sergeant Topaz thinks I murdered your sister. I didn't.'

I waited for the explosion. There wasn't one. Instead, in a calm voice, he said, 'Topaz is a dickhead. Polly might be alive. Maybe she took off, like my brother. Maybe you know something about that.'

'Fred,' I said, growing uneasy and fearing that the temporarily composed person before me might blow up in my face at any moment. 'I didn't have anything to do with Polly's disappearance, and I don't know where she is now. Why would I come here if I had anything to hide?'

'Because you're scared of me.' The mad sometimes speak the truth because they don't understand the social advantages of lying.

'If that were true, Fred, wouldn't I stay out of your way?'

'Not if you're not very smart, but think that you are. Not if you think you can talk me out of thumping you.'

My good eye quickly glanced from left to right. The fence between us was reassuringly high and extensive. I was safe from Fred's fists for the moment.

'What's your name again?' he asked, and screwed up his face.

'It really isn't a hard name to remember,' I said. I did not refresh his memory. That would have felt too much like giving in.

Without warning, and as if he'd been hit by a jolt of electricity, he leapt to the wire with the speed of a predator and curled his long fingers through it. His hands seemed even more enormous than when I had first seen them at the Drummond house. I drew back involuntarily, the way you do when a caged animal throws itself at the bars in a zoo.

'Listen,' he said. His tone was now weirdly conspiratorial. This mercurial shift of emotional states was frightening. 'I was only winding you up, all right? I know now that you didn't kill Polly. And I know that she's dead, too. Topaz is right about that. She hasn't run away. She's dead. And I know who killed her.'

'How do you know?' I asked nervously. I suddenly thought that my original suspicion had been right. He knew who had killed his sister because he had.

'I just know, that's all, and they'll pay. The coppers won't catch them, but they'll pay.'

'"They?"'

'What?'

'"They." You said, "they'll pay".'

He smirked at me.

'Bad grammar, huh?' he said.

He stepped back from the fence, undid the buttons of his fly, and urinated copiously and insultingly practically at my feet. He did not turn his stream directly on me, but he shook his penis vigorously when he had finished, and in the process — and I'm sure not accidentally — propelled a few drops through the fence. At least one drop landed on my face, at the corner of my mouth. I was rigid with revulsion.

'We only came down to refuel,' he said. 'I'm going up again.'
He turned and walked back towards the Wackett.

'Who's *they*?' I shouted after him. 'Who's *they*?'

Too late, I realised that I had not wiped away the droplet of
his piss. It rolled into my mouth, filling it with the acrid taste
of Fred's micturition. I had become a magnet for his disgusting
body fluids.

I watched him speak with his flight instructor before they
clambered into the cockpit. It trundled down the runway and
climbed into air as if it were stumbling up invisible steps. I
retrieved the bicycle from where it was leaning against the fence
and threw my leg over it. The Wackett rumbled, stuttered, and
was suddenly silent. I looked up, and saw it frozen for a second
against the sky. Then it dropped like a stone into the Mary
River. It shattered as if it had hit concrete, and the pieces sank
from sight.

The bodies of the instructor and Fred Drummond were
retrieved later that day.

Chapter Four

SO MANY QUESTIONS

IN ORDER TO AVOID THE NASTY SURPRISE of the unexpected visit from Peter Topaz — he seemed to be a master of these — I cycled straight from the airfield to the police station, feeling with each turn of the pedals a growing resentment towards him and the world in general. The fates themselves were conspiring against me, and I allowed myself an absurd little burst of fury, expressed as an obscenity and directed at Fred Drummond, who had had the gall to fall to his death within minutes of speaking to me.

Topaz wasn't at the station. The surly creature behind the desk, who was afflicted with an adenoidal problem which only surgery or death could correct, said that he'd been called out to help search a patch of scrub on the outskirts of town. There had been the report of a body of a woman being seen there. This turned out to be mischievous, so Topaz was not in his usual state of half-suspended laconia when he arrived back. He was frankly pissed off. In my increasingly paranoid relations with him I immediately panicked and thought that he would assume I had been responsible for the vexatious false sighting. When he came into the station his anger was still so fierce that he didn't acknowledge me with the carefully crafted smile I had come to realise was his trademark. He simply indicated with a nod that I should follow him.

We sat in an airless room where the trivial emotions of small-town criminals had rendered the atmosphere so stale that I found it difficult to breathe. Topaz sat opposite me and waited for me to speak. He didn't have to wait long. I blurted out, 'I didn't make that call.' I sounded like a frightened schoolboy trying to duck the blame.

'I didn't think that you did. Why would I think that?'

I recovered my composure.

'I see. So you're quite happy to believe that I could kill someone, but you don't think I am sufficiently anti-social to make a nuisance phone-call.'

He was not in the mood for conversation.

'Why are you here? Come to confess?'

'Fred Drummond is dead.'

That stopped him. I didn't know, until this moment, that news of death could be a mood elevator. Topaz's annoyance fell away and he leaned forward, his eyes enlivened by the thrill of the hunt.

'What have you done with his body?'

It was my turn to be pulled up short. My God, what kind of a person did Topaz think I was?

'I didn't kill him,' I said, my voice flying an octave above its normal range. 'I went to the airport, just to speak to him. To clear things up. To get him to see that I had had nothing to do with Polly's disappearance. Nothing. I spoke to him, and he said that he knew that already, or rather that he knew it now, and that he knew who'd done it and that he was going to get them. He said "them". Then he pissed, practically on my shoes, and went up for a training flight. The motor cut out and the plane crashed into the river. That's what I know. And that's all I know.'

Topaz stood up and went into the outer office. I assumed he was making a phone call. He returned and said, 'The RAAF is searching the river.'

If I'd been able to fold my arms in a triumphant 'So there!' I would have done so. I had to settle for arranging my features into a facial equivalent.

'I suppose you think I sabotaged the aircraft,' I said.

'The RAAF will investigate what went wrong. It's not a police matter.'

'Poor Mrs Drummond. Who'll look after her now?'

'There's another son. He's up north somewhere. We'll find him and let him know.'

Having been energised by the electric possibility that I had been about to confess, he smiled at me before saying, 'You can go.'

Before leaving, I turned and said, 'I'm not guilty of anything, you know.'

He just made a steeple with his fingers and said, 'We're all guilty of something, Will.'

Two days after Fred's accident, Polly's body was brought down from the water tower. That it might have been a suicide was ruled out of contention. The *Chronicle* gleefully reported that the ladder that led to the rim of the tower was ten feet off the ground. Another ladder would have to have been used to reach the attached ladder. No such ladder was found lying at the scene, and so it was assumed that whoever had brought it there had taken it away with him after he had dumped the body. Given the weight of a dead body, the suspect must have been strong and, presumably, male. There was an unsubtle suggestion in the report that the murder must have been committed by a newcomer to the town. A local would not have fouled his own water supply. Short of actually naming me, the reporter could not have alerted his readers more obviously to my position as chief suspect. This was what I said when I put the paper down in the kitchen of the George Hotel the morning after the discovery of Polly's body. Tibald, Annie, and Augie were the only people there to hear my indignation. They had the decency to reassure me, quite firmly, that they did not believe that I was the culprit.

'The town is full of strangers, Will,' Annie said.

'That's right,' said Augie. 'There must be a thousand RAAF people here for a start. We don't know what that girl got up to or who she knew. Pardon me if that sounds offensive or disrespectful.'

I looked at Augie Kelly. There was a change in him. The growing reputation of his hotel had propelled him into a fierce regime of personal hygiene — his hair was trimmed and carefully oiled, and his face was shaven with a barber's professional closeness. He was comprehensively shevelled. Even his shoes were polished, and the hair which spilled from his shirt collar clipped.

'No one here really thinks you're a killer, Will,' said Annie. 'It's too absurd.'

She put her hand on my good arm, reassuringly.

'Not even Bill Henty?' I asked.

'What about me?' Henty had come into the kitchen just as I had spoken his name. He was wearing khaki shorts and had a towel draped around his shoulders. He had been exercising vigorously, and was sweating profusely.

'They've found that girl's body,' said Annie. 'I was just assuring Will that none of us believe he's got anything to do with it. Not now that, you know, she's actually dead.'

Henty wiped his face with one end of the towel and sniffed.

'Like Tibald said, we're all capable of murder.'

'Bill,' Annie said. 'You don't really think …'

'Let's wait and see. That's all I'm saying. What do you say, Tibald?'

Tibald turned from the stove and said that as far he was concerned a man was innocent until proven otherwise. I was glad to hear him say this — it seemed to be a retreat from his earlier position — but the effect was spoiled when he added that sometimes this tenet was difficult to justify.

Henty then said, smugly, 'Augie, get us a beer, will you? I can't go into the bar like this.'

I got to my feet, threw Henty a contemptuous if bruised glance, and went up to my room. Before leaving, though, I leaned down and kissed Annie lightly on the cheek.

'Thank you,' I said quietly. She reached up, covered my hand with hers, and gave it a squeeze. Through all the hideousness, and despite my rising anger at Henty's words — and, for some reason, his bare, obsessively sculpted chest exacerbated that anger — through all this, that small squeeze sent a charge through me that travelled directly to my private parts. I had to stop myself from saying out loud that Annie Hudson did indeed resemble Greer Garson.

I lay on my bed, trying to get things in order. I knew that Topaz would arrive soon with more questions and impertinent accusations. I was surprised that he hadn't come last night. He couldn't arrest me, although he no doubt wanted to. At any rate, I assumed that he couldn't arrest me. I was a bit murky on this area of the law and whether it applied anyway in such a remote town. He would surely need some substantial evidence before he consigned me to the earthen-floored hell of a Maryborough jail. I was not, however, confident about this. Perhaps suspects were thrown into prison here as a matter of course.

My arm was aching, my eye was tender, and I had a headache that felt as if all it needed was a gentle push to result in bleeding from the ears. I also had an erection. The images flooding my brain, and by extension my penis, were, my God, images of me making love to Annie Hudson. What was wrong with me? Was I aroused by a woman's pity? Knowing that women responded positively to wounded men, I suspected that Annie's sympathy was partly the result of my injuries. I could not explain my own attraction to her so neatly. She was, after all, receiving the priceless gift of Peter Topaz's nocturnal emissions. I wasn't sure of this, but I had every reason to believe that it was so. My sudden desire was not unreasonable, or inexplicable. She was, after all, a woman of considerable charms. My attraction could hardly be an expression of some kind of as yet undescribed fetish.

I was about to relieve myself of this unwanted, but not unwelcome, bout of erotic yearning when there was a knock on the door. It opened before I had a chance to call 'Wait!', and Augie Kelly entered to the sight of me fumbling with my flies. At least I had brought nothing forth.

'It is customary to wait until you're invited in,' I snapped. If I hadn't been so cross, and therefore obviously guilty of something, he would not have realised that he had caught me in flagrante delicto solo, as it were.

'Sorry,' he said, and then, in an attempt at conciliation, 'It must be difficult with only one hand free. You should get someone to help you.'

It would be an understatement to say that I was flabbergasted by his lewdness. I suppose he thought he was being blokey, or letting me see that he was a man of the world, unfussed by the libidinous pursuits of others. Well, I wasn't going to behave like a shy teenager.

'And who would you suggest, Mr Kelly? Do you have a sister who is looking for work?'

He laughed the laugh of a man who was sisterless.

'I don't think you need to look any further than Miss Hudson,' he said.

Those weird, green eyes missed nothing. I had underestimated Mr Kelly. Perhaps, though, he was alert to what had passed between Annie and me because his own interest in her had not gone unnoticed by me. Jealousy improves eyesight. Indeed, it improves upon eyesight. I pushed the pillows against the bed-head and propped myself up.

'What can I do for you, Mr Kelly?'

'Please, call me Augie. There's no need for all this formality. I just caught you having a toss, for God's sake.'

I coughed uncomfortably, and to cover my embarrassment said, 'It's an unusual name, Augie is.'

'It's short for Augustus,' he said, letting me off the hook, but letting me know that that was exactly what he was doing.

'Augustus Kelly,' I said, and thought it was rather too grand a name to wear in a town without trees. I didn't say so because I didn't think I had the upper hand. He pulled a chair up and sat at the foot of my bed.

'Even if people stop coming,' he said suddenly, 'you can stay here.'

I was surprised by the intensity with which he said this. There was a tiny, almost imperceptible tremor in his voice.

'People won't stop coming, Augie. If anything, they'll come in droves, hoping to get a glimpse of Jack the Ripper. It's a bargain. They get a good meal and a shiver of horror, and all for a few bob. It's better than the pictures.'

'I'm just saying, you can stay here, whatever happens.'

There was that tiny tremor of emotion again. Had he been drinking?

I felt grateful for this show of support, especially as he seemed so sincere about it, but I changed my mind when I looked into his murky eyes. He was acting. He was good, but he was acting. I knew what Kelly was up to. He thought that I would be out of the way soon, that I would be carted off to jail. That would ensure that Tibald would stay. Without me the troupe would disband, and they would all need jobs. Augie would have an already broken-in workforce at his disposal.

'To be perfectly honest, Will,' he said, reading my mind and retreating from his sentiment. 'Tibald is the real reason you don't have to go. The man is a genius. I just tasted this soup thing he's made for tonight. Everyone gets just a mouthful. We're not even counting it as a course.'

'It's called an *amuse gueule*,' I said coolly.

'That's what he called it, but I don't speak Latin.'

'It's not Latin. Look, never mind.'

Augie's frank admission of the basis of my remaining welcome had taken a good deal of the warmth, even if it had been acted warmth, out of the earlier gesture.

'He's made it out of chokos. Can you believe that? I hate chokos, but this is …' He groped for the word.

'Sublime?' I offered, wishing that he would take his hairy arms and return to the kitchen.

'Exactly,' he said, and his face was lit momentarily by the

rapturous recollection of the taste of Tibald's choko reduction. 'I'm getting the boiler fixed,' he added, 'so we'll have hot water. Soon.'

'Any moment you'll be telling me people want to stay here.'

'But they do. I've had several RAAF officers interested in moving their wives across from the Royal. But we're not ready for that yet. It's all a bit rundown.'

'But it's good enough for a murder suspect.' And his leading lady, I thought, but didn't say it. Augie smiled. Although it wasn't quite as calculated as the Topaz smile, it lacked the generosity of the real thing.

'Yes, Will,' he said. 'It's good enough for a murder suspect.' With that he patted my knee, stood up, and said, 'It's probably a good idea if you don't help at dinner yet. Your eye is, well, it's unsightly and … people eating, that sort of thing.'

'Fine,' I said.

❧

Augie Kelly had barely closed the door when three short, sharp raps preceded the entry of Peter Topaz. He was brusque and to the point.

'This is now officially a murder investigation, and I need you to accompany me to the station.'

Wearily I rolled off the bed and held out my good hand as if to receive handcuffs.

'Don't be melodramatic,' he said. 'This isn't a Hollywood gangster picture.'

I walked with Peter Topaz from the George to the police station. He said very little. He seemed preoccupied. The silence made me uncomfortable, which perhaps was what was intended. I felt conspicuous, too, with my arm in a sling and with a police escort. Several people stared at us, and I fancied that more than one of them whispered to their companions.

'This is humiliating,' I said. 'I've done nothing wrong. It looks like I'm being taken in for questioning.'

'You are being taken in for questioning.'

'Outrageous,' I said sulkily.

'Why don't you do yourself a favour and accept the fact that you were the last person to see her alive and that we might be interested in that small fact.'

'I was not the last person ...'

'Shut up, Will.'

He said this so savagely that I was shocked into silence.

I took Topaz's coolness towards me personally. It might seem odd, but it bothered me that his certainty about my guilt was getting in the way of his liking me. As we approached the police station I had the ghastly realisation that I had been looking forward to impressing him with our production of *Titus Andronicus*. Let me tell you, your chances of showing off are severely diminished by the possibility that you might have murdered someone.

Inside the police station, Topaz put me in the room where he had interviewed me previously. He left, and I sat for ten minutes breathing its foetid, dead air. I presumed this was a police device for unsettling a suspect. It worked. When he returned he brought with him a tall, unnaturally thin man with dark, straight hair in need of a trim, and with a prominent Adam's apple. He was wearing a suit. It was not a very good suit, but a suit nonetheless.

'This is Detective Sergeant Conroy,' said Topaz. 'He's heading the investigation, and he'll be asking the questions.'

Conroy had large, brown eyes, and one of them quivered in its socket in the most disconcerting manner. He took in the person before him — me — and sat down. Topaz sat at his side, but slightly behind him. Before Conroy spoke, he cleared his throat noisily.

'I 'spose you're gonna tell me we're pickin' on you because you're with the circus.'

Who on earth did he think he was talking to? I felt a rush of indignation that he would mistake me for one of those squalid, shifty, slightly sinister circus types. Hadn't Topaz briefed him at all? These thoughts crashed through my headache and came out in the form of an incredulous 'Whaaaa?'

Conroy, who had affected to be checking some notes, looked up at me.

'Is something wrong?'

'I am not,' I said, trying to summon the dignity that would support what I was about to say, 'I am not a member of a travelling circus. I am an actor. Do I look like some swarthy gypsy?'

'To be frank, Mr Power, just at the minute you look like shit.'

'Obviously, you're not seeing me at my best.'

I caught Topaz's eye and detected a smirk.

'We won't keep you, Mr Power,' said Conroy. 'This isn't a formal interview. We're not keeping a record of it. I wanted to introduce myself, get a few details from you, and let you know that you're not to leave town for the time being. OK?'

The 'OK' was spoken with the condescension usually reserved for the very young or the very, very old.

'Just ask your questions and get it over with,' I said resignedly.

At the end of my informal interview with Detective Sergeant Conroy, I felt wrung out by the conflicting emotions raging within. On the one hand, I felt mortified by Conroy's failure to make even the slightest feint at an assumption of my innocence; and on the other, I felt a sort of elation at having been able to provide him with a list of alternative suspects. There was

Smelt, who'd come with Polly to the first dinner at the George, and there was the chap who'd told Polly to warn Fred about the money he owed — the same chap who had inadvertently rescued me from Fred's fists. There was Fred himself, of course, although his being dead was inconvenient. Apart from anything else, he was the only other person who could have corroborated that when I left the Drummond house Polly was still alive. Mrs Drummond could not be relied upon to give an accurate account. The fact that Polly had left soon after wasn't helpful, but Fred would have told the police eventually what he told me — that he knew I was innocent and that he knew who was guilty. There were the circus people and the RAAF people …

'Thank you, Mr Power,' Conroy said when I ran all this by him. 'We are not stupid.' He made a play of writing down the names of the individuals I had mentioned, but it was clear that his heart wasn't in it.

'And I,' I said, 'am not guilty.'

He managed an ugly little grin when I said that, and his quivering eye seemed to quiver just a little bit more.

By the time I reached the point where I was to cross Kent Street it was four o'clock, and the bicycle exodus from Walkers Engineering had begun. I scanned faces as they whizzed past in their hundreds, but I did not see the man who had belted Fred Drummond so viciously at the ACF dance. He was bound to be among the riders, but spotting him would have been like trying to identify a particular bird in a flock of flamingos. I didn't have any clear notion of what I would do if I saw him. It occurred to me, though, as the moving blur of cyclists passed, that I could not sit back and allow Topaz and Conroy to build a case against me unopposed. I had an advantage over them. I was able to eliminate their chief suspect. I wasn't hamstrung by the limiting belief that this murder had been committed by William Power.

When Kent Street had been cleared of cycle traffic I crossed it, and before I had reached the opposite footpath I had made the decision that I would nail Polly's killer. I was able to think confidently of nailing the killer because it was broad daylight. and I had not properly considered that the process might be a dangerous one. My bravura was, I realised later that night, attached to the absurd belief that I could organise clearing my name along the lines of a three-act murder mystery. Standing on the corner of Kent Street I had been swept away by the imagined climax of presenting the culprit to Topaz and Conroy, trussed and bleating his guilt, in a brilliant *coup de théâtre*. Reclining in the tepid waters of the bath that night, it occurred to me that the person who had killed Polly Drummond might resist discovery, and would, quite likely, use any means to do so, including killing again. The chap seeking to nail him might be a prime candidate. I would need help, and I believed that I could call on Arthur's loyalty to assist me.

I didn't linger in the bath. The cast on my arm had taken most of the pleasure out of a good, long soak. I could tell from the noise coming up from downstairs that the dining room was full. Arthur wouldn't be back in his room for two more hours at least. I used the time to try to sort out a plan. I made a list of people I wanted to talk to. It was a small list of three.

—Man on bicycle.

—Smelt.

—The person Polly visited after we had watched the circus come to town.

This was discouraging. I had no idea how to find the person whose name I knew, let alone the other two. I also jotted down, 'Search Drummond house'. Polly had said that she kept a diary; such a diary might contain a vital clue, or the names of her friends. It would have been unnatural, also, if I had not been curious to read her impressions of me. The police may have already found this item, but I had no way of knowing this, and there was every chance that they had overlooked it. Just reading my jottings made me nervous. I believed, though, that this was something I had to do, and how difficult could it be? Mrs Drummond slept deeply, that much I already knew, and she wasn't exactly compos mentis. I could hold a bagpipe rehearsal in Polly's bedroom and it wouldn't register.

When I told Arthur my plans, he was enthusiastic but a bit wary about the house search. 'If you get caught you'll be charged with burglary on top of everything else. My God, they'll think you're a one-man crime wave.'

'I won't get caught and I'm not stealing anything. It's more of an unannounced visit than a break and enter.' I failed to mention that his being with me was a part of the plan. He wasn't ready to hear this. He then made a brilliant suggestion.

'You should go to the funeral tomorrow.'

'Is it tomorrow?'

'The notice is in the *Chronicle*. It's for both of them. It would be good to see who turns up.'

The funeral was a big affair. It would have been cruel to expect Mrs Drummond to bury her children on separate occasions, so there were two caskets in the aisle of the Lutheran Church in John Street. The church was crowded. There were many uniforms there, but the majority of mourners were civilians. I arrived late, not wanting to draw attention to myself, and stood in the shadows at the back. I was not the only latecomer, and was soon hemmed in. An order of service had been distributed at the door, and when I ran my eye over it there were no names that were known to me. It provided me, though, with a more complete list of people I would need to talk to.

The eulogies for Polly were quite moving. A young woman, Shirley Moynahan, who said that she was her closest friend, spoke of Polly's love of the movies and her generosity. It was a pity somebody hadn't given her words (she read them) a quick once-over. This would have eliminated the poor grammar, which rather spoiled the effect — for me, anyway. She broke down halfway through, and had to be helped to her seat. There were three other speakers for Polly. Only one person spoke for Fred. This was an air force officer who gave the unfortunate impression that he didn't know Fred all that well. Indeed, he seemed anxious to let the assembly know that Fred wasn't actually a good friend, but more a subordinate under his command. This was a duty eulogy, not a cry from the heart.

Mrs Drummond didn't speak. She was protected from the hideous, wrenching tragedy of the double burial by her madness. At least I thought this until I saw her face as she walked behind the coffins as they were carried out of the church. She looked stricken. There was no protective madness here, just the raw and savage truth of almost incomprehensible grief. As she passed, she caught my eye, and she stopped. One hand went to her mouth, and the other pointed at me. It trembled in the air, and many eyes followed the direction of the pointing finger. Because of the crush of people around me, it couldn't have been clear to observers whom she was indicating. A sudden shriek echoed through the church. It sounded like the word 'Him!', but it was entangled in the frightful sounds that wrapped themselves around it as they emerged from Mrs Drummond's throat. She fell to the ground, and in the confusion I pushed my way out of the church and into the grey day outside. Before I had reached the gate, a voice called out, 'Wait a minute.'

It was Augie Kelly.

'What are you doing here?' I asked, puzzled. He had made a serious effort to present himself as the sophisticated hotelier he felt he had become.

'Paying my respects,' he said. 'It doesn't hurt to be seen at these things in a small town. Show you care, that you're part of a community. That sort of thing.'

'So you see all these grieving people as potential clients.'

'If they breathe, they eat, and they might as well eat at the George.'

He had the grace to laugh. I couldn't laugh with him because Mrs Drummond's hysterical outburst had unsettled me, and it was still ringing in my ears. How many people had realised that her finger had been pointed at me? How many would report this terrifying *J'accuse* to the police?

Augie walked with me back to the George. We made small talk about the hotel and how everything was going so well. He pretended to be interested in *Titus Andronicus*, but I knew that he was hopeful its premiere would be delayed as long as possible. He hadn't thought about who he would employ to wait on tables when we were performing. I was able to reassure him that my injuries were interfering with rehearsals, which would almost certainly mean a postponement of opening night.

When we reached the George, I went into the kitchen to see Tibald. Walter Sunder was there. I hadn't seen him for a couple of days and I assumed he had been immersed in learning the script. He suddenly seemed like an old man, much older than his sixty-five years.

'I'm not well,' he said, and left the kitchen.

'What's wrong with him?' I asked.

'He wants to leave,' Tibald said, without looking up from his surgical preparation of a bullock's heart.

'Why?'

'He's tired, and he doesn't want to work for a man who murders young women.'

Tibald's tone was as neutral as if he had asked me to pass him the salt.

'Oh, really?' I said, exasperated. 'I thought he'd have more sense.'

Tibald looked up when I said that.

'Why?' he asked. 'Because he's older than the rest of us? That's not sixty-five years of accumulated wisdom, you know. It's sixty-five years of accumulated stupidity.'

'Still, I'm disappointed. I'll talk to him.'

Tibald shrugged and went back to the bloodied mess that would cause small moans of pleasure to escape from diners that night. I could not beard Walter immediately. It was imperative that I speak to Arthur. He did not yet know that I had woven him into my scheme. His wariness about my involvement in a burglary escalated into dismay when I told him I needed him to come with me to the Drummond house that night.

'We've only got two arms between us,' I said. 'That's the bare minimum required for burglary.'

There were several arguments that Arthur put forward in favour of staying safely at the George. He pointed out, quite reasonably, that after the trauma of the funeral Mrs Drummond would surely have company. I said that the people who were at the funeral were there for Polly. Possibly some were there for Fred, and probably a good number were there because in Maryborough a funeral constituted a day out. Mrs Drummond was so peculiar, I argued, that even if she did have friends to support her she would probably order them out of the house at her earliest convenience, with the charge of being a papist hurled at their backs. Arthur wasn't convinced.

'All right,' I said. 'I won't ask you to come into the house with me. Wait at the gate and warn me if anyone arrives.'

'And how will I do that? Whistle something from Gilbert and Sullivan? Cough in Morse code?'

'I have to do this, Arthur. I don't care how insane it seems. My life might depend on this. Please don't throw obstacles in my way.'

This was the first time I had spoken aloud the dread that had been percolating through me ever since Topaz first voiced his suspicions.

'They could hang me, Arthur. They could pin this on me and hang me.'

I had been standing up while Arthur sat on the edge of his bed, but when I heard myself utter the word 'hang' I felt weak at the knees and had to sit beside him.

'All right,' he said quietly. 'I'll do it. I'll come with you. But I'm not going into the house. And they can't hang you in Queensland. There's no death penalty here.'

I should have felt relieved to hear that. But I didn't.

At 2.00 am we went downstairs quietly and passed through the dining room on our way to the front door. Just as we were about to reach it, it opened, and two figures entered. We dropped below a table. The figures stopped within a few feet of us and moved together in an embrace.

'Not here,' said Adrian. 'Upstairs.'

The other man laughed softly and said, 'I hope you can take nine inches.'

'I can give it, and I can take it,' whispered Adrian, and the two of them headed upstairs.

'Honestly,' I said. 'Living opposite the wharf, Adrian's like a kid in a toy shop.'

Outside, the air was cool and moist, and it was so dark I could barely see my hand in front of my face. Thick clouds obscured the moon completely and there was not even the faintest wash of light. There was barely a breath of wind. The Mary River slapped against its banks, and the vague odour of its swampy edges wafted on the air. We moved quickly up March Street, away from the wharf where, even at this hour, people were working. By the time we'd crossed Alice Street, not a soul stirred. In less than fifteen minutes we had turned into Queen Street and we were only a block from the Drummond house in Richmond Street. When we reached its gate, we stopped and spoke for the first time since setting out.

'We're here,' I said unnecessarily.

'That's exactly what Polly said that time we came here.'

The house loomed in the darkness, the trees that softened its outlines by day forming frightening shapes by night. The palms on either side of the staircase looked like shadowy sentries. We opened the gate, expecting it to creak alarmingly. Its well-oiled hinges swung soundlessly.

'This is as far as I go,' whispered Arthur. 'That was the deal.'

I walked around the side of the house, not wanting to enter it from the street. The back stairs were not as grand as those at the front. They were steeply pitched with a rail that had become splintery over time. They had been well made, though, and did not offer any complaint as my feet met them, one by one. My heart was racing, and I had to pause to gather my nerve. The silence, which should have been my ally, felt threatening, as if it contained something secret and nasty. I had brought a torch with me, with all but a narrow line of its face blacked out. I turned it on and directed the feeble beam towards the doorhandle of the back door. I hadn't given much thought to what I would do if the doors were locked. I was counting on Mrs Drummond being too batty to bother. I tried the knob and it turned, the tongue sliding smoothly out of its catch. I pushed gently and the door opened inwards. The house exhaled a waft of warm, slightly stale air ... and something else. I couldn't place it, but my nose is a sensitive instrument, and there was an odour, drifting among the household smells, that was sweetly metallic. I closed the door gently. The click as the latch fell into place sounded to my nervous ear like a gunshot. My senses were so alert, so taut with the fear of discovery, that I felt rather than heard a movement in a further room. It was almost as if I were feeling the sudden tensing of someone else's muscles. I strained eyes and ears for the faintest indication that I had been heard. Nothing. I must have been mistaken.

With the sliver of torchlight pointed at the floor I walked slowly across the kitchen and entered the room where Polly and Fred had fought. My pulse quickened inexplicably. Some instinct was racing ahead of sensory awareness, warning me that all was not as it should be. The room was empty, but there it was again, a rustle from one of the rooms on the other side of the living room. It was little more than a vibration in the air which reached me like a tiny shock wave. I understood instinctively that this was not Mrs Drummond moving about. The sound was too minimal, too furtive, too disciplined, too aware of me. Someone else was searching the house. A person keeping Mrs Drummond company would not choose to move about in complete darkness. I switched off my torch and tried to suppress the panic that was rising in me. Moving slowly into the deepest darkness of the living room, I waited.

I didn't have to wait long. The door to the hallway opened, its whiteness reflecting the minimal light available. I wondered if the sling on my arm offered a pallid sail that would give me away. A figure that was no more than a shadow entered the room. He stood for a moment as if listening. I was certain it was a man. How could he not hear my heart beating? He was like darkness gathered and shaped into human form. I sensed that he was staring into the blackness where I stood, deciding what to do. My eyes lost his outline for a moment. He merged into the night around him and then he was gone. He slipped into the kitchen, and I heard the back door click shut behind him. He made no attempt to soften the sound. I took a few shallow breaths. My extremities had turned cold, and my guts were churning. Nausea flooded my body, and I sat down in the nearest chair. It was the chair Mrs Drummond had fallen asleep in the night I was here.

I willed myself to stand up and enter the hallway from which the bedrooms radiated. Common sense told me to leave, to follow the intruder's lead and get away from the house. Uncommon sense compelled me to find out what he had been looking for. I switched on the torch again and picked my way towards a half-open door. I edged my way in, and was instantly aware of a concentrating of the odour I had detected on entering the kitchen. There was no sound of breathing, so I supposed that this was not where Mrs Drummond was sleeping. I moved towards the bulky shape of a bed, and as I approached it the smell got stronger and my shoes slipped on something wet on the floor. The weak torchlight illuminated a glistening puddle of a liquid which appeared black, like oil. I knew immediately that it was blood, and dropped the torch as the awful jolt of horror struck me. Without thinking, I dropped to my knees and scrabbled about for it with my free hand. It had rolled under the bed. I could see its narrow beam. Lying flat, I wriggled towards it and grabbed it with fingers now sticky with blood. My shirt and trousers clung wetly to me, having mopped up a good deal of the blood on the floor. I stood at the foot of the bed, my mind blank. I couldn't shine the torch towards the pillow because I didn't want to see what I knew was there.

'Will?'

Arthur's voice came from the doorway. I could form no words but uttered an incoherent, animal sound. He switched on the light to reveal a tableau of indescribable violence. It took a moment to adjust to the burning glare of the overhead globe, and then the full force of the scene assaulted my eyes. I saw Mrs Drummond, propped on pillows, her throat so savagely cut that her head lolled to one side, attached only by a few tenacious sinews. Her bed was awash with her blood, and the floor ran with it. I also saw Arthur, staring not at Mrs Drummond's body, but at me. I realised when I looked down at myself that I was drenched with blood, and it must have appeared that I had grappled with the victim.

'No,' I said, 'No. I dropped the torch. See, there. There!' I pointed to a patch of smeared blood on the floor. 'It went under the bed.'

There was desperation in my voice. Arthur looked at the smear, then back at me, and I saw that he believed me.

'Someone came out of the house,' he said, 'and brushed past me. I thought something was wrong.'

'What will we do?' My voice cracked — the physical expression of how close I was to breaking down.

'We can't be the ones to report this,' he said. 'They'll arrest you if they know you were here. We have to make sure they don't find that out.'

I was powerless to argue or to act. I looked at him dumbly.

'Don't move,' he said sharply. His eyes roamed the room. There was a chest of drawers near the door. Taking a handkerchief from his pocket, he opened a drawer, using the cloth as a barrier against fingerprints. He pulled out a sheet, folded it into a square, and put it on the ground. He took another piece of cloth — a towel this time — from the drawer, and threw it to me.

'Take off your shoes, but not your socks, and throw them onto the sheet.'

I followed his instructions, not understanding what he was doing.

'See where you've left shoe prints? Wipe them away with the towel, then wipe your hands as much as possible and throw the towel onto the sheet.'

I mopped away the impressions left by my bloodied shoes.

'Now, don't walk in any more blood, but come across and stand on the sheet.'

I followed his directions without a murmur. He examined each foot to see whether or not any blood had soaked through to the woollen socks. It hadn't.

'Now listen to me carefully, Will. You have to hold the torch. It's got blood on it. You mustn't touch anything on the way out, and we have to wipe every surface you touched on the way in.'

He gathered the corners of the sheet together and wiped the doorhandle and the door's surface with his handkerchief, then wiped the light switch and flicked it off.

'Torch on,' he said.

I tried to recall everything I might have touched, but I was certain that the only surfaces I had come into contact with were the doors and the chair in the living room. He wiped its arms and then all the doors. The handle on the door through which I had entered the house was the last item he cleaned.

'We're destroying evidence the murderer might have left,' I said.

'Can't be helped.'

At the bottom of the stairs, breathing fresh, night air, my thoughts became more ordered.

'This can't be happening.'

'You can't go back to the hotel like that. Someone might see you. The river is at the end of the street. You'll have to wash there.'

Richmond Street ran down to the Mary River, or rather it petered out in a riot of scrub and riparian vegetation. Getting to the water would mean struggling through the tangle of bushes on its banks.

'Surely I can wash this off back at the George.' The sound of the river was intimidating, and the idea of sinking into it at night was unnerving. What predatory wildlife was lurking there? It was not a river that welcomed bathers. Rather, it sought to bar them with its fortifications of roots, vines, and mud — and its occasional shark, swimming into fresh water to rid itself of parasites. Arthur was firm.

'You're covered in blood. It's in your hair, on your face and I bet it's soaked through your clothes onto your skin. It's like dog shit. It's got wings. You look like you've been wallowing in the belly of a slaughtered bullock. You can't risk being seen like that. You need total immersion.'

He laid the sheet on the ground.

'Get undressed and put everything on the sheet. Everything. I'll get rid of them.'

'These are good pants. I've only got one other good pair.'

'I see. Well maybe you can wear them on the way to your jail cell.'

I began to undress.

'I can't walk back naked.'

'I'll go back to the George, get you a change of clothes, and be back here in half an hour. We don't have any options, or has that escaped your notice? You must have enough coupons to cover a pair of trousers.'

'It's not the coupons I'm worried about. It's the money. We're not exactly rolling in it.'

When I had thrown all my clothes onto the sheet, I began to shiver. It wasn't a particularly cold night, but my thermostat was responding in advance to my body entering the Mary River. I realised that Arthur had been right. The blood had soaked through the cotton of my shirt and trousers. I could feel it coagulating on my skin. Perhaps I was imagining it, but the chill which came up from the river did not settle on my body evenly. The blood, where it had dried, formed a sort of carapace against the cold.

'Sling,' Arthur said.

'What?'

'Sling. Take off the sling. It's caked.'

I took it off. The cast felt suddenly heavy. How on earth was I going to keep it dry?

Arthur gathered up the sheet.

'I'll get rid of this,' he said. 'I'm not sure how, but I'll think of something. I'll be back soon. Stay in the bushes.'

'I wasn't planning on ringing doorbells.'

Arthur headed off down Richmond Street. I called him back.

'Hey, Arthur.'

He came back, his bundle tucked under his one arm.

'Thanks. Thanks. I wouldn't like you to think I don't appreciate your help.'

He nodded and turned away again. I pushed my way into the scrub that stood between me and the river, and had gone only a few feet before my vulnerable body was scratched and irritated by branch and sharp-edged leaf. My feet were cut by jagged stones and tree roots. As I struggled towards the water the ground softened and the scrub gave way to grasses. Clay turned to sucking mud, into which I sank up to my knees. When I finally felt the chill of water, I was exhausted. I waded out until the river flowed over my chest. It was numbingly cold and the water tugged at me, wanting to take me with it. I held my plastered arm above my head, and with my free hand began the soapless task of cleaning Mrs Drummond's blood from my body.

I scrubbed hard, shuddering from the cold, but also from the hideous clarity with which her mutilated image returned. I ducked my head under to clean the matted blood from my hair. My first attempt at this almost unbalanced me. On my second, I simply bent my knees and kept the plaster upright, like a bizarre periscope. I held my breath for as long as I could, kneading my fingers through my hair, and came up gasping. I performed the manoeuvre one more time, and when I thrust my head out of the water it struck, with force, a tree branch being carried along by the current. Temporarily stunned by the blow, I dropped my plastered arm into the water. I felt my scalp release a rivulet of blood. My mind was a crowded, noisy place of panicky voices, and in one corner a sharp, insistent pain was asserting itself against the general clamour. The river was supposed to wash me clean. Instead it had inflicted yet another difficult-to-explain injury.

I returned to the bank the way I had come, sustaining more cuts, scratches, and bruises in the process. I sat down and waited for Arthur — cold, sore, and aching, and harassed by mosquitoes and an entomological encyclopaedia of insects. I was sure my body had become a surveyor's map of slashes and welts. When Arthur called my name, I don't think I have ever been more grateful to see a person. The bottom end of Richmond Street does not offer the amenities of Eden and is not the place to spend any more time naked than desperation demands.

I stank of the river, but Arthur cautioned against having a bath until the morning. He was right. The gurgle of pipes would draw attention to the fact that I had not been tucked up in bed — which is where I would be saying I had been when Mrs Drummond's body was found and the coppers came calling.

At an unsuspicious hour I bathed and shaved and washed my hair, and sluiced out the rank scum left behind. I was annoyed by the number of lacerations my body had sustained. Any one of them might erupt into infection. I would have to keep them cleaned and swabbed with peroxide. Most importantly, I would have to present myself at the hospital and explain how I had managed to saturate the inside of the cast. With teeth gritted I would have to accept the matron's suggestion that this, too, was the result of drunkenness.

At ten o'clock I endured the disapproval of the matron at the hospital as the cast was cut from my arm with vicious-looking shears. It was reset, and I was admonished that if this happened again I would have to suffer the discomfort and possible ghastly infection that might follow. There was a war on, and plaster didn't grow on trees. I held my tongue, allowing the assassination of my character as though it were a balm to my spirit. I might accept this woman's apology when the truth was finally told. Might. Through my indignation, I noticed again that she had splendid breasts.

I called the cast together at midday and told them that there was to be a line reading in the dining room at two o'clock. They groaned. The hall was not available because it was Saturday, and local urchins would be hurtling about its floor on roller skates. It had been days since the last rehearsal, and my troupe had become used to the seductively measured pace of small-town life. It occurred to me as I was talking to them that I had only a vague idea how each of them filled the day. I'd been distracted and hadn't paid any attention to their activities. I knew what Adrian did at night, but not what he did during the day — he slept, I supposed, like some species of nocturnal marsupial. Bill Henty exercised all day. I'd seen him setting out most mornings on some long-distance run. I hadn't felt any inclination to join him, despite his snide suggestion that it would do me no harm. Anybody who ran miles every day with nothing to show for it but wiry thighs was running away from something.

I knew what Tibald did. Annie? Trysts with Topaz? I didn't know for certain whether or not she had seduced him yet, but she'd had seventeen days in which to do it and I couldn't see either of them holding back. I felt a twinge of new jealousy about their friendship. I thought now that I could rely on Annie being a quiet advocate for me, if only because she thought I was too weak to commit a murder. As I looked at her sitting with her legs crossed elegantly and her neck arched sinuously, I realised that my feelings about her had always been deformed by the pressure I had exerted upon myself to resist being attracted to her. She was a lousy actress, I wasn't prepared to surrender that assessment, but she had something better than talent. She had the capacity to arouse lust.

Walter Sunder was at the meeting in the dining room. He sat with his arms folded, and he wouldn't meet my eye. I hadn't yet had a chance to talk to him about his decision to leave, but the strain of the previous night's events had exhausted my desire to convince him to stay. I had come to the conclusion, even as I was talking, that we could do without him. He wasn't a great actor, not even a good actor. He was serviceable, and it was useful to have a man his age to play the porter in *Macbeth* or Polonius in *Hamlet*. He didn't bring any new insights to his roles, but he said the lines, didn't fall over, and looked his age. More than that would have required talent he didn't have.

'Walter has decided to leave us,' I said, and there was not a trace of acrimony in my voice. This was not news to anybody. Clearly, Walter had let everybody know that he was leaving and he would not have neglected to say why.

'We wish him well in his retirement.'

He snorted quietly.

'What will you do?' I asked.

'I'm staying here.' There was more than a hint of defiance in his voice. 'Tibald needs help.'

'The company can't pay your board if you're not a part of it.' It was impossible not to sound churlish, but I saw no reason why we had to carry him. The thought of the 25 shillings and ten coupons I would have to pay for new trousers was nagging at me.

'Don't worry your head about it,' he said, and rose to leave. 'That's between me and Augie, and it's taken care of.'

He left the room.

'This means more rewrites,' I said, 'but this afternoon's reading is still on. I'll take Walter's part for the time being. I presume that everybody is line perfect by now. You've had plenty of time to get it off by heart.'

'It's a bit hard if you keep changing it,' said Kevin Skakel. Skakel was a dark horse, almost literally. He was in his late twenties, and had thick hair that was ink-black, and olive skin. Pale-blue eyes were thrown into high relief by the colour of his skin and hair. His features were the mismanaged melding of an Irish and continental heritage. At least that was the assumption I made. He was Catholic and attended mass regularly. Individually, there was nothing at all wrong with his features, but together they seemed ill-suited. Annie disagreed.

I know this because soon after Kevin joined us she told me that she thought he was interestingly put together and almost handsome.

'I couldn't make love to him, though,' she had said airily. 'I like men to have two good feet. And I'd prefer that they didn't go to church. I don't like the idea of being talked about in Confession.'

Kevin Skakel didn't speak up much, but his reserve was not shyness. Despite the limp that his clubfoot gave him, he carried himself well. He wasn't surly, but he was closed off somehow. I didn't really know him, and I don't think anybody else did either. He didn't give off an aura of loneliness, but he spent much of his time alone. He was perfectly happy to engage in conversation, but he never initiated one, and I never heard him offer an observation without first being pressed for one. He gave nothing away, which is why his remark about the changes I was obliged to make to the script were so singular.

'I can't force Walter to remain in the company, Kevin,' I said evenly. 'We all have to wear the consequences of his leaving, and we still have a show to put on.'

He turned his head slightly to one side and raised his eyebrows fractionally. It was a minimal gesture of disapproval, but also of acceptance. He offered no other comment. Here, I thought, was yet another person I could not trust.

The read-through went surprisingly well. I say 'surprisingly' because Bill Henty's hostility, although unexpressed, was expressive nonetheless, and Kevin Skakel was even more reserved than normal. They were professional, determinedly so, but even Miss Helen Keller would have noticed the *froideur*. I was relieved to discover that everyone had his or her lines down. They had not been slacking off. This was a timely reminder to me that the Power Players were not amateurs. At the end of the read-through the cast dispersed, but Annie Hudson remained behind.

'That was good,' she said. 'I always like this stage. You can see how it fits together, where the relationships are. I've got a good sense now of how to play her.'

I didn't want to deflate this bubble of enthusiasm by saying that the way Annie played her characters was indistinguishable, one from another. Lady Macbeth and Connie, the bad-breath girl? Same person. Until very recently I might have humorously pointed this out, but that was before I had been afflicted with the intensely pleasurable torture of wanting to sleep with her. I would have to seduce her. The thought made my stomach lurch. Did she know me too well? Did she look at me the way a loathsome, annoying brother is looked at? Could I compete with Topaz? My confidence drained away at a rate of knots and I marvelled, not for the first time, at how easily a woman can unman a chap.

'Will? Why are you staring at me like that? Stop it. It's giving me the creeps.'

I snapped out of my reverie.

'Oh, sorry. I was miles away. Looking through you, not at you.'

'Thanks very much. That's very flattering,' she said, and smiled. 'I'm having lunch out at Teddington Weir tomorrow, with Peter. Why don't you come, let him get to know you better.'

This was such a remarkable suggestion that I let out an involuntary laugh.

'You can't be serious.'

'Why not? After all, he wouldn't think you were capable of murder if he could see for himself how ...' She was hurrying to a mildly offensive observation, but stopped short. This left her sentence dangling, needing the descriptor to complete it.

'So he could see for himself how what? How weak I am? Is that what you were about to say?'

'No. Well, yes, but not exactly. I was going to say how civilised, how decent, you are — how you wouldn't raise your hand against anyone and especially not against a woman.'

She reached out, put her hand on my neck, and looked closely at my face. Inexplicably, and embarrassingly, my eyes welled with tears. She turned discreetly away, picked up her script, said, 'Think about it', and left. Without her knowing it, her tent had been pitched well inside the fortified walls of my emotional keep.

The dining room was quiet. Voices and laughter came from the bar, but here I was alone. In a few minutes the setting up for dinner would begin. I had pushed the vision of the almost decapitated Mrs Drummond into a far corner of my mind, but now it appeared before me, untrammelled and disconcerting. It was after 5.00 pm. Her body must have been found by now. Topaz would turn up soon, and I wondered if I had the strength to tolerate his questions and insinuations without giving something away. And what about Arthur? Would he be steady? My hand began to shake slightly and I felt light-headed, as if I might faint. My body had a tendency to go into delayed shock at moments of high anxiety. As last night's abattoir colours and odours flooded my memory, a terrifying fact presented itself. There was someone out there who had killed two women. This person had looked through the darkness to the place where I had been standing, and he had decided to let me live.

'Why?' I asked Arthur when I went to his room later. 'Why didn't he attack me?'

'I can think of lots of reasons. Firstly, you can't be sure he really knew you were there.'

'I am sure. I felt his eyes on me, and they were like dank hands running over my body.'

'Even if he did know you were there, he couldn't risk a fight. He might lose, or get hurt. But if you couldn't see his face, he couldn't see yours. Besides, having someone else in the house at the time might suit him. Being there doesn't make you a witness; it makes you a suspect.'

*

Topaz called for Annie the next day. I was sitting with her and Arthur and Adrian on the second-storey verandah, outside Annie's bedroom. We were tinkering with the script. Adrian was the first to see Topaz riding towards the George down Wharf Street. The legs of his trousers were sensibly secured with clips. He was out of uniform, but his eyes were always in uniform.

'Here's your boyfriend,' Adrian said.

'And don't you just wish he was yours,' Annie replied.

'Yes, indeed,' he said, and they both laughed.

Annie jumped up and waved.

'Come up,' she called as he leaned his bicycle against the downstairs railing.

Topaz came through Annie's bedroom and eased himself out of the low window on to the verandah. His obvious familiarity with the room sent a spasm of resentment through me. He greeted everyone with a wide smile, but when he nodded at me the edge of the smile retreated a little, so that I would know that he did not greet murderers warmly. Annie, feeling perfectly at ease, kissed him on the mouth. He did not resist or make any attempt to disguise the nature of their relationship. He returned her kiss and put his arm around her waist.

'Let's go,' he said. 'It's a long ride.'

'Tibald's made us lunch,' she said. 'Isn't he a dear?'

She turned to me.

'Will, are you coming?'

Topaz stiffened at these words and shot me a glance that was unambiguous in its intent. He needn't have worried. I had no desire to join them. The thought of watching them bill and coo made me sick.

'No,' I said. 'I don't think that would be a good idea.'

It was only after they had left, as I was watching them ride away, that I realised that Mrs Drummond's body had not yet been found. My god, how long was it going to take? Was there really no one who would call on her to see how she was doing? A little rush of elation went through me. Maybe it would be days before she was found. With the days getting warm and with the ravenous appetites of Maryborough's insects, and who knows what else, establishing the exact time of Mrs Drummond's death would be difficult. With the passing of a few more days, accuracy would be almost impossible.

Chapter Five

SO FEW ANSWERS

DETECTIVE SERGEANT CONROY called at the George on Monday morning. He came into the bar where I was sitting. There was nobody else there, as the George did not serve alcohol until after 11.00 am. When I saw him I assumed that the body had been found, and I girded my loins for the first remark. I half-expected him to arrest me. However, it quickly became clear that Mrs Drummond was still propped on her pillows. This visit was designed to embarrass and unnerve me, but it did neither. He must have been sorely disappointed to find me alone, with no one to witness any discomfort I might feel.

'Just checking a few details,' he said.

'I don't know how many times I have to repeat it, Sergeant Conroy,' I said.

'Detective Sergeant,' he said, his vanity pricked by my error.

'When I left the Drummond house, Polly was still alive.'

'We don't dispute that, Mr Power. It's one of the few facts we agree on. It's what happened next that is of interest to us.'

'And there our ways must part because I have no idea what happened next, except that I came here and went to bed.'

'And nobody saw you.'

'And nobody saw me. It was late. What was I supposed to do — knock on people's bedroom doors and announce the joyous news that I had got home in one piece from the pictures? If I had killed her, don't you think I would have organised an alibi?'

'I never try to second-guess a murderer, Mr Power.'

I shook my head in weary resignation.

'Is there anything else you want to ask me?'

'Perhaps tomorrow,' he said.

'I'll be at Wright's Hall most of the day, rehearsing.'

'We may require you at the station. We'll let you know.'

With that, he left. So this was how it was going to be. They had no evidence, but they thought they could harass me into a confession.

I had cancelled Monday afternoon's rehearsal. I had other plans — like saving my skin. I wanted to speak to the young woman who had given Polly's eulogy and who had described Polly as her closest friend before breaking down. This was Shirley Moynahan, and she had worked with Polly at Manahan's, the department store in Adelaide Street. I went in just after the 11.00 am test siren had sounded. I discovered, with a perverse tinge of pique, that I had overestimated my notoriety. I thought that I would draw stares as the man most likely to have murdered Polly Drummond. No one spared me a second glance. My looks had improved, of course. My eye had gone down and showed only faint bruising. The scratches left by Polly's fingernails had healed, and my other injuries were hidden under my clothes.

I asked at the front counter for Shirley Moynahan. A woman, in her late sixties by the look of her mean, desiccated face, directed me to Ladies' Lingerie.

'She's popular,' she said. 'You're the second person today.'

I took a stab in the dark. 'I'm just following up some of the detective's questions.'

'I told that Conroy not to upset Shirl. She's had a rough trot. I hope you're not going to upset her either. You coppers never know when to stop.'

'We're just trying to find answers, Mrs …?'

She didn't provide her name, and I thought that I had overplayed my hand. I should have moved on quickly and not replied to her remark. I did not want to be caught out in a lie about who I was.

'You're not from round here,' she said, and she cocked her head in a way that was skin-crawlingly salacious. 'Brought you up from Brisbane, have they? That'd be right. Conroy couldn't work out the size of his underpants without help. I told him, I said, if he wanted to solve Polly's murder all he had to do was arrest that actor, or was he from the circus? Anyway, the one who took her to the pictures.'

'Really? What do you know about this … actor, did you say?'

'I think he was an actor, but he might have come in with the circus. They're all the same. Well, Shirl said that Polly told her that he was keen on her. She knocked him back and he went berserk. It's obvious, but Conroy can't see it.'

'Berserk, you say?'

'I've told all this to Conroy. Don't you people talk to each other?'

'I spoke to him earlier. And no, he didn't mention it, but we were discussing other aspects of the case.' This at least was the truth.

A customer took my informant from me and I made my way towards Ladies' Lingerie, more than a little disturbed by the revelation that I was the front runner as far as this well-short-of-perfect stranger was concerned. If she were representative of the general populace then I was in serious public relations trouble.

I recognised Shirley Moynahan, even though she had her back to me. It was the defeated slump of her shoulders. When she was delivering her eulogy I had noticed that they were rounded, as if the world's unpleasantness bore down upon her and formed an invisible yoke. She was plain, and that's all there was to it. Her hair was badly cut in that ubiquitous victory bob, encouraged by propaganda, that suited one girl in a hundred and which depended anyway upon a skilful hairdresser if it was to appear anything other than drab. I didn't think that even the skills of Mr Sydney Guilaroff himself would have saved her. The overall effect, confirmed when she turned around, was lumpen. Her nose began well but ended badly, and her lips were so thin as to be hardly there at all. Her eyes, which might have rescued her, let her down by being a dull, flat brown with none of the shifting facets of a true hazel iris. They were surmounted by two strong eyebrows, which would have benefited from a judicious shaping and thinning. Clearly, she had decided long ago, even though she was only twenty-four, that trading on her looks was simply not an option. I hoped for her sake that she had a talent in reserve that would assist a visitor in overcoming the unfortunate first impression she couldn't help but make.

She was assisting a customer, selling her a garment that looked almost orthopaedic in its shapelessness. She took the money and coupons, and then noticed me. Her hand flew to her mouth and she quickly looked away. The customer left, happy I presume, to have purchased a foundation garment sufficiently robust to deal with the demands she would make upon it. I walked to the counter and introduced myself, unnecessarily, as she obviously already knew who I was. I raised my hand in a calming motion, and she flinched as though she thought I might strike her.

'Miss Moynahan, please.'

I tried to convey in those few words enough information to reassure her that she was quite safe, and that she was not face-to-face with the man who had murdered her best friend. I drew on all my acting experience to get the cadences exactly right.

'I'll scream,' she said.

I took a few steps back.

'All right,' I said. 'Look. I'm way back here. Please just hear what I've got to say and then I'll leave.'

She digested this and nodded. Her eyes darted around the lingerie department. There was a well-dressed woman at the far end. A RAAF officer's wife, probably. Her presence gave Shirley courage.

'I did *not* kill your friend,' I said. 'I've never killed anything in my life, not even a rabbit. I was one of the last people to see her alive, that's true, but I wasn't the very last person. That was the person who took her life.'

Shirley Moynahan began to sniffle and then to cry. I moved towards the counter and said quietly, 'Shirley, your friend was a lovely woman, and she deserves to have the person responsible brought to justice. I am not that person. If you knew anything about me you would know that.'

I opened my eyes as wide as a doe's and filled them with enough tears to make them glitter. She saw then that she need not fear me, not here in the lingerie department.

'She liked you,' she said. 'Polly said that you were good friends with Cary Grant. Is that true?'

I had to think rapidly. Would a harmless lie help put her further at her ease?

'Well, I don't know about good friends. Acquaintances, really.'

'She said you liked her, that she might get to meet Cary Grant.'

For goodness sake!

'I did like her. Very much. But I didn't know her very well. We only went out once before …'

She gulped back a sob.

'Yes,' she said. 'Before she died.'

'Can I be honest with you, Shirley? May I call you Shirley?'

'Yes, please.'

She straightened up, prepared to accept the precious gift of my honesty.

'The police,' I said, 'the police think that I'm guilty, and they're not the only ones. I'm sure lots of people think the same thing. Can you imagine how that makes me feel?'

'Hunted,' she said, and her face told me that she had slipped into a melodrama of her own imagining.

'Yes. Exactly. Hunted. The police are so sure of my guilt that if I don't find the answer myself they'll make a case against me and send me to trial. I could spend the rest of my life in prison for a crime I didn't commit.'

That hand flew to her mouth again.

'I need help,' I said, and sounded helpless. 'I need your help. Please.'

I thought this was nicely judged, a perfect balance of need and determination.

'How can I help you?' she asked, with an agreeable note of despair in her voice.

'We can't talk here,' I said. 'When do you finish?'

She hesitated, and I knew that she was reluctant to meet me privately, despite the softening of her attitude.

'When you finish work,' I said, 'I could meet you in King's Cafeteria.'

She was visibly relieved. Even if I were the killer I would be unlikely to strike in a busy café.

'Three-thirty,' she said. 'I'll meet you there.'

'I'll buy you a milkshake,' I said, and bestowed a radiant smile upon her. She took a ball of filthy cloth from her pocket and blew her nose noisily.

With a few hours to spare, I walked to Wright's Hall, let myself in, and tried to ignore the threat hanging over me by imagining a performance of *Titus Andronicus* here. We had played in less salubrious places, although never with the possibility of arrest hovering in the wings. We were a reduced company, two players short — Tibald and old Walter Sunder. I could collapse several minor characters into one, knowing that the majority of the audience would only understand one word in ten anyway. I was walking back and forth in the area that would be our stage, blocking our movements in my head and configuring one or two dramatic tableaux. So intensely was I concentrating that I did not hear Peter Topaz come in. I discovered him standing at the back of the hall when I whirled around, practising a movement I intended to make in Act 111.

'I've already spoken to Conroy today,' I said.

His footsteps echoed as he walked towards me. The acoustics were not ideal for Shakespeare. He stopped, and turned his cap in his hands.

'What if I told you I've changed my mind, that I thought you were innocent,' he said.

'I'd say that you've been listening to Annie, and that your dick and your brain have changed places. Or maybe this is a new tactic. You tell me you think I'm innocent so I let my guard down. Is this one of Conroy's bright ideas? Get Power's confidence. Catch him out. Whatever, I don't believe you.'

'All right. I can see that this looks transparent. I'm not denying that Conroy thinks we've got our man. That's partly because he thinks you're an arsehole. All I'm saying is that now I'm not so sure.'

'About me being an arsehole, or innocent?'

Without missing a beat, he said, 'Innocent. If you killed Polly, there are too many things that don't add up.'

All I felt when I heard this was anger. Perhaps I should have been relieved, and grabbed him in a bear hug and told him all about the body of Mrs Drummond growing more putrid by the hour. I did not, however, believe him.

'Listen,' I said. 'Stop mucking around with me. This innocent bullshit doesn't wash. So Annie says I'm a nice guy. So what? You know nothing about me. Nothing. What's my background? Huh? You have no idea. Maybe my past is strewn with corpses. Don't stand there now and tell me that you suddenly have a gut feeling, or a cock feeling, that I didn't do it. I don't actually mind that much that you think I'm a murderer. I do mind that you think I'm a moron.'

He looked down at the ground and fidgeted with his cap.

'To tell you the truth, Will, Annie has never said that you were a nice guy. She does believe you're not guilty, though, and she did try to convince me. It wasn't her who changed my mind. It was Mrs Drummond.'

That pulled me up short.

'You spoke to her?' I asked, knowing that the interview couldn't have taken place recently.

'Of course,' he said. 'Several times. She's not a good witness, but she told me something that you didn't and I wondered why. She said that the night you were there Polly and Fred had a fight, a "rip-snorter" she said. Punches, kicks, the works. Is that true?'

'What if it is?'

'I wondered why you didn't mention it. All you said was that Fred was nuts. I thought Mrs Drummond might have been making it up, but she repeated it to me the next time I spoke to her. She said that you tried to break it up. Fred didn't mention it when I interviewed him either, but of course he wouldn't because it makes him look bad. I called on Mrs Drummond the day after Fred died, and she was rambling and said that he was being punished. I asked her what he was being punished for, but that was as much as I could get out of her. She just kept repeating, "punished ... punished ... punished." Then she decided I was a papist, and starting screaming at me to get out of the house and that I would join her son in hell. I went back to my notes, and I couldn't find anything in them about a fight in what you said, and I couldn't figure out why until Annie said something offhand. She said that it was easy to embarrass you; that you blushed easily. It was a passing remark, but it occurred to me that the spectacle of a woman you were attracted to flailing about on the ground with her brother might be sufficiently mortifying to warrant omission. I don't mean mortifying for you. I mean that you found it embarrassing for her. If you killed her, why would this small moment of shame still bother you enough to hide it?'

'Wouldn't it be nice,' I said, 'if you believed any of what you have just said? It has such an authentic ring to it. Considered, logical, in some ways even incontrovertible. It had it all. The initial error, the regretful re-think, the revelation of innocence. I'm looking for a replacement actor. You'd be a shoe-in if you were interested.'

'You're letting your feelings for Annie cloud your judgement.'

I betrayed the truth of his acuity by letting out an involuntary gasp.

'I'm not a moron either, Will.' He put on his cap and strode to the door of Wright's Hall. Before he left he turned and said, 'You were born in Ballarat. Your father was a banker, and died when you were sixteen years old. You have two younger brothers, and you had a sister who died when she was an infant. Your mother lives in Melbourne with your second-youngest brother, Brian, who is a teacher, and his wife. Your other brother, Fulton, is in the army and is currently posted to Darwin. Your mother's name is Agnes. Her maiden name was Sinclair. Your past is not strewn with corpses.'

With that he walked out, leaving behind the scent of Lifebuoy soap.

'Arsehole,' I said to the empty room.

At 3.30 I was sitting in King's Cafeteria drinking a lime milkshake and waiting for Shirley Moynahan. She still hadn't shown up at four. I thought she must have lost her nerve, but she came in at five past four and apologised for being late. She had been dealing with a difficult customer who didn't understand that she couldn't just hand over coupons and be given underwear in return. This story might have been true, but she had also used the time to inexpertly apply make-up. For my benefit? Well, she wasn't trying to impress the girl making the milkshakes.

'I'm sorry about before,' she said, 'but I've been frightened of my own shadow ever since Polly was killed. I have nightmares.'

She lowered her voice. 'I sleep with the light on.'

This shared intimacy, if it was intended to titillate, was wide of the mark. I could see no immediate advantage in sleeping with Shirley, and whoever eventually took up that challenge could only be aided and abetted by darkness.

'Are you frightened now?' I asked.

'No, no, I'm not. It was just the shock of seeing you.' She leaned across the table and in a conspiratorial tone said, 'I don't believe that you killed Polly.' She looked around, anxious that no one should overhear her. 'I think Fred did, and then he killed himself in that plane.'

'How can you be sure?'

'I wasn't until I met you. I'm sorry, but you had to be a suspect, Will.' She called me "Will" with the casual air of a long-standing friend. The whole affair had become a movie for her. Who did she see herself as? Bette Davis? Barbara Stanwyck? More like Marie Dressler, I thought.

'Now I know,' she said, between slurps of her milkshake, 'that my original suspicions about Fred are correct.'

'How do you know?'

'Polly was scared of him.'

I had seen no evidence of this. Quite the contrary. Polly had launched herself at Fred with no hint of trepidation. I let Shirley go on without challenging her assertion.

'Polly didn't talk about it much. She said … she said …' Here she faltered, as if what she was about to say might offend my delicate sensibilities.

'She said that she had to lock her bedroom at night because Fred would, you know …'

She flushed scarlet at the picture of incestuous lust she had painted.

'He never did anything, but he tried once or twice.'

'There's another brother, isn't there?'

'Joe. He's the oldest. He left a few years ago. I didn't know him. Polly didn't talk much about him.'

'What about Mr Drummond, Polly's father?'

'There was an accident when we were about ten years old. Mr Drummond's car hit a tree.'

She was hiding something behind this curious construction. I guessed what it was.

'Joe was driving, wasn't he.'

'How did you know?'

'Just the way you said it, as though there was no driver at all. He would only have been … what? Fifteen or sixteen?'

She nodded.

'Yes. I think he must be about thirty now.'

I let this information sink in. The Drummond family was unusually prone to dying violently.

'Mrs Drummond went a bit batty after that. Joe had to be the man in the house. He left in the end.' Her voice trailed off.

'Tell me about Smelt.'

'Jimmy? Why do you want to know about him?'

I didn't want to interfere with her certainty about Fred's guilt and frighten her into silence. Even if Fred had killed Polly he certainly hadn't cut his mother's throat. Dead people have great difficulty holding things like knife handles.

'It's just that Polly seemed quite close to him.'

Shirley laughed, and the laughter had the unfortunate effect of distorting rather than brightening her features.

'She only went to that dinner with him to make Patrick jealous.'

'Who's Patrick?'

What she said next really took me by surprise.

'Patrick Lutteral. Her fiancé.'

I cupped my chin in my hand and tried to disguise my interest.

'She never mentioned him,' I said, and remembered suddenly the deep kiss, with the promise of more, we had exchanged at her gate.

'Well, she wouldn't. It was sort of a secret. They didn't want Mrs Drummond to find out. Pat's a Catholic.'

'Did Fred know?'

'Yes. He hated Pat. Said he was a bludger and a coward. He's a porter in the railway, and that's a reserved industry. Not everyone can join up.'

There was raw vehemence in her voice as she defended Patrick Lutteral. It blazed so suddenly that I suspected Shirley Moynahan of harbouring strong feelings about her best friend's fiancé.

'Does anyone else know about the engagement?'

She shrugged.

'A few people. Patrick's mates, probably. He would have told them. Not his parents though. They wouldn't want Pat marrying a Protestant.'

'Do the police know?'

The question unsettled her. She lowered her gaze for a moment, and then met my eyes directly.

'I didn't tell them. I suppose I lied to Sergeant Topaz.'

'Why didn't you tell him? It's a fairly important piece of information.'

'They'd been having rows, Pat and Polly. Polly wanted to get married right away so that she could move away from Fred and her mother. Pat wanted to wait. He wanted to soften up his parents, try to change their minds about marrying a non-Catholic. Polly said he was weak and that he should lead his own life, and who cares if they couldn't get married in the

Catholic Church. He wanted her to convert. She wouldn't. Well, imagine her mother. She'd explode. So then she told him that if he didn't love her enough to marry her no matter what, she'd just better look around for someone who did. That's why she went to the dinner with Jimmy Smelt.'

'And that's why she went to the pictures with me.'

'Yes, partly, but she really liked you. She told me. She came round after you'd been at the circus thing. She said you knew Cary Grant.'

Shirley finished her milkshake and sucked up the dregs.

'Did you think the police might suspect Patrick if you told them about the rows?' I asked.

'Of course. And that wouldn't be fair, because Patrick shouldn't be a suspect.'

Her tone was matter-of-fact — an unashamed declaration of Patrick Lutteral's innocence. Such certainty could only arise from infatuation. I would have to meet this Lutteral and try to gauge for myself his potential for bloody violence.

'Did Patrick know that Polly was going to the pictures with me?'

'Oh, yes. I told him.'

She realised immediately that she had said something she would rather not have said.

'I ran into him,' she stammered, stumbling towards an explanation, 'and he asked what Polly was doing and so I told him. What's wrong with that?'

This last was a little petulant, and it was obvious that she was lying. She hadn't run into Patrick Lutteral by accident. She had sought him out and told him all that Polly had told her. It was mischievous. It wasn't difficult to surmise that Shirley had entertained the hope that Patrick might throw Polly over and turn his gaze in her direction. She offered so much more than

Polly. She was a virgin for a start. Had to be. She was Catholic, too, and she adored him.

'Where can I meet Patrick?'

'I don't think you should talk to him about all this. He's very upset. About Polly.'

I spoke to her firmly.

'Would you rather the police spoke to him? I'm sorry, Shirley, but I have to speak to him. He might know something that will help me.'

She was quiet for a moment, turning over in her mind which way to play this. She must have known that now I had Patrick's name and occupation it would be a simple matter to find him. If I was going to talk to Patrick, she wanted to be there.

'All right,' she said, and I sensed that I had gone down in her estimation by forcing her into this position. She agreed to bring Patrick to the side door of St Mary's Church in Adelaide Street at 6.00 pm the following day.

Next day's rehearsal was interrupted by the arrival of a policeman I had not seen before. He was a man in his fifties, and he wore no stripes on his sleeve. To still be a constable so late in life spoke volumes about what happens when low intelligence meets lack of ambition. He was bald, or nearly so, and had skin as tanned as leather. His pate was dotted all over with beads of sweat which he mopped constantly.

'Detective Sergeant Conroy wants to see William Power at the station,' he wheezed.

'And you are?' I asked imperiously.

'Constable Valentine.' He grinned idiotically. 'I'm to escort you.'

Sending the station's lowest-ranking and most ostentatiously unimpressive officer was Conroy's less-than-subtle reminder of his low opinion of me. It wasn't Valentine's fault that he was half-witted — he'd probably been dropped on his head as an infant — so I resisted the temptation and refrained from taking the mickey out of him on our way to the station. In fact, Constable Valentine was agreeable company. Despite having a catalogue of reasons not to be, he was a happy man, and his happiness placed him beyond the reach of parody.

When we reached the police station Conroy was unable to see me immediately. I'd expected this and was determined not to be annoyed by it. Conroy would get no satisfaction from me. He would be shown that my patience was inexhaustible, and that if he thought he could break me in this way he had another think coming. I occupied my time by quietly singing 'The White Cliffs of Dover' over and over again, until the constable behind the desk asked me to desist. I declined.

'Think of it as singing to keep all our spirits up,' I said, and crooned, 'There'll be bluebirds over the White Cliffs of Dover, tomorrow, just you wait and see,' for the umpteenth time. Conroy passed through the outer office where I was sitting and did not acknowledge me. He spoke loudly to the desk clerk. I closed my eyes and raised the volume of my melodious rendition, and gave no indication that I was aware of his presence.

'He won't shut up singing that fucking song,' said the desk clerk.

'I don't hear anything,' Conroy said, 'except a sound like there's something wrong with the drains.'

He left and didn't return for half an hour. He then asked me the same questions he had asked previously. I gave him the same answers, but without rancour and with a considered air as if it was almost a pleasure to provide him with the information he sought.

'I hope you don't think I'm badgering you,' he said snidely.

'Not at all. It is one's civic duty to assist the police, and I am pleased to perform that duty when called upon to do so. Please don't hesitate to call me back if you think of any new questions or if there is anything you haven't understood.'

His eye quivered in its socket as if my words were an electric prod touching the vulnerable white.

'You can go,' he said, and I admired his measured tone.

There was no point returning to Wright's Hall now. The cast would have left. It was almost five-thirty. Shirley and Patrick were due at St Mary's at six. I could use the half hour to explore the church.

The front entrance to St Mary's was set well back from Adelaide Street. The façade was simple, with a stained-glass window set above a rather severe gabled doorway. Decorative elements on the exterior were few, which is why the unecclesiastical figure of a cockerel perched atop the roof drew the eye. Two women emerged from the church, chattering and laughing. They paid scant attention to me. They were followed by Shirley Moynahan and a young man, who, when he saw me, stopped Shirley and lifted his chin in my direction.

My first impression of Patrick Lutteral was that Polly would have had him for breakfast. He was timid. He was good looking I suppose, but they were the soft, half-formed good looks of a boy, even though he must have been twenty. His reddish-blond hair was straight and combed neatly away from his face with the squeaky precision of an altar boy. I would not have been in the least surprised to learn that his mother had combed it for him before he left the house. His mouth was full and sensual, and it made me slightly nauseous to think that it had visited Polly's lips, just as mine had. Shirley's demeanour in his company confirmed my suspicions about her feelings for him. Perhaps she wasn't wrong to have hopes in relation to this young man. He might be persuaded that her constancy and piety were adequate substitutes for the pleasures of the flesh.

In the few seconds it took for them to reach me, I concluded that Patrick Lutteral would face two choices in his life — marriage to Shirley Moynahan and their consequent dry, joyless and procreative couplings, or the priesthood, where his boyish, rosy-hued face would decline into the jowly visage of a middle-aged monsignor, his cheeks florid with exploded capillaries and his eyes deadened by envy of the sad and harmless sexual misdemeanours of his dull parishioners.

'This is Patrick,' Shirley said, and added unnecessarily that they had both just been to confession, where Shirley had probably unburdened herself of the impure thoughts she entertained about her unimpressive companion.

'I'm William Power.' I held out my hand. Patrick did not reciprocate.

'So, we start as rivals,' I said. 'That's fine by me, but it's not to your advantage to be so sour. Polly wasn't interested in me. She was using me to get at you. It puzzles me that she would do this, but there you are.' I saw no reason to obfuscate.

'We can't talk here,' Patrick said, and his voice was unexpectedly deep. 'Someone will see us.'

I followed them around to the side of the church, where we stood in the shadow of a door which was not in regular use. I didn't beat about the bush.

'No doubt Shirley has told you why I wish to speak to you.'

'She also told me that they think you killed Polly. Why should I think otherwise?'

'Because it is entirely possible that you killed her.'

Shirley exhaled a high-pitched shriek of outrage. Patrick coughed in disbelief at this bold and brutal assertion.

'I had no reason to kill Polly,' I said. 'I didn't know you existed, let alone that you and Polly had an understanding. You on the other hand had a good reason. Jealousy.'

'I don't have to hear this,' he said, rallying, and made to walk away.

'You'd better talk fast,' I said, 'because the only way I'm not going to the police with the information about your engagement and your arguments is if you can convince me that you didn't do it. I'm not playing a game with you. I don't have that luxury.'

He whirled back towards me, and his eyes were wide and glassy with rage.

'You kissed her!' he hissed. 'You kissed her!'

There was an awful moment of silence as we all realised the implication of his uncontrolled remark.

'My God,' I said. 'You were there. You followed us. It was so dark. You must have been very close.'

For one horrifying moment, there in the side portico of St Mary's Church I thought I was looking at the unlikely murderer of a young woman and her deranged mother. Then he began blubbering, and my certainty collapsed.

'I saw you,' he said between wracking sobs. 'You kissed her.'

Shirley put her arm around his shoulders and said, 'Ssssh.' It was a truly grotesque little pietà.

'You followed us,' I said again, hoping the exaggerated incredulity in my voice would prompt something more substantial than a choking cry. He calmed down sufficiently to exchange weeping for pique.

'Shirley told me about you. Yes, I followed you. You were so caught up that you didn't even notice, and I was so close behind you that I could have touched you. Polly knew I was there. She knew. That's why she kissed you. She knew I'd see it. Why else would she kiss you?'

'Perhaps she wanted to. I have been in situations where I have been kissed irrespective of lurking fiancés.'

'You're old enough to be her father.'

'Only if I fucked her mother when I was sixteen,' I said.

Shirley recoiled and Patrick's mouth dropped open.

'This is a church,' he said. 'You can't say that kind of filth here.'

'I'll risk the thunderbolt. How dare you follow us like some lunatic. How long did you hang around for? Long enough to kill her?'

I knew this pathetic creature couldn't have murdered Polly and have had the self-possession to dispose of the body so imaginatively. He certainly could not have stood in the living room of the Drummond house, having just slashed Mrs Drummond's throat and looked so calmly at the shape he perceived standing only a few feet from him.

'No,' he said, and withdrew three paces from me. 'No.' He looked wildly at Shirley and said, 'No,' again, but he knew that he had put himself in a terrible position, as terrible as my own.

'What else did you see?' I asked, and my voice was hard.

'I saw Fred light a cigarette, and then you went inside and he followed. I waited for a bit, and then you came out.'

'Then what?'

'I followed you. I thought I'd say something to you, but I didn't.'

'Polly left the house after I did. That was when she was killed.'

'I wasn't there! I didn't see! I was following you.'

His voice was becoming hysterical. Shirley stepped between Patrick and me. With her face empurpled, her eyes bulging, and a vein at her temple pulsing, she spat her words at me.

'Leave him alone! Leave him alone!'

Shirley flew at me, her hands clawing my face. I raised the arm resting in the sling and warded off her nails. She landed no blows, and Patrick encircled her with his arms from behind. She didn't struggle against him, but fell back on his puny chest, subdued, even ecstatic. If Patrick chose the priesthood, this was as close as she was ever likely to come to sex. They were breathing heavily, not in any erotically charged way. Both were simply shocked and exhausted by the unexpected release of unruly and fierce emotions. I left them there, propping each other up in the portico. Patrick Lutteral hadn't killed anybody, unless a vicious Mr Hyde was resting quietly beneath his flaccid exterior.

The following night, Wednesday, was a full moon. The dining room was full. It had become the place to eat for RAAF officers and their wives and mistresses. Augie walked around the room like the maître'd at a grand establishment, pausing occasionally to explain a particular dish to a customer who was unfamiliar with terms like *rognons de veau flambés* and *cervelles au beurre noir*. Augie himself had to work from notes. I was still not helping out at table service, but I was in the kitchen doing as much as I was able to with the use of only one arm. At the end of the meal Topaz arrived, and he and Annie went for a walk in the brilliant moonlight. He stayed out of my way. At any rate, he chose not to speak to me when he saw me.

On Thursday the front page of the *Chronicle* carried the news that the Duke of Kent had been killed in an air crash. The war in the Pacific could not compete with a royal death. That afternoon, Mrs Drummond's body was found by a neighbour who had sniffed the air and followed the rank odour of putrefaction to its awful source. After six, undisturbed days I could only imagine the sight which met her eyes when she pushed open that bedroom door. Mrs Drummond's body would have been a swarming colony of beetles and maggots, and human in its general outline only. Her head may well have fallen free from its tenuous grip on the torso and rolled away in disgust from the feeding frenzy beneath it.

Conroy did not send one of his slow-witted minions to tell me the news. He came himself, and he was scrubbed and shaved as if he were inviting me on a first date. It was after five o'clock, and we had returned from that day's rehearsal. There was a short, sharp rap on my bedroom door, and Conroy entered before he had been invited to do so. He was accompanied by a uniformed officer who I had seen around town but whose name I did not know.

'We've found her,' he said.

I had been mentally preparing for this moment for days. In a beautifully underplayed reading I said, 'Found who?'

He narrowed his eyes and said in a voice taut with irritation, 'Mrs Drummond.'

This was no time for sarcasm or a smart remark. I arranged my features into a portrait of perplexity and concern.

'You've found Mrs Drummond? I didn't know she'd gone missing. What happened? Did she wander off? Is she all right?'

'She's dead, as you very well know,' he said sourly.

'Are you accusing me of something?'

Conroy didn't flinch.

'I haven't accused you of anything,' he said. 'Yet.'

'And what am I supposed to make of that "As you very well know"?'

'You can make of it whatever you like.'

I began to work myself up into a white-hot furnace of indignation, and as I spoke I was careful to drop in well-placed indications that I did not know how long Mrs Drummond had been dead. Conroy would be alert to the merest hint of prior knowledge.

'I have been harassed and embarrassed and inconvenienced by you for days now. You have no evidence against me, and yet you persist in focussing your investigation on me while the trail that would lead you to Polly's killer gets colder by the day. Now you have a second corpse, and you head straight back to me. This time I have an alibi. I was with people all day today and all day yesterday, and I can account for last night as well. If you'd been looking in the right place for Polly's killer instead of wasting your time on me, Mrs Drummond might still be alive.'

I addressed these remarks to both Conroy and the policeman with him. I could tell from the expression on the uniformed man's face that this interview had departed from an expressed plan. He kept shooting looks at Conroy which suggested he was curious to hear how Conroy would deal with this. There was an unmistakeable, but barely perceptible, smile about his lips which betrayed his detestation of Conroy and revealed that he was enjoying the fact that things were not falling neatly into place. To Conroy's credit, he did not bluster or express his frustration, except in the quickening of his eye quiver.

'I have not said anything about the time of Mrs Drummond's death, and I am not fooled by your assumption that it was today or yesterday. Senior Constable Harvey here might be, but I assure you I am not.'

This gratuitous dig at his companion was proof enough that an antagonism existed between them. Senior Constable Harvey said nothing in his defence, but the colour rose in his neck and the muscles along his forearms tensed.

'Why don't you arrest me, if you're so certain of my guilt?' I asked.

'This is not Nazi Germany, Mr Power. When I have the evidence against you it will be my pleasure to arrest you, and I will make sure that I do it personally. I am a patient man.'

I wanted to put my face close to his and scream, 'You moron! How could I sever a woman's head with only one hand?'

I didn't. Instead, I lifted an eyebrow and said, 'You need more than patience to catch murderers, Detective Sergeant Conroy. You need intelligence.'

The slightest of smirks on Constable Harvey's face indicated that in him I might have found an ally.

The gothic extravagance of Mrs Drummond's death could not be kept from the people of Maryborough. Friday's *Chronicle* didn't spare its readers the graphic details. The reporter hadn't gone to the woman who had found the body, but had interviewed instead her 'close friend'. This person, unencumbered by the trauma and revulsion suffered by the eyewitness, was able to inject into her description a prurient note of shuddery glee which elevated or depressed the report, depending on your point of view, almost to the level of a blackly comic entertainment.

> A close friend of the witness said that the deceased's head had been detached from the body and was found on the other side of the room.

So I had been right about that.

> Detective Sergeant Conroy, in charge of the investigation into the disappearance and murder of the deceased's daughter, Miss Polly Drummond, was not prepared to speculate on any connection between the two crimes. The deceased's son, Mr Fred Drummond, also died recently in what was believed to be an aircraft accident.

When laid out in cold, black print, the mortality rate in the Drummond family made remarkable reading. The sense of these killings being some kind of vendetta against a particular family was the only thing that stood between the townspeople and panic about a maniac in their midst.

There was nothing in the newspaper report about suspects, and I had come to accept that my role in Polly's death had not been discussed more seriously than as a piece of idle gossip, and then not very widely. There was certainly no whispering campaign being waged against me. Indeed, on occasions when discussion of the gruesome details by dinner patrons had been overheard by members of the company, the consensus was that it was a simple matter of murder/suicide, with Fred identified as the culprit. Adrian had heard mention of me only once, and not by name. Somebody had said that that drunk actor who had fallen off the stage at the ACF dance had something to do with it. Someone else at the table had said that he wasn't an actor, that he was with the circus, and that he would have been more interested in Fred than Polly. This was useful misinformation, but it got up my nose nonetheless. I was relieved to have it confirmed that I had been worrying unnecessarily about my notoriety, but I was annoyed to discover myself depicted as an alcoholic circus performer with homosexual tendencies.

With the discovery of Mrs Drummond's body it was certain that Fred's reputation would be rescued. That, of course, meant that people would be looking for a substitute suspect — and, despite the hopelessly murky sense in the town of who I actually was, I was in the box seat to be that suspect. This was made clear to me by Annie Hudson, who took me aside at the end of Friday night's service and said that Topaz was concerned about how people might react to me now. Ill-informed gossip spread faster than cholera, and he could not guarantee that there would be no leaks from the police station about my being questioned in relation to both murders. In fact, Annie said, such leaks were not only inevitable, they were calculated.

'Peter said that Conroy would have no objection to you being alienated and isolated.'

'His concern is touching, but I don't trust him. Am I supposed to believe that he has suddenly developed a fondness for me?'

Annie looked puzzled.

'Don't be silly, Will. Peter doesn't like you. He can't stand you, really. He thinks you're a pompous, arrogant, self-serving ponce. But he also thinks someone else is responsible for these crimes, and that Conroy has got it wrong.'

'How much of this posturing is for your benefit and how much is out of a concern for justice?'

Annie, exasperated, said, 'Honestly, Will, you are your own worst enemy. Peter is willing to overlook what a prick he thinks you are and try to help you, and all you can do is whinny like some jealous, snotty-nosed schoolboy.'

'Why would I be jealous of Topaz?' I asked, sounding perilously like the schoolboy as described.

She avoided answering that, and said instead, 'Peter is prepared to challenge Conroy directly and appear with you in public. If people see the two of you laughing and acting like you're the best of friends, the word will spread and maybe take some of the heat off you.'

'Or maybe he hopes I'll let something slip if he gains my confidence.'

'You know, Will, it's bloody incredible! You really do think that everyone around you is stupid, don't you? Even if Peter was trying to trap you, there's nothing for him to catch in the trap.' She paused, ominously. 'Is there?'

She was right. The more I resisted Topaz's efforts, the more it looked like I had something to hide.

'I'm sorry,' I said. 'You're absolutely right. I have nothing to lose and everything to gain. I just don't like to be taken for a mug. Tell Topaz I'll meet with him.'

'Good,' she said. 'You can sit together and fake friendship. We'll see who's the better actor.'

Chapter Six

MEETING CHARLOTTE

SATURDAY MORNING was warm and still, and by 10.00 am the temperature hinted at the summer ahead. Peter Topaz arrived and we sat for a while with Annie, on the verandah outside her bedroom. The talk was small.

'Augie is fixing up the Ladies' Lounge,' Annie said. 'Soon there'll be hoity women in there ordering Pimms and discussing their friends' taste in hats.'

Topaz laughed indulgently. I was uncomfortable. Quite apart from anything else, Annie's assessment of how Topaz felt about me was getting in the way of easy banter. I also believed that we were unevenly matched, in that his dislike of me was greater than my dislike of him. As a general rule I prefer it to be the other way around. It went deeper than that, too. My dislike of Topaz was situational, based on his original supposition that I was a murderer. His dislike of me was personal, and grew out of his strange misreading of my character. He was under no pressure to change my mind about him. I felt, perhaps foolishly, under considerable pressure to change his mind about me. This feeling coexisted, confusingly, with a lingering suspicion about Topaz's motives. I thought it best to get a few things out in the open.

'Annie says you think I'm a ponce,' I said.

He was unfazed by the remark.

'Well, Will,' he drawled, 'that doesn't make me Sherlock Holmes, does it?'

'All right,' intervened Annie. ' We all understand that you're not the best of friends, but let's get this over with, and Will, stop being such a pain in the arse. Peter's sticking his neck out for you.'

I raised my hands in acquiescence, but said nothing.

'We're going to the Ladies' Lounge at the Royal,' Topaz said. 'The three of us. Then Annie's leaving, and you and I are going for a friendly stroll around town, stopping at the Engineers' Arms on the way home.'

'Why are you doing this?' I asked. 'Really.'

'Conroy's a smart man, but even smart men have blind spots. He wants to get out of here. Go to Brisbane. If he tidies this case up quickly he's in line for a promotion and a transfer. It's hard to get Brisbane to notice you if you're stuck in a small town where not much happens. A double murder is good for the CV.'

'You want him to go?'

'He's a good detective, but a move to Brisbane for him would be good for both our careers. I don't want him to screw up this case, and if he keeps going after you he will screw it up.'

'If you really believe that Conroy's got the wrong man, you must have some idea of who the right man is.'

'Must I? Fred was a possibility, but I thought at first that you were a better one, until more information came in. You were never a possibility for Mrs Drummond. That was way outside your pathological potential.'

'You make that sound like an insult.'

'That's because you always put your ego before your common sense. Most people would be happy not to be called a psychopath. You feel slighted, as if a skill of yours is being impugned.'

'Boys, boys,' said Annie. 'Let's go and have a drink, for Christ's sake.'

Annie and Peter Topaz walked arm in arm. I fell back, but Annie looped her arm through mine and we walked thus, the three of us linked. Occasionally Annie threw her head back and released a peal of laughter. An observer might well have thought that we were a jaunty trio.

The Ladies' Lounge of the Royal Hotel was busy. Well-dressed women wearing clothes that fell far short of the austerity restrictions drank gin slings at two shillings a pop, while their husbands drank beer in the main bar. We sat at a table, and Topaz offered to pay for the first round.

'Oh, no,' said Annie. 'Let me. To celebrate.'

'What are we celebrating?' I asked.

'I haven't told you yet. I've got a job on 4MB. Advertisements and doing the Women's Session in the morning.' She dipped her chin and added, sotto voce, 'It pays incredibly well and it's only half an hour a day, so it won't interfere with rehearsals.'

I mustn't have been smiling.

'You're not cross are you, Will? It just sort of fell in my lap. The producer was at dinner the other night, and we got talking and he said he needed an actress and that I'd be perfect, especially as people already know me. And just think, I'll be Johnny-on-the-spot if anything comes up for you.'

Topaz turned to me and said, 'And if you fall over on radio, nobody can see you, so that's got to be a good thing.' He smiled broadly and slapped me on the back.

'I'll have a whiskey,' I said, choosing the most expensive spirit from the list.

'A pink lady for me,' said Annie, and handed Topaz the money. He went to the bar to order.

'When do you start?' I asked, struggling to keep any peevishness out of my voice.

'I've already recorded three commercials, and the first Ladies' Session is next week. Do try to be good about it, Will. A girl needs an income.'

'The company pays you,' I said.

'Oh yes, but three pounds a week, Will. Really, it's not a king's ransom, is it?'

'It's all we can afford at the moment.'

Topaz came back with the drinks. He had decided on a whiskey, too. He nodded to several women on his way across the room.

'Now,' he said, 'what shall we talk about?'

'Anything except the war,' said Annie. 'It's bad enough having to hear about it on the radio day in and day out.'

Topaz reached across and clasped her hand.

'I'm sure he's fine. If he wasn't, you would have heard.'

'You're sure who's fine?' I asked.

'Annie's brother, John. He's flying with the RAF in England.'

'Please,' said Annie, 'let's talk about something else. We're supposed to look like we're enjoying ourselves.'

I was frankly amazed by this little nugget of information. I had never thought of Annie in any sort of family context, but then I didn't think that way about anybody in the company. I suppose they all had siblings tucked away somewhere.

Topaz raised his glass in a toast and said, 'To your new job.'

I followed automatically, raised mine, and said graciously,

'Yes, Annie. Well done.'

It's astonishing, when one recalls events, how momentous occurrences are set in motion by the smallest of actions. Whenever I now hear the clink of glasses, raised and touched in celebration, I associate it with the horrifying consequences of my meeting Mrs Charlotte Witherburn. I had just sipped my whiskey when a woman wearing an extremely well-cut outfit — it must have cost her at least 50 guineas, perhaps more — came to our table, leaned down, and kissed Topaz lightly on the cheek.

'Thank you for speaking to Harry. I think things are better than they were.'

'Let me know if they get worse.'

Clearly there was an understanding between them to which we were not to be privy.

'These are friends of mine,' he said. 'Annie Hudson and William Power. Mrs Charlotte Witherburn.'

I stood up.

'Oh, yes,' she said. 'Miss Hudson, the actress. How lovely. And Mr Power. You're with the circus, I think someone mentioned.'

'No. I'm an actor. My company is in town preparing a play. Shakespeare.'

'Bringing culture to the barbarians.' Her mouth formed the arc of a smile. There was no laughter in her eyes, and I didn't think there had been laughter there for a very long time. She looked in her late thirties, with dark hair carefully and artfully curled. Her skin was pale, but not pallid, simply protected from the devastating desiccation of the Queensland sun. She had once been very beautiful and, although she was still remarkable, there was something in her face suggestive of decline. There was a great sadness about her that I found intriguing and erotically charged.

'Won't you join us?' I said.

Our eyes met and I felt a kind of spasm, deep in my brain, almost like a short circuit. I stopped breathing.

'I don't want to interrupt your conversation,' she said, in a voice that had had money spent on it. 'And I have left a friend at a table. Thank you, but I must go back to her.'

Charlotte Witherburn returned to her table, but before she had sat down I had undergone a shattering transformation. When I now looked at Annie Hudson I saw a charming, amusing, rather coarse woman who bore a striking resemblance to Greer Garson, but who aroused nothing in me. Nothing. She was as sexless as a sister, her attractiveness noted, acknowledged, but disempowered. I did not now see Peter Topaz as a rival, but as a copper who was in the unfortunate position of having to publicly support a suspect he did not like. I experienced a rush of affection for him. It may have been the whiskey, which I had finished in one gulp.

'Will, are you all right?'

Annie's voice called me back from the abstracted plateau of sudden infatuation to the reassuring banality of the Ladies' Lounge of the Royal Hotel.

'Yes,' I said. 'I'm fine. I'm perfectly fine.'

We sat for an hour, chatting inanely but comfortably. Topaz asked about the company, how it worked, what plays we had performed. All the while I kept an eye on Charlotte Witherburn. When she and her companion got up to leave she looked across and waved a farewell.

'Who is she?' I asked, and I could not entirely disguise the eagerness in my voice.

'She's married to Harry Witherburn.'

'Should that mean something?'

'Timber and sugar. He's probably the richest man in Maryborough.'

'She seems unhappy.'

'She is unhappy.'

That was as indiscreet as Topaz was prepared to be, while he was sober at any rate, although I couldn't imagine that he would ever get so drunk that he would drop his guard.

'I have to go,' said Annie. 'I'm recording this afternoon.'

She kissed Topaz, patted my arm, and left, her departure watched by many pairs of eyes.

'I think it's time we were seen in a less salubrious pub,' Topaz said. On our way out, he stopped at two tables and chatted briefly. At each of them he said, 'This is a friend of mine, William Power.'

At least two of the women raised their eyebrows in mild surprise, but shook my hand without compunction. As we set off for the Engineers' Arms in March Street, I said, 'Listen, Peter. I want to apologise. I've been a prick.'

'Is that the whiskey talking, Will?'

'Fair go. I've only had two. I realised in there that you really were sticking your neck out for me and that there's nothing in it for you.'

'I'm not a knight in shining armour, Will. There's plenty in it for me. Conroy's transfer for one thing.'

'Still, I am grateful. I know I don't seem very grateful, but I am.'

'I understand your distrust, Will. I've never had someone accuse me of being a murderer to my face, but if I had, I wouldn't take to it too kindly.'

'Can I trust you, Peter?'

He stopped walking and faced me.

'No. I am not your friend. I'm a copper. If I learned anything to your disadvantage, I'd use it. You should keep that in mind. You can trust me in this, though. I'm not laying a trap for you. You didn't do it.'

'My God,' I said. 'You know who did. Don't you?'

He continued walking. At the door of the hotel he said, 'I don't have any evidence.'

'And what's Conroy's view on this?'

'He said that the smart money was on that fucking nancy-boy actor. I think those were his exact words.'

He smiled and pushed open the door. I followed him into the bar.

The Engineers' Arms was crowded and noisy. There weren't many uniforms in here. Topaz had chosen it because it was a pub favoured by locals, most of whom worked up the road at Walkers Engineering. A few of them greeted him. A few others turned away, obviously unhappy to have a walloper, even an off-duty one, in their bar. We stood against a wall, exchanged a shouted word now and again, and performed a reasonable impression of two mates socialising.

'I need a piss,' I shouted.

I followed my nose to the urinal and, having relieved myself into the evil-smelling trough, stepped down and was about to leave when a man blocked the doorway. There was a belligerent air about him that was familiar.

'Gedday,' he said, and in an extraordinary feat of compression managed to gorge the word with menace. He detached himself from the doorway and stood at the urinal.

'You're that actor,' he said as he released a stream of beer-induced urine into the trough. At least he hadn't accused me of being with the circus. I looked at his broad back, the shoulders rounded as he emptied his bladder.

'I need to talk to you,' he said.

'I don't think we've met,' I said.

He swivelled, took one hand off his cock and offered it to me. His hand, that is.

'Mal Flint,' he said.

I raised my hand and gave him a sort of half wave, rather than clasp his recently occupied paw.

'William Power,' I said.

He finished, did up his flies, and said, 'We have met. You were with Polly Drummond that time in the street and Fred was beating you to a pulp when I stepped in.'

'I suppose I should thank you then, Mr Flint.'

'Nah. I wasn't rescuing you, mate. I was getting Fred, is all. It was good that he was distracted. Made it easier to lay the little bastard out.'

Violence hovered around Mal Flint like a force field. I could see that his solution to any problem would be a vicious one. Someone gets up your nose? Thump him, stomp on him. A sheilah steps out of line? Give her a backhander, show her who's boss.

'I understand Fred owed you money.'

'He owed me fifty quid, the little prick.'

I wanted to get out of the toilets, away from the acrid smell of ammonia, but Mal Flint wasn't moving.

'The coppers have been to see me,' he said. 'Your mate in there. He came round askin' questions. Now how would he know Drummond owed me money unless a little bird who overheard something told him?'

'If you haven't done anything, you don't have anything to worry about,' I said lamely.

Between clenched teeth he said, 'I don't want any coppers stickin' their fuckin' beaks into my business, and if you know what's good for you you'll tell that cunt Topaz to back right off.

It'd be a pity if your other arm got broken, wouldn't it. How'd you wipe your arse?'

He shoved me with the flat of his hand, not forcefully, but as a kind of physical exclamation mark.

When I returned to the bar, Topaz was nowhere to be seen. The barman, who saw me looking around, indicated that he'd gone outside, onto the pavement. He was talking closely and quietly to a young man of about eighteen or nineteen. When they saw me, the young man pulled away from Topaz and walked quickly up March Street. The speed of his departure was so singular that I asked Topaz who he was.

'Just a bloke,' he said.

'He ran off like a startled rabbit.'

'No one likes being seen talking to a copper.'

'Except me, apparently.'

'It's a topsy-turvy world,' he said, and laughed briefly.

'I've just had an extremely unpleasant experience in the urinal,' I said. He raised his eyebrows and turned his head to one side.

'It's not what you're thinking. I had a run in with an ape named Mal Flint. Know him?'

'Ape is a bit flattering for Mal Flint. I wouldn't have thought he was one of the higher primates. I know him.'

'He threatened me. Said that he'd break my other arm unless I told you to back off. Oh, and he called you a cunt.'

'Mal Flint is a brainless thug. Stay out of his way.'

'Fred Drummond owed him a lot of money. Fifty pounds. Why?'

'Flint runs a two-up game and dog fights and God knows what else. Fred was a big loser.'

'Is it possible,' I said, 'that the two murders are not connected? I can't see why Flint would kill Polly, although he's strong enough to take her up that ladder. But what if he went to the Drummond house, looking for his money, and was disturbed by Mrs Drummond? Would he be capable of cutting an old lady's throat?'

'Listen, Sherlock,' Topaz said. 'Don't start playing amateur detective. You'll get into all sorts of trouble. You could get yourself killed. I don't think our culprit, whoever he is, is particularly squeamish about how he deals with people who get in his way.'

'I'm right though, aren't I? About Mal Flint. You think that's a possibility. That's why you went round to see him.'

'Since Polly's death I have spoken to dozens of people. Do you really think I've been sitting on my arse doing nothing? Flint was just one of them.'

At that point, Flint himself came out of the pub. He passed by us and spat on the ground.

'He's a dangerous man, Will. Don't go poking around Flint.'

I watched Flint's retreating back. He looked over his shoulder once, and the malevolence in his eyes made me think that severing a human head would cause him no more concern than decapitating a chook for the Sunday roast.

Buoyed by whiskey and beer, I was not affected by Walter Sunder's surly presence in the kitchen during preparation for dinner. He sliced carrots and chopped onions, and shot me the odd, sideways glance. At six o'clock Tibald turned on the radio to hear the BBC news. As a crisp voice calmly enunciated that Stalingrad was expected to fall, I went in search of Augie Kelly. He was in the dining room, with Adrian, and laying the tables. I asked to speak with him privately.

Augie had a small office, not much more than a cupboard under the stairs, but it sat two people comfortably. It smelled of new paint, and was either feminine or military in its neatness.

'What do you know about Mrs Charlotte Witherburn?'

'She's rich. Wouldn't be seen dead here. Not grand enough.'

'You've met her?'

'Now where would I meet a woman like that?'

'You seem to know a lot about what she thinks for someone who's never met her.'

'Oh, I get it,' he said, leaning back in his chair. 'She's a looker. Am I right? Or am I right?'

I did not dignify this with a response.

'What about her husband? What do you know about him?'

'I've heard talk at the bar. He didn't get rich by being nice to people. He's got enemies, and the word is he'll go after anything in a skirt. I've never met him either. Seen him, though. Strutting around the place. Looks like a bulldog. If she's a looker, she married him for his money, not his looks. Why all the questions?'

'I met her today, with Annie and Topaz. At the Royal.'

He looked a little hurt.

'Well, the Ladies' Lounge here isn't up and running yet. Maybe Mrs Witherburn will come here for a drink when it is. She'll give the place a bit of class, Augie.'

'And you're going to get her here, are you? You don't think she's a bit out of your league?'

The sudden hostility in his voice was unexpected.

'I've barely spoken three words to the woman. What are you so annoyed about?'

He calmed down immediately.

'Sorry,' he said, as the blush of anger which had stained his cheeks receded. 'I can't stand those sorts of people.'

'I had no idea you were such a volcano of class resentment. I thought she was charming.'

'That's nice. But what did she think of you?'

He ended the conversation by returning to the dining room. I said aloud to no one, 'What the hell was that all about?'

The melancholy figure of Charlotte Witherburn floated in and out of my dreams that night. I woke with no specific memory of these dreams except for the discordant image of a creature, half man, half bulldog, mounting her. There was no excitement attached to the image, I hasten to add, only loathing.

It was Annie who raised the subject of Charlotte Witherburn, at breakfast that Sunday morning.

'Will and I met the richest woman in Maryborough yesterday,' she said. 'Charlotte Witherburn. Her husband's a stinker, apparently.'

'I see them at Mass,' said Kevin Skakel. 'They're always together, but I've never seen them speak to each other. That woman has got some clothes, let me tell you.'

'Do they always go to the same Mass?' I asked, dismally attempting nonchalance.

'Ten o'clock Mass. Every Sunday. They'll be there today.'

'Well, I heard that he bashes her.'

We all turned to look at Adrian.

'That's the word on the waterfront, is it?' I said.

'No need to get snippy. I'm just saying what I heard. He cheats on her and he thumps her.' He pursed his lips in a caricature of haughtiness and added, 'My source, I assure you, is impeccable and also well endowed, although that might not be quite relevant.'

Kevin Skakel, who despite his church-going never revealed the slightest disapproval of Adrian's morals, said, 'I'd believe that. She moves like a martyr.'

So he'd noticed it, too. I wondered if Mrs Witherburn had

made an appearance in his dreams as well as mine.

We went our separate ways after breakfast. I walked down to the courthouse and around Queen's Park with Arthur. I kept him informed of all that had happened, and held nothing back, not even my unsettling reaction to that briefest of meetings with Mrs Witherburn. I also expressed my relief that he would not be called upon to lie to the police and back up my alibi.

'That might still be necessary,' he said. 'We don't know what's going on in the investigation. They aren't amateurs.'

'Arthur, I have to see Charlotte Witherburn again. Will you come with me to St Mary's?'

'I should say no. I should know by now that going anywhere with you is bloody dangerous.'

'Come on,' I coaxed. 'The church is just around the corner, and it's nearly ten o'clock.'

I had already begun walking towards it. Arthur followed and caught up with me.

'Why do you want to see her?'

'Because, because, because, because, because.'

'She's a married woman.'

'An unhappily married woman. I just want to see her. I want you to see her, to tell me if I'm mad for thinking that she's the most beautiful woman I've ever seen.'

'You've gone troppo,' was all he said.

People were arriving at St Mary's in large numbers. Some were going straight in; others were hanging about the door, chatting. Arthur and I waited by the gate in Adelaide Street. Just before ten, a car pulled up — the only one to do so. Everyone else had arrived by bicycle or on foot. The passenger door opened and Charlotte Witherburn stepped out, followed immediately by the driver, who I took from his resemblance to a bulldog to be her husband. She was taller than he, and she paid him no heed as they entered the churchyard. Harry Witherburn was the ugliest man I had ever seen. His lips were fleshy and pulpy, and glistened beneath a cauliflower nose. His eyebrows were bushy, nature having decided to grow hair there instead of on his head. The mean, black marbles that were his eyes offered shuttered windows to his soul, and on either side of that obscene mouth jowly pouches hung. How could she bear to be touched by him? He must have been fifteen years her senior, and those years had not been kind to him. He wore the marks of every epicurean indulgence all over his flabby, undisciplined body. They entered the church without speaking to anyone.

'Well,' I said. 'What do you think?'

'I didn't get a good look at her. Nice hat, though. He's no oil painting.'

'When they come out, I'm going to speak to her.'

'I'm not hanging around for an hour. My advice is don't speak to her, but you're not going to listen to me. You can tell me about it later.'

I entered the church halfway through the service and stood at the back. Charlotte and Harry were sitting in the front row, right on the aisle. They would be the first to approach the altar rail and receive communion. Harry Witherburn was obviously a man who expected to be first in everything. I left the church before the end of the Mass and waited by the car. To my surprise, Mr and Mrs Witherburn did not emerge together. Charlotte came out alone. He must have loitered in the nave talking to someone. She hurried towards the car, hesitating when she saw me, and then coming over, her hand extended.

'Mr Power, how nice. Were you at Mass?'

'Technically, no.'

'Goodness me, you sound like a Jesuit.'

Over her shoulder I saw her husband barrelling towards

us. His face was unreadable. It was incapable of registering emotion. Whether he was experiencing an orgasm or having a stroke would only be determined after the fact. Mrs Witherburn swung round on him and circumvented whatever he was about to say by speaking first.

'Harry. This is Mr William Power. He's in town with his acting company.'

Harry Witherburn looked me up and down, and made a small noise somewhere between a grunt and a dislodging of phlegm.

'He and his actors are going to do scenes from Shakespeare at our Red Cross fund-raiser.'

I did not give away that this was news to me.

'Well, that'll be bloody boring,' he said. 'But you do what you like.'

He got into the driver's seat and started the motor.

'So that's arranged then,' she said. 'I'll let you know the date.'

They were gone before I had the chance to utter a single word.

✑

By Sunday evening everyone had been told that we had been requested to do scenes for a Red Cross fund-raiser, and claims for the performance of a preferred party piece had been staked — every actor has a party piece.

'We'll decide the program later,' I said. 'We don't even know the date yet.'

'Charlotte Witherburn, Will,' said Annie. 'It'll be at their house, and it's the biggest house in town. Think what publicity this will be for *Titus*. My God, people might actually come.'

Later that evening, Augie grudgingly admitted that he might

have been wrong about Charlotte Witherburn. But when I told him that she had made the offer out of the blue, and that she had deliberately created the impression that it had been arrived at after some discussion, he said, 'So she's using you against her husband.'

He seemed satisfied with this diagnosis. I was not. Augie, of course, was touching a raw spot. I was not unbruised by the recent revelation that it was not solely on the strength of my charms that Polly had expressed an interest in me. To be used by her to inflame the jealousy of the barely pubescent Patrick Lutteral had not made a significant contribution to my self-esteem. The meaning behind Charlotte Witherburn's look when she had so daringly declared that the Power Players would appear at her benefit was of an entirely different order. There may be, as the great man said, no art to find the mind's construction in the face, but what I saw in Charlotte's face was a desire to escape. This was no thoughtless, adolescent game of 'Marry me quickly'. This was sadder and perhaps more dangerous than that.

I looked at myself long and hard in the mirror before I went to bed that night. My face had healed. The only evidence of Fred's blow was a slight discoloration of the eyelid, only apparent when the eye was closed, and a red fleck below the iris. I wished it wasn't there. It was unsightly, but I didn't think it would prejudice Mrs Witherburn against me. Just before I fell asleep my confidence deserted me, and I thought that after all I may have over-interpreted what was the briefest of exchanges and the most ambiguous of looks.

I changed my mind the following morning when Arthur knocked on my bedroom door and said that Mrs Charlotte Witherburn was waiting to see me in the dining room downstairs. I made a detour to the bathroom to comb my hair and check that I hadn't missed any bits when I'd shaved that morning. Damn that red fleck.

When I entered the dining room she was silhouetted against the window so that at first she seemed as insubstantial as a shadow.

'Mr Power, how lovely.'

'Please, call me Will.'

'Charlotte,' she said as we shook hands and laughed lightly, as though the exchange of names was some obscure witticism. She looked about the room.

'I've never been here.'

'Well, why would you? It used to be run down. Well, more run down.'

'I've heard about the food, of course. Harry would never come.'

She paused.

'Or has he been?'

With that simple question she laid bare the intimate truth that her marriage was a charade.

'Not that I'm aware of,' I said. 'I'm sure I would remember his unusual face.'

'His face is actually his best feature.'

'Oh dear,' I said, and smiled.

'I was expecting this place to be rather louche,' she said. 'But this is a nice room. I hope you don't mind my calling on you. Pete Topaz told me your company was staying here, and I wanted to let you know that I was serious about the Red Cross benefit. It's next Monday. Is that too soon?'

'No, no, not at all.'

She called him 'Pete'. How close were they?

'Is there something in particular you would like us to do, Charlotte?'

'I'm afraid my knowledge of Shakespeare is too thin to make any useful suggestions.'

She moved a little closer to me, and the sweet smell of her

perfume made me a little dizzy.

'I must apologise for the boorish behaviour of my husband yesterday. He is not a cultured man.'

I assured her that I had not taken his words personally, and hoped that perhaps we could change his mind. She laughed.

'Oh, no,' she said. 'That hope is doomed to be dashed. He may not even be at the fund-raiser. He finds such things boring. Perhaps you could come to the house tomorrow and see where you will be performing.'

'Shall I bring the company?'

'I don't think that will be necessary. Shall we say eleven o'clock? We'll have lunch'

She presented me with a card with an address printed on it.

On her way out she almost collided with Augie, who had walked in unaware that anybody was in the dining room. He was carrying a pile of tablecloths, several of which fell to the ground.

'I'm so sorry,' Charlotte said, and bent to help him retrieve them.

'This is Mr Augie Kelly,' I said, 'the proprietor. Augie, Mrs Charlotte Witherburn.'

'I've heard so much about your dining room,' she said. 'I must come one night.'

If Augie had intended a rebuke, it remained unspoken. Charlotte left, and as the sound of her car receded he said, 'She's not as uppity as I thought she'd be.'

'Augie, she's stunning.'

At 11.00 am I pushed my borrowed bicycle up the drive of Witherburn, an extravagant and gleaming Federation mansion, white against the deep green of the gardens around it. The house

was girdled with a wide verandah of elaborate timber fretwork, with front steps that could be approached from the left or the right. The lower branches of the steps met at a landing and continued from there to double doors of intricate lattice. These doors gave access to the verandah, and beyond them lay the main door. The right-hand side of the house swelled out to form a sort of grand rotunda. The roof above it resembled a giant circus tent made of metal, and sitting right on top of it was a small lookout, circled with a wooden railing.

I turned the handle of the door at the top of the stairs and opened it. There was no one on the wide verandah. Ahead, an elegantly carved door was open. A house of this size could not be run without servants, but there was no sign of them. I took a few paces inside the house and called.

'Hello!'

Charlotte emerged from a side room immediately.

'Will, come in.'

I knew from the silence that we were alone, and the thrill of this was so intense that my first words were an incoherent babble about how beautiful Witherburn was.

'My husband likes people to know that he is a rich man. Would you like a drink?'

'It's a bit early for …'

'It's never too early for champagne. It should be drunk first thing in the morning and last thing at night.'

We sat on the verandah drinking expensive champagne, and it seemed that the ease between us was the ease of two people who were already lovers. So it was without any uncertainty or tentativeness that we made our way to Charlotte's bedroom and made love.

We lay side by side afterwards, unsurprised at what had happened. We had moved together with the unthinking trust of familiarity — Charlotte seemed almost reassuringly bored — and when she said that we would have to get dressed because the staff would be returning soon, I thought, yes, of course. We could not lie about naked, and risk discovery. The haste with which Charlotte drew on her clothes was proof of her nervousness on this point. We straightened the sheets and made the bed, and returned to our seats on the verandah, where we drank the remaining champagne and Charlotte spoke about her marriage.

'I've never committed adultery before,' she said, and in her uninflected tone I recognised that this was the truth.

'My husband and I do not make love. We have separate bedrooms. You weren't lying in his sheets.'

'Why do you stay with him?'

She looked at me quizzically, as if the answer to this were perfectly obvious.

'We're Catholic,' she said. 'Divorce is impossible.'

'Does he treat you badly?' I asked.

'Oh yes,' she said matter-of-factly. 'He's a violent man and sometimes he …' Her voice trailed off.

Anger welled within me. I reached out to touch her, but as I did so I heard a noise in the house, and a moment later a door at the end of the verandah opened and a woman appeared.

'Are you ready for lunch, Mrs Witherburn?'

'Yes, thank you, Joyce.'

'I'll bring it out.'

Joyce must have come up the back stairs without our hearing her. She brought us a tray of sandwiches and a pot of tea, and withdrew. Charlotte didn't introduce me. When we were alone she poured the tea and said, 'My husband was having an affair with that girl who was murdered.'

She took one of the small triangles of bread and bit into it.

My stomach lurched and a maelstrom of emotion began to turn within me.

'I knew that girl,' I heard a voice say, and it was my own, but somehow separate from me.

'Yes,' Charlotte said, 'I know, but it wasn't your child she was carrying. It was Harry's.'

Her face was impassive.

'How do you know this?' I whispered.

'About two weeks before she died, before you had arrived in town, she came to see me. She said that she was pregnant and that Harry had dumped her as soon as she had told him. He wanted her to get rid of it. She said no.'

'Why did she tell you this?'

'She wanted me to know what kind of a man Harry was. She thought I would be shocked, that I would fall into a swoon. I told her that I knew already what kind of man my husband was.'

'What did Polly want from you?'

'Nothing. Absolutely nothing. She made no demands, no threats. Nothing. She said that she wouldn't expose Harry, that she was going to get married, and I suppose her husband would think the child was his. She was only six weeks pregnant. I rather liked her. There was something admirable in her pride. I suppose I admired it because I had surrendered mine long ago.'

'Charlotte, does Peter Topaz know all this?'

'Yes, of course. As soon as that girl's body was found I told him all I knew. Harry denied that the child was his, but he could hardly deny the affair. There were any number of people who knew. Even the girl's brother. He came here, too. He spoke to Harry, or argued with him. He wanted money to keep his mouth shut about the baby. Harry practically threw him down the stairs. I thought he was going to kill him.'

'Do you think your husband killed Polly Drummond?' I

asked quietly. She didn't answer, but stood up and walked to the verandah railing.

'That's him now,' she said, and I heard the sound of a car crunching gravel in the drive. I stood up and watched as the car stopped and Harry Witherburn got out. He looked up at us and gave a strange, abbreviated, ugly laugh before heading up the steps.

'*Why* do you stay with him?' I whispered.

She turned eyes bleak with defeat towards me and said, 'Where would I go?'

When Harry Witherburn opened the doors at the top of the steps he passed through to the front door of the house without speaking to us. He cast a brutish glance our way and disappeared inside.

'You'll come again,' said Charlotte.

'Of course,' I said.

She kissed me lightly on the lips and followed her husband into the dark interior of Witherburn.

I cycled to Wright's Hall, where the company was rehearsing in my absence. I was glad to be distracted from the tumult of feeling that had been unleashed by my visit to Witherburn.

'It's a huge place,' was all I said.

At midnight I knocked on Arthur's door. He was lying on his bed, reading, wearing only a pair of khaki shorts. In my presence he was unselfconscious about his ruined torso, but he rarely allowed anyone else to see it. I had become so used to it that the puckered skin and truncated shoulder no longer caused me a sympathetic shudder at the pain he must have endured. I told him everything that had happened that day. Everything.

'And Topaz knows all this?'

'He doesn't know I made love to Mrs Witherburn.'

He was exasperated by my literal-mindedness.

'He knows all the other stuff? He knows that Polly was pregnant and that Harry Witherburn was the father?'

'Yes.'

'This is why he doesn't suspect you any more. He's got far more convincing suspects to sort out.'

'But Conroy knows, too. Peter tells him everything. Why is he still on my case?'

'They could be divvying up the suspects. Each of them putting pressure on a different person. Or maybe Witherburn is a mate of Conroys.'

'All right, let's just go through some of the possibilities here. Now, we know that Polly was pregnant. The post-mortem would have revealed that to the coppers, but Charlotte told them anyway. Harry Witherburn was the father.'

'She said he was the father. That doesn't mean he was, even if they were lovers. He might not have been the only one. You almost got there yourself. It might have been Patrick what's-his-name.'

'Lutteral. Unlikely.'

'You can't know that for sure. It might have been Fred.'

'That's unpleasant.'

'Nevertheless, if what Shirley Moynahan told you is true, it's a possibility. Or it might have been someone we don't even know about yet.'

'Harry Witherburn had the most to lose.'

'Maybe. But if you're a religious prig like Patrick Lutteral and your fiancée tells you she's pregnant and that you'd better marry her in a hurry, you might react badly. Of course, if they've never actually had sex and he found out that she was pregnant to someone else, well, who knows what he might do. Witherburn is definitely not the only candidate here.'

'If you'd met Patrick Lutteral, you'd know he couldn't have done it.'

'I've met enough religious types to know that they are the last people on earth you'd trust. Scratch a zealot and uncover a pervert. Don't make Conroy's mistake and settle on a suspect and be blind to other options. Our problem is, Will, that we don't know enough about Polly Drummond. Her life holds the key to her death.'

'What about Mrs Drummond? Was she killed by a different person? Mal Flint?'

'He could have killed Polly, too.'

'Why?'

'Like I said, we don't know enough about her. Maybe she was fucking him, too. I agree that the two murders seem very different, but that might be deliberate. Someone could be trying to create the impression that there are two killers out there.'

'When I came in here,' I said, 'I thought I had a grip on all this. Now I'm more confused than ever.'

'Does Mrs Witherburn think her husband had anything to do with Polly's death?'

'I asked her that. She didn't answer, which I suppose means yes. You don't think she's in danger, do you?'

'I think she's been in danger since the day she married him, and if you're not careful you'll be in danger, too.'

'We're getting closer, Arthur.'

'No, we're not, Will. We're just uncovering more people who might decide that the world can do without you.'

I hardly slept that night. All I could think about was Charlotte in that huge house, with her husband crouching like a black spider in some dark corner of it. I woke fatigued and did not go down for breakfast. At eight-thirty Augie came to my room and said that there was a man downstairs who wanted to see me.

'Did he give a name?'

'No. No name. I don't know who he is. Never seen him before. I told him to wait in the bar.'

I had a strange foreboding as I pushed open the bar-room door. The man had his back to me and was seated at the empty bar, smoking. When he heard me come in, he stood down from the stool and faced me. He was my age and height, and his clothes sat uncomfortably on a lean body, hardened by work. His face was tanned, but the most remarkable feature about it was the eyebrows, which were ginger, although his close-cropped hair was dark brown. I had never seen him before, and yet there was something about him …

'Are you William Power?' he asked.

'Yes. And you are?'

'My name's Joe Drummond,' he said. 'So you're the murdering prick I've heard about.'

He pulled a pistol from his trouser pocket and pointed it at my chest. The last thing I remembered was the shattering report as he pulled the trigger. I felt no pain, but fell into a well of darkness, and continued falling until all sensation stopped.

PART TWO

Chapter Seven

FREEDOM AND CAPTURE

'WHY AREN'T I DEAD?' That was the first question I asked the splendidly breasted matron when I woke, yet again, in the Maryborough Base Hospital.

'By rights, you should be, Mr Power. The man who shot you was expecting you to remain upright. It seems that as soon as you saw his gun you began to faint. You crumpled just as he pulled the trigger. The bullet went through the muscle at the top of your shoulder, above the collarbone. It was meant for your heart. There's no permanent damage, but that left arm will be out of action for a bit longer.'

Was there a whiff of mockery when she said that I had begun to faint at the sight of the gun? Would she rather I had stood proudly and taken the bullet where Joe Drummond had intended it to go?

'Where's Joe Drummond?' I asked.

'Who's Joe Drummond?'

'The man who shot me.'

'I'm sorry, Mr Power, you'll have to ask Sergeant Topaz that. You're becoming a regular. Usually we only see circus people when there's been a tumbling accident or someone falling from a horse.'

'I'm not with the circus,' I said wearily. 'Why does everyone in this town think I'm with the circus?'

'Perhaps they think you look disreputable,' said Peter Topaz as he came into the ward.

'Where's Joe Drummond?' I asked again.

'He's in custody. It might surprise you, but we do actually take a dim view of people pointing guns at other people and pulling the trigger.'

I moved slightly to make myself more comfortable, but a sharp stab of pain forced me to remain still. I felt as if I must have gone white, and experienced a rush of nausea.

'Are you going to be sick, Mr Power?' asked the matron with unnecessary sternness.

'No,' I said grimly, and by a sheer act of will held the contents of my stomach in check. I thought she'd had enough entertainment at my expense already.

'I need a statement from you.' Topaz paused and scratched his chest between the first and second button of his shirt. 'I also need to know if you intend to press charges.'

This was one of the most extraordinary remarks I had ever heard.

'I would have thought that attempted murder was a crime, even in Queensland,' I said.

'Well, strictly speaking, it is. But perhaps this was more in the nature of an assault, or an accident.'

I was dumbfounded.

'He shot me,' I said. 'If I hadn't ducked, I'd be a dead man.'

The matron made a noise that sounded unpleasantly like a chortle.

'If Joe Drummond had wanted to kill you,' Topaz said, 'you'd be lying on a slab in the mortuary. He doesn't miss. He would have summed you up as a fainter as soon as he saw you and made the necessary adjustments.'

'You're serious, aren't you? You really don't want me to press charges.'

Topaz gave the matron a look that indicated that he wanted her to leave. She took the hint without demur and withdrew.

'Frankly, Will, I don't want you to press charges.' He didn't take his eyes off me as he waited for my response. Another little stab of pain quelled a sudden urge to give energetic expression to my astonishment. I settled for weakly asserting that Topaz obviously was disappointed that Joe Drummond had missed and that he was hoping to give him a second go at shuffling me off this mortal coil.

'I want you to meet him,' he said.

'Thanks. I've already met him. We didn't really hit it off.'

'The person who killed Polly and her mother, if it was the same person, will never be caught if Joe Drummond is locked up.'

This remarkable little aperçu penetrated the fog of nausea that had enveloped me since I had agitated my wound by moving.

'You'll have to explain that,' I said. 'I'm obviously too dim to understand how that could possibly be true.'

Peter Topaz looked from side to side, and the movement was so mechanical as to be almost a pantomime parody of a person anxious not to be overheard.

'I can't guess at the motive, but we have three dead

Drummonds and one live one. Joe Drummond might be a source of some interest to our killer.'

Topaz sat on the end of my bed. His weight shifted my body painfully. My involuntary wince did not encourage him to stand up. In fact, he made another unnecessary movement.

'You want to use Joe Drummond as bait?'

'Yes,' he said matter-of-factly. 'But he's no sprat, I assure you. He's willing. More than willing.'

'I see. So since he shot me you've convinced him that I'm not the murderer.'

'He didn't take much convincing. He said that the moment he saw you he knew you probably didn't do it.'

'But he pulled the trigger anyway.'

'Well, when you point a gun at someone there's a sort of adrenaline juggernaut that makes retreat difficult. He feels bad about shooting you. Really, he does.'

'I'm looking forward to him feeling a lot worse.'

'Oh, come on,' Topaz said. 'What do you want, an eye for an eye? You want to shoot him in the shoulder?'

'No. I want the law to do what it's supposed to do and punish people who shoot me.'

'The quality of mercy …'

'Oh, please!'

Topaz shrugged. 'I'll let you think about it. Joe's in the cells, and that's not very pleasant, I assure you.'

'Perhaps you should put him in a suite at the Royal.'

He held up both hands. 'All right, all right. You're obviously not in a reasonable frame of mind at the moment. But think about it. At least think about meeting him, and then decide whether to press charges or not.'

After Topaz left I stared at the ceiling and tried to douse the spark of anger that threatened to flare inside me. I closed my eyes and relaxed into the imagined speech of a judge thundering a lengthy sentence at the bowed and chastened head of Joe Drummond. This pleasant reverie was interrupted by Annie Hudson, who grabbed my foot through the bed sheet and shook it.

'You have to drop the charges against Joe,' she said sharply.

'I'm very well, thank you for asking.'

'I know that. I asked the matron. You have to drop the charges against Joe.'

'Joe? Joe? You're on first-name terms with the man who tried to kill me? Has everyone gone mad? Is the fact that I've been shot of any interest to anybody?'

'Oh, really, Will. Why does everything always have to be about you? Joe Drummond is sweating in a disgusting cell when he should be out helping to catch the person who murdered his mother and his sister. You're lying here in the lap of luxury and ...'

This was too much. I forced myself into sitting upright, ignoring the pain this caused, reached behind me with my good hand, grabbed the pillow, and threw it forcefully at Annie's head. It caught her in the face. She was prepared to take this as a joke until she saw the look on my face. She realised then that the emotion behind the throw was not jocular. My fury did not make her cower. It had the reverse effect. She walked to the table beside the bed and lifted the jug of water that was sitting there. With a movement that was both deft and brutal, she upended its contents over my head. The shock of the chill made me gasp.

'I'm just sorry it wasn't a bedpan full of urine,' she said.

The matron came from nowhere and ordered Annie out of her hospital.

'I'm sorry about the sheets, Matron,' Annie said as she swept out, 'but I'm sure you've wanted to tip something over him yourself.'

The matron did not disagree, which was offensive enough, then she began replacing my wet dressing rather too roughly. I was pushed and pulled in all directions with little regard for my physical comfort. She removed the sling, my shirt, and the bandages on the gunshot wound.

'Gently!' I yelped.

'I am busy enough, Mr Power, without you adding to my workload.'

'Excuse me,' I snapped. 'I did not tip water over myself. It wasn't me who let a madwoman in here outside visiting hours.'

'You're going home later this afternoon. You can get up now and sit in the waiting room until the doctor discharges you.'

I wasn't given any choice in this matter. I was bundled out of the sopping bed, and its sheets were stripped before I had a chance to protest.

'Circus people,' she muttered.

I was expecting that someone would come in the truck to pick me up. Petrol had become difficult to get in Maryborough, but I knew that we had at least a quarter of a tank left, and the short drive from the George to the hospital would hardly drain it. No one came, however — not even Arthur. On the uncomfortable walk to the hotel I consoled myself that Annie had probably driven from the rehearsal hall when she had made her unpleasant visit, and that everybody was doing the right thing professionally by choosing to work on their pieces for the benefit. I didn't for a moment think that I had been abandoned by the company. I wasn't, after all, very badly injured, and Charlotte's fund-raiser was only a few days away. Performing well there could add significant numbers to the box-office.

As I walked I was engaged in a little rehearsal of my own. What was I going to say to Annie? Despite my feelings for Charlotte, I could not entirely expunge from recent memory my alarming sexual lurch towards Annie, even if it had not developed beyond a moment of disrupted onanism. All thoughts of Annie, positive and negative, vanished when I entered the dining room of the George Hotel. A silhouette sat against a far window, upright, but somehow broken at the same time. Charlotte stood as soon as she saw me. She put out her hand to stop my headlong rush towards her.

'Oh, Will,' she whispered, and the pain in her voice was as palpable to me as the pain in my shoulder.

'What is it?' I asked.

She moved so that a panel of light fell across her face. One eye was red and bruised, and her lip, oddly swollen, was cracked at one end. Under the pressure of her words a thin ooze of blood had broken through the lipstick she had used to disguise the damage.

'We're both in the wars,' she said, and smiled faintly. I reached up to touch her face, but she pulled away from me and her eyes darted nervously over my shoulder, as if she was expecting to see someone there.

'The red-headed man,' she said. 'I don't like him. I don't like the way he looks at me.'

I had seen the way Augie Kelly looked at women, and I could not argue with Charlotte's revulsion. There was, however, a more compelling issue at hand.

'Did your husband do this to you?' I asked.

'Why, yes, of course,' she said, and she furrowed her brow quizzically as if she thought the question peculiar or unnecessary.

'Did he find out about us?'

'No. I don't think so. I don't know. He may have. He doesn't really need an excuse.'

'Will you come up to my room? We can talk freely there.'

'Oh, no,' she said. 'Not here. Not in a hotel. I'll come for you tomorrow at eleven. We'll drive somewhere.'

She was suddenly anxious to leave. When Augie Kelly entered the room, she said, in a voice pitched too high to be convincingly casual, 'Thank you, Mr Power. Those pieces sound perfect. I'm sure people will be most entertained.'

With her head lowered she hurried out. A moment later the sound of her car's engine reached us and then receded as she drove away.

'Walked into a door, did she?' Augie said, crassly.

'The only way her husband can get an erection is by thumping women. Perhaps you're familiar with the condition.'

'All right, all right. Keep your shirt on. It's none of my business.'

I sat down, suddenly tired.

'Christ, Augie, what a mess, what a fucking mess.'

Augie left but came back almost immediately with a beer.

'The others will be back soon,' he said. 'Do you want me to keep mum about Mrs Witherburn's visit?'

'No. Why should you? You heard her. She was here about the fund-raiser.'

'OK. I'll be more specific. Do you want me to keep mum about what she looked like.'

I realised that I was being drawn into a kind of intimacy with Augie, but I felt I had to call on him to keep quiet.

'Yes. If you wouldn't mind. It's nobody's business.'

'Just ours,' he said.

I didn't want to give Augie the impression that I considered him a mate who could expect further confidences from me. Arm's length was my preferred distance where Augie Kelly was concerned. Charlotte would not have been happy to hear Augie appointing himself as the guardian of her reputation.

'I know you don't want to hear this,' he said, and his tone indicated that, as a friend, he felt able to speak the words I apparently didn't want to hear. 'I know you don't want to hear this, but don't get mixed up with the Witherburns. You are a trouble magnet, and Harry Witherburn is real trouble. He's a powerful man, and if he thinks you're messing around with his wife he'll squash you like a bug.'

I let Augie run through his gratuitous and impertinent advice without interruption. The fact that he felt able to give it made it clear that he had made the shift from considering me as a client to adopting me as an intimate. I would have to be careful in future not to encourage him further.

'I am not involved with his wife,' I lied.

'Why is she coming tomorrow?' he shot back.

'She's showing me Teddington Weir,' I said off the top of my head. 'I expressed an interest in seeing it, and she offered to drive me there. We need to discuss the program for her fundraiser.'

As I said this I decided that Teddington was, in fact, the ideal destination. On the weekend it was a popular place to swim and court, but it was sufficiently far out of town to ensure that on a weekday nobody would be there.

'Will, if you don't want to admit to adultery with Charlotte Witherburn, that's fine, but it's perfectly obvious that there's something going on between the two of you. If I can see it, Harry Witherburn can see it. That's all I'm saying.'

I was aware that that was not all he was saying. He was exercising his imagined, new-found privilege of casting moral aspersions in my direction. Adultery is such an ugly word, and I was about to say so when the rumble of the truck arriving from Wright's Hall brought our conversation to an end.

The troupe came into the dining room, but before anybody had a chance to inquire after my health Annie stood before me, arms akimbo, and said, 'Well?'

'Well what?' I gripped my beer, knowing that it was not beyond her to pour it into my lap.

'Joe Drummond. What are you going to do about Joe?'

'I'm not going to discuss that with you.'

'Now, Will.' Adrian stepped forward. 'He sat here quiet as a mouse after he shot you. He just waited for the police. He didn't even drink the beer that Augie got for him. I talked to him and he was quite charming. No one that good looking should be in jail.'

'Oh, for God's sake, Adrian,' I said. 'And what was I doing while you were plying him with beer and having a lovely little chat?'

'You were unconscious. It's not as if you could have joined in.'

I decided to assert my authority before this became any more exasperating or ridiculous.

'I'm not going to discuss this any further. I want to meet you all here at 8.30 tomorrow morning to finalise choosing your pieces for the fund-raiser. I won't be at the rehearsal in the morning. I'll join you in the afternoon. Thank you.'

Ignoring this clear dismissal, Bill Henty said, 'And where will you be while we're working?' As was usual with him, there was an ugly note of aggression in his voice.

'I'll be at the police station laying formal charges against the man who attempted to kill me,' I said. I looked at Annie when I said this. Henty sniffed and left the room. The others followed, with Annie turning at the door to say, 'Selfish. Nasty. Vicious.'

'That's the title of your autobiography, is it?' I said.

Arthur remained behind and sat opposite me.

'I suppose you're going to tell me now that Joe Drummond is misunderstood, that he's not a murderous thug. I can't believe that he was offered a beer.'

'No, I'm not going to tell you that.'

I was expecting more, but nothing came. He was looking at me in a most disconcerting way.

'Say it,' I said. 'Say whatever it is you want to say.'

'All right, but let me finish before you interrupt or storm out in high dudgeon.'

I nodded agreement.

'I don't know the first thing about Joe Drummond,' he said. 'Maybe he's a maniac. Maybe he's an arsehole. Maybe he's distracted by grief. I don't know and in some ways it doesn't matter. OK, he shot you. That was foolish and dangerous and criminal, and he should be held to account for it. If you decide to press charges that would be perfectly reasonable and understandable. Don't pay attention to Annie's carry-on. She's responding to his vulnerability. She does that, and just at the moment Joe Drummond is more vulnerable than you are, and Peter Topaz has been softening her up about him. However, and it's a big however, Joe Drummond is safe when he's in jail, and that's bad for you. You need him to be out and unsafe. The next target.'

I signalled that I wanted to interject at this point. 'And what if he's got a different idea about who should be a target? He's already had a practice shot at me. What if he's after a bullseye?'

'That's why you need to talk to him. Obviously you're not going to take anybody else's word for it that he made a mistake. You have to hear it from him, and you can judge for yourself whether you trust him or not. I won't lie to you, Will. Peter Topaz asked me to talk to you.'

I narrowed my eyes as an expression of disapproval.

'I wouldn't have agreed to do it if I didn't think he had a point. Conroy's not crossing you off his suspect list, and no one's making much headway in solving this. If it's someone out to get the Drummond family, having the last one out of reach protects everyone except you. And Joe Drummond has said he's willing to sit in that house and wait for the killer to show his hand.'

I said nothing, but because this was coming from Arthur the rage that was swelling within me did not spill into the room. What he said made hideous sense. Somehow I had to get past the incredible lack of concern for my welfare which all this interest in Joe Drummond seemed to imply.

'Well?' Arthur said.

'All right, I'll talk to Drummond. But I'm not promising anything, and I want Topaz there in the room. And I want Drummond restrained.'

'You could do it now. Topaz would still be at the station.'

'No,' I said emphatically. 'The least Drummond can do is spend one night in the cells. I'm sure it's not his first and, until I'm convinced he's not a threat, it won't be his last.'

The following morning the cast gathered as requested in the dining room. Tibald was there too. He felt that his rendition of Falstaff's 'Chimes at midnight' speech was peerless, and that a one-off at Witherburn would not interfere with his cooking.

'Perhaps Mrs Witherburn would appreciate a platter of decent hors d'oeuvres,' he said, knowing that the offer would secure his place. It would also introduce more people to the wonders of the Canty cuisine. Annie had opted for Portia's 'Quality of mercy' speech. She looked daggers at me when she announced her choice, as if I might learn something from the text. Bill Henty had gone for the 'Band of brothers' speech from *Henry V*. I had half thought I might do this myself, but I let him have it. Adrian, who liked burying himself under a mountain of make-up, had settled on Polonius' 'Neither a borrower nor a lender be' from *Hamlet*; and Kevin Skakel, oddly, had decided against Shakespeare and wanted to do William McGonagall's 'Tay Bridge Disaster', a poem he considered to be one of the masterpieces in the language. That really tells you all you need to know about Kevin Skakel. As I said later to Arthur, I thought Kevin might have suffered a club brain as well as a club foot. Arthur had chosen two of the sonnets, and I was thinking of something from *Coriolanus*. The others had gone for crowd-pleasers. I wanted a piece that might challenge an audience.

'I'll join you at the hall later,' I said. I did not tell Annie that I had decided to talk to Joe Drummond. I wasn't going to give her the satisfaction of supposing, wrongly, that I had caved in to pressure from her.

'You can drop me off at the police station on the way,' I said. 'I just have to go up to my room to get my copy of *Coriolanus*'.

I took a few minutes to unearth it, and when I returned to the dining room I discovered that they had left without me. I walked to the police station. When I entered, the desk was unattended. I coughed, but no one came, so I went outside and walked down the side of the building to where I presumed the cells were. There were only two cells housed in an outbuilding which looked as if it had been constructed last century, and it probably had been. Peter Topaz was there, unlocking the door. On the ground beside him were two plates of food. Flies had settled on them as he grappled with the lock.

'I've changed my mind,' I said.

Most people would have jumped or shown some surprise at

an unexpected voice from behind. Topaz didn't flinch.

'Good', he said, and bent down to pick up the plates. 'If you wait in the office I'll bring Joe in as soon as he's eaten his breakfast.'

Topaz came back to the office alone.

'He won't be long,' he said.

'I want him handcuffed, and I want you in the room.'

'The handcuffs aren't necessary, and of course I'll be in the room. You needn't worry, he's not going to jump you.'

'If he's not cuffed, I'm not talking to him.'

Topaz sighed heavily, but agreed to constrain Drummond for the duration of our encounter. He led me into the familiar interview room and returned to the front desk, where I heard a muffled conversation between him and whoever had now arrived for duty. When he came back into the room, he sat opposite me and had the decency to ask after my health.

'How are you feeling, Will? A bit sore, I imagine.'

'I feel fine. I've got a hole in my shoulder which might turn septic, and I'm about to meet the arsehole who put it there. Why wouldn't I feel fine?'

'What changed your mind?'

'Someone whose opinion I respect pointed out that there were advantages in not pressing charges. It's exactly what you said, of course, but it sounded more reasonable when it came from someone I admire.'

'How did Arthur lose his arm?'

Topaz had a way of asking questions that came out of nowhere. I suppose it was a technique designed to wrong-foot suspects.

'You'll have to ask him yourself,' I said.

'Is it a secret?'

'No, but I don't like discussing my friends behind their backs.'

'Fair enough. He's pretty adept with the one arm, isn't he?'

I didn't reply to this. I had no idea whether he was insinuating something or simply expressing admiration. There was an awkward silence. At least I found it awkward. Topaz seemed perfectly at ease. A knock on the door was followed by the entrance of the simple-minded constable who had escorted me to see Conroy a few days previously.

'I've got Joe here,' he said.

Topaz rose and opened the door fully. I suddenly felt sick with nerves. Joe Drummond came into the room, and his appearance took me by surprise. I was expecting an angry, surly, hostile brute. Joe Drummond, with his hands behind his back and with eyes red-rimmed from lack of sleep, did not look dangerous. He looked wounded in some profound way. He sat down and was forced to lean forward slightly because his handcuffs pressed against the back of the chair. I began to feel ashamed that I had insisted on seeing him like this. He was unshaven, and the sour smell of the malodorous cell in which he had spent the night clung to him. His eyes, startlingly blue against the red-streaked whites, met mine without embarrassment. Despite his circumstances, I saw no weakness there, but I saw no danger either.

'I'm sorry,' he said simply.

I didn't know how to respond to this. I had imagined that I would lacerate him with words, but I found myself unable to offer anything more than a small gesture of acceptance with my good hand. I turned to Peter Topaz and said, 'There's been a mistake. The incident was an accident. We were fooling around with the gun, and it went off.'

It was clumsy and utterly unconvincing, but it was a legal nicety that Topaz needed to hear.

'Accidents happen. Of course,' he said, turning to Joe Drummond, 'you'll be charged with discharging a firearm within the town limits, but if Mr Power has no objection, you'll be released as soon as the paperwork is done. If you stand up, I'll take off those cuffs.'

As Joe's hands were freed I wondered for a moment if he would suddenly be transformed into the avenging lunatic I had pictured him to be. He merely rubbed his wrists and quietly said, 'Thank you.'

He had said four words in all, and he was now a free man.

*

Within half an hour, Joe Drummond and I left the police station together. Only a few hours previously I wouldn't have thought this possible. Topaz was not with us. I suppose he wanted to avoid any suspicion that he had been involved in this most irregular state of affairs.

We walked a short way down Lennox Street without speaking. There is a natural social reticence between shooter and shot. I broke the silence by asking him what kind of breakfast was provided by the Maryborough police force. I realise that this was almost perversely banal, considering what might have been said, but I had had very little experience in making small talk with people who had recently wanted to kill me. Joe Drummond circumvented the need for small talk by saying, 'I haven't been home yet. I don't know whether they've cleaned it or not.'

It was understandable, I suppose, that his focus should have shifted to what he might find at the Drummond house, but I thought it incumbent upon him to perhaps spend a little more time exploring how I felt about what he had done to me.

'Mr Drummond,' I said.

'Joe,' he said, without slackening his pace and without looking at me.

'Joe. There are one or two things we need to discuss, don't you think?'

He stopped suddenly and turned to me.

'Yes, there are.' I could tell that he was gathering strength with every breath he took. 'Now is not the time. I'm sorry I jumped to conclusions about you, but my family, my entire family, is dead. I'm grateful that I'm out here and not locked up in that shithole, but right now I can't think straight about anything. I have to get home.'

A block further on I said, 'I'm going this way.'

He nodded and said, 'You know the house. Come tonight.'

This struck me as so ludicrous that I actually laughed.

'Bring someone with you if you're frightened of me,' he said. 'Come armed and point the thing at me while we're talking. I don't care, but come.'

I didn't have the option of saying that this was out of the question because he strode off before I could marshal my response. While I was standing there watching him walk away, he turned and shouted, 'The breakfast was shit!'

I arrived back at the George just before eleven o'clock. I was on the point of pushing open the door to the dining room when Charlotte's car pulled up. She was wearing a pale pink, silk scarf, tied under her chin and circling her head, and sunglasses. In profile she looked like a haughty film star. When she turned her face to indicate that I should get in beside her, I could see even from outside the car that her lip was still swollen.

'Where shall we go?' she asked.

'Teddington Weir,' I said. 'Do you know the way?'

She laughed.

'Oh, yes. That's where my husband raped me two weeks before we were married.'

The car pulled away. She took her hand off the wheel and squeezed my hand. As we drove past the courthouse her hand fell to my thigh and moved without impediment to my groin. The dull ache in my shoulder receded against the rising tide of physical pleasure. Like many of the best things in life, masturbation is somehow more enjoyable when someone else does all the work.

It only took us fifteen minutes to get to Teddington Weir. Once we had turned off at Tinana, the road to the weir was deserted. Cane fields flourished on either side, and an occasional house was visible from the road, but we did not see a single person. The weir had been a good choice. We wouldn't be disturbed or observed.

Teddington Weir was two bodies of water. The upper reservoir with its fish ladder and brutal concrete water courses was less attractive than the lower reservoir. This was a large body of water fringed on all sides with dense vegetation. To reach it we climbed down an embankment, using the unofficial steps created by frequent, week-end visitors. A path ran alongside the water, although trees and shrubs obscured it for much of its length. Here and there small areas had been cleared or trampled, and we slipped into one of these. We disturbed a goanna, which climbed a tree in no particular hurry. Halfway up it decided that it had given enough ground and sat quite still, pressing itself against the trunk so that if you looked away and back again, it took a moment to locate it. We were alone, apart from the goanna and a drongo that sat above us on a branch, observing us, with its bright eyes the colour of breathed-on-embers.

Charlotte removed her sunglasses and revealed her bruised eye. I experienced a rush of tenderness and desire so sudden and strong that it made me dizzy. She allowed me to touch her injured face gently and to kiss her damaged mouth with infinite care. The physical urgency between us grew and was satisfied before we had said more than a few words. I don't think I am deceiving myself when I say that Charlotte enjoyed herself at least as much as I did, and possibly more. I jarred my arm rather. It was afterwards that I began to feel that we were being watched. I looked about, got up, and pushed aside nearby foliage.

'What's the matter, Will?'

'Nothing,' I said. 'Nothing.'

The sensation that another pair of eyes was observing us was so vivid that they might have been fingers touching me.

'Will?'

Charlotte put her face close to mine. She kissed my eyelids and my mouth, and sucked gently on my earlobes.

'Will you help me kill Harry?' she whispered.

Her words sank into the porches of my ears with the swiftness of the poison used to dispatch Hamlet senior. I pulled away from her. My face must have betrayed my astonishment, not to say shock, at her suggestion, but she remained impassive.

'We would be happy together,' she said. 'We would be rich.'

'It's murder, Charlotte.'

'Yes. The worst of sins. But will God punish the just killing of an evil man?'

'It's not God I'm worried about. It's Topaz and Conroy.'

Charlotte's eyes filled with tears, and she seemed to suffer a kind of collapse from within.

'I can't live like this anymore,' she said. 'Every day I'm more afraid than I was the day before. Every day the humiliations grow. I can't even bring myself to tell you what he does to me.'

'But murder, Charlotte.'

'Yes,' she said, and she bit each word off. 'Yes. Murder.

Revenge. Punishment. Justice.' Her face softened suddenly, and she added quietly, 'Salvation. Rescue.'

It may have been that her extraordinary words so electrified my system that every cell was on high alert, but I knew that I had heard a footfall and a rasp that was surely an intake of breath. The sounds came from everywhere and nowhere. They seemed to emanate from the air around us. Had the watcher — for now I was certain that there was a watcher nearby — heard what Charlotte had said? Charlotte seemed unaware of the intrusion. She was searching my face for a reaction to her remarks. I was suddenly overwhelmed by a terrifying sense that a malevolent force lurked nearby, its vibrations spreading like a toxic mist from the trees, the bushes, from the weir itself. The hair stood up on the back of my neck and I felt an onrush of panic. My breath came in short, shallow gasps.

'We have to leave here,' I said.

I put my hand on Charlotte's arm, and my fear spread like a contagion into her body. Colour drained away from her face.

'What?' she said, 'What is it?' and her voice quavered slightly.

'There's something here. Someone. We have to leave.'

With our movements made shuddery and uncertain with inexplicable terror, we scrambled up the incline and made it back to Charlotte's car. Charlotte fumbled at the ignition. The engine turned over, but it didn't catch. There was no one outside the car, and no possibility that anyone could emerge from the undergrowth and take us by surprise. Nevertheless the atmosphere was alive with malice. Charlotte tried the ignition again and made a small, whimpering noise when it again failed to catch. The third time, it coughed into action. She engaged first gear noisily, and we pulled away from Teddington Weir.

The further we left the weir behind us, the calmer the air

inside the car became. At the turnoff into Tinana, Charlotte stopped the car. Throughout the drive she had checked the rear-view mirror. We had not been pursued.

'What was it?' she asked. 'What was that?'

'There was someone there, Charlotte, and he wanted to hurt both of us.' I was aware that I was sounding a little dramatic, but I'd just had the fright of my life.

'Hurt?'

'Kill, Charlotte. He wanted to kill us.'

'Maybe what I said frightened you and then it just took hold.'

I shook my head.

'No. I felt there was someone else there, watching us, almost as soon as we arrived.'

'No, Will. I think I frightened you, and panic is catchy.'

She looked straight ahead.

'I meant what I said, Will. Will you help me?'

Her head fell forward and she began to cry. At first the sobbing was a whimper, but it swelled symphonically into a body-wracking expression of inconsolable despair. I couldn't bear to see her like this.

'Charlotte, there has to be another way.'

Her sobs subsided and she turned her face, puffy with tears and battery, towards me.

'I've seen murder in Harry's eyes, Will. He will kill me unless I stop him. I won't let him kill me, not like he killed Polly Drummond.'

Even in the midst of the maelstrom of emotion that had enveloped the car, this last statement was a conversation stopper. For a moment the only sound of which I was conscious was Charlotte's swallowing.

'Does Topaz know this?' I asked.

She shook her head.

'He suspects, of course. But I know.'

'Can you prove it?'

'When he kills me, Will, will that be proof enough? I know because he told me.'

There was a steeliness in her voice that I had not heard before. It was the mere glimpse of a ruthless heart, and perhaps I should have taken heed of it then and there. So fleeting was it that I convinced myself that I had been mistaken.

'Help me,' she said quietly.

'Yes. We'll find a way out of this.'

She must have known that I didn't mean murder, but Harry Witherburn had less than a week to live from that moment

Chapter Eight

UNPLEASANT ENCOUNTERS

CHARLOTTE DROPPED ME a few blocks from Wright's Hall. We hardly spoke during the short drive from Tinana to town, and she didn't kiss me when she stopped to let me out. She touched my hand and smiled. She was concerned about being seen. I didn't believe that Charlotte really wanted Harry dead. My grasp of Catholic theology might be weak, but I didn't think that someone who wouldn't contemplate divorce would choose murder as the less soul-imperilling solution to a bad marriage.

When I reached Wright's Hall I saw Kevin Skakel limping about outside. He was declaiming the 'Tay Bridge Disaster' in an execrable Scottish accent. It was a tragedy that his clubfoot had kept him out of the army, because his personality lent itself to following orders. The revelation that Annie had a brother had set me wondering about the ties that bound the rest of the company. I don't say that it occupied much of my thinking time, and I suppose if I'd really wanted to know I could have just asked. It never seemed to be the right time to do this though.

'Kevin,' I called as I pushed open the gate. He stopped mid-declamation and held his hands up to his eyes against the glare.

'Will,' he said when he realised who it was. He came over to me. His olive skin shone with a patina of sweat. 'I meant to ask you how you were feeling this morning, but I didn't get a chance.'

It was unusual for Kevin to initiate conversation. The McGonagall must have roused him from his customary reticence.

'Well, Kevin,' I said. 'I'm just about as well as can be expected under the circumstances.'

'There's a rosary at St Mary's tonight. I'll say a prayer for you.'

It occurred to me that anyone who thought McGonagall was a greater poet than Shakespeare was in more urgent need of celestial help than I was, but I was gracious and said that I was sure God would bend an attentive ear to Kevin's pleas.

'I'm not praying to God,' he said. 'I'm praying to St Jude.'

'I don't understand the workings of the Church of Rome, Kevin, but if my dilemma is part of St Jude's portfolio, well and good.'

'He looks after hopeless cases,' he said, and smiled so ambiguously that I began to think that I had underestimated Kevin Skakel.

He followed me into the hall where Tibald, Annie, Arthur, and Adrian were watching Bill Henty perform his *Henry V* speech. For some reason he was doing it without his shirt. This was typical. Henty took every opportunity to display the torso he had honed with constant running and endless sit-ups. Abdominal muscles are no substitute for a personality, I thought.

'"We few, we happy few, we band of brothers,"' he was saying, but in such a lacklustre way that he would encourage desertion among the troops rather than fierce loyalty.

'Energy!' I shouted. 'More energy! You want this tiny army to take on the might of France!'

Henty, who always seemed much older than his twenty-eight years, stopped his recital. He looked at me with those unsettling dual-coloured eyes of his: one green, one brown.

'Why don't you show us how it's done?' he said, his voice a carefully modulated mix of boredom and resentment.

'All right,' I said. 'I will, but I'll do it with my clothes on, if that's all right. I don't think the text is illuminated particularly by doing it topless.'

I performed the speech where I was standing, and I moved through the lines assuredly, gathering momentum as I went until I practically raised the roof with that final cry of 'St Crispin's Day!' All this with the use of only one arm.

My performance was met with a sneer from Bill Henty. Tibald coughed and said that it was, perhaps, too big for such a small hall. I might have said that he was, himself, too big for such a small hall, but I held fire.

'I thought it was excellent,' said Arthur.

Annie cast him the kind of look you lavish on a traitor.

'I suppose,' she said, 'you feel good after destroying someone's life.'

'Joe Drummond is free,' I said wearily, 'but you needn't think it had anything to do with you, or even with him especially. It was purely self-interest.'

Annie's face lost its rigid, sour aspect immediately, and her features settled back into the cosy, reliable, and undeniably sexy familiarity of Greer Garson.

'Now,' I said, 'let's see your pieces. Annie, you first.'

'No, Will,' she said. 'You go first.'

I realised that I had left my copy of *Coriolanus* in Charlotte's car. I didn't yet have my piece off by heart, but I improvised where I was uncertain. I may not have had the words down pat, but the emotion was all there. Bill Henty didn't run through his piece again. He sat sulking by the side wall, occasionally doing an ostentatious press-up. I was happy with them all, except for Kevin Skakel and his 'Tay Bridge Disaster.'

> Oh! Ill-fated Bridge of the Silv'ry Tay,
> I must now conclude my lay
> By telling the world fearlessly without the least dismay,
> That your central girders would not have given way,
> At least many sensible men do say,
> Had they been supported on each side with buttresses,
> At least many sensible men confesses,
> For the stronger we our houses do build,
> The less chance we have of being killed.

There were tears in his pale eyes as he finished his recital. How could a man who was not hearing-impaired be so deaf to language?

Although it was only three o'clock, Tibald said that he had to get back to the kitchen. Walter Sunder had been left behind, now that he had resigned from the company, and he ought by now, Tibald said, to have finished the tasks he could do unsupervised. We called it a day. It had certainly been a long one for me.

In the truck on the way back to the hotel I began to grapple with the idea of going to see Joe Drummond that night. I could take Arthur with me and maybe let Topaz know, although I imagined the police would be watching the Drummond house. They would hardly bait the trap and leave it unattended.

I was expecting Arthur to resist my request that he come with me to see Joe Drummond, but he was not in the least reluctant. Annie, who was now all sweetness and light, said that she would cover for him at dinner and we set out for the Drummond place at 8.00 pm. There was a strong wind with the scent of rain on it, but the sky was mostly clear. If there'd been any street trees in Richmond Street, they would have been soughing. There weren't and, consequently, they weren't.

When we reached the Drummond gate we, or rather I, hesitated. I was losing my nerve. The house rose behind it, a dense shadow with a presence that was almost animal. I looked across the street, hoping to see evidence of a police observer — the red glow of a cigarette perhaps. There was no one I could discover and, anyway, might it not have been the killer, come to complete his murderous hat-trick?

I am a much braver man in daylight, and I don't mind admitting it. Coming to see Joe Drummond suddenly seemed like a very bad idea indeed. Even if he had no designs on my safety, whoever was after him would not have to wrestle with his conscience before turning his weapon on me. I muttered this to Arthur.

'I think Joe might be a little more difficult to subdue than his sister or his mother,' he said. 'And if the killer is watching he won't make any attempt when there are three people he'd have to deal with. Besides, somewhere here there must be a copper. It might even be Topaz.'

We climbed the stairs to the front door and knocked. It opened, but no light revealed the opener. He stood back from the door, in darkness. He made no sound. I felt the familiar fizz of fear begin its rise within me. Was this man Joe? Why had I come here?

'Come in,' the figure said. It was Joe. We entered the house and in so doing moved from moonlight into a darkness so complete that the house might have been sitting at the bottom of a well.

'Wait here,' he said. A few seconds later the door to the living room opened and a rectangle of pale yellow illuminated the corridor sufficient to light our way. The doors along the corridor were closed, but neither Arthur nor I gave any indication, not even by the smallest glance — not that Joe would have detected it in the gloom — that we knew which room had been his mother's.

Inside the living room, a single candle provided the only light.

'Power's off,' said Joe.

I introduced him to Arthur.

'How'd you lose your arm?' Joe asked bluntly. I had never heard anyone ask this question to Arthur's face, and to ask it after having been introduced for the first time struck me as singular.

'In a farming accident,' Arthur said, and his tone indicated that he thought the question perfectly natural and that he was unoffended by its directness.

'What a bastard of a thing to happen,' Joe said. 'I knew a bloke up north lost both his arms. Had to get his mates to help him take a piss.'

Arthur laughed. 'The meaning of true friendship.'

Joe sat, and Arthur and I followed his example. It was difficult to read Joe's expression in the dimly lit room.

'You met my brother,' he said, 'and you had a bit of a fling with Polly. You're almost one of the family.'

'Yes, I met your brother and, no, I didn't have a bit of a fling with your sister.'

'You took her to the pictures.'

'Yes. Once. I don't think that means we're related.'

'You know,' he said. 'I owe you. I shot you and you got me out of the clink, and you've come here tonight.' He leaned forward, made a steeple with his fingers, and added. 'I am grateful, but I have to tell you, you're a bit of a prick. Did you know that?'

'Well, Joe,' I said, 'if you were hoping for a beautiful friendship perhaps you should revise how you introduce yourself. Shooting people is not a social skill.'

Arthur coughed ostentatiously in an attempt to short-circuit what was becoming a pointless slanging match which Joe did not have the vocabulary to win.

'What did my sister see in you?' said Joe, with a deliberation that was particularly offensive. I decided to employ the clarifying astringent of truth to this conversation.

'Polly wasn't interested in me. She had other, more compelling motives for being seen in public with me. She was engaged to a singularly unimpressive weed called Patrick Lutteral, only he was baulking at bolting down the aisle with her and so Polly thought she might hurry him along by demonstrating that he had competition.'

I gave him a moment to take that much in and then continued.

'She was in a hurry because she was pregnant.'

I was expecting some protestation at this point, or some indication that the information was startling. I was, after all, speaking about his murdered sister. He did not react in any way that was detectable in the flickering light of the candle.

'Go on,' was all he said.

'Patrick may have been the father, but I doubt it. He's grimly Catholic. There were other candidates.'

I let that plural sink in.

'She was Harry Witherburn's mistress, and she told him that she was carrying his child.'

I stopped again. I was saving the best for last.

'If what Polly told her silly friend Shirley Moynahan is true, it's quite possible that Fred was the father.'

I had thought that this accusation would bring Joe to his feet, but his reaction was shockingly minimal. He leaned back in his seat and closed his eyes. When he opened them, the candlelight caught what might have been tears trapped in his lashes. I regretted then wounding him with what amounted to little more than the gossip of a jealous shop girl. A twinge in my shoulder immediately assuaged my guilt.

'Do you think Witherburn killed her?' he asked.

'Probably,' I said. I was aware that Arthur had turned his head sharply towards me. There must have been such certainty in my voice that he suspected that I had held something back from him. I had, of course. I had not told him that Charlotte had openly accused her husband of the murder. Her extraordinary and obviously hysterical request that I help her to dispose of the odious Harry Witherburn had made me cautious about sharing her remarkable confidence.

'I take it,' said Joe, 'that you're not so sure that he killed my mother.'

I resisted the sudden urge to swing round towards the room where Mrs Drummond's headless body had lain rotting for so many days. Perhaps he sensed my arrested movement.

'She died in one of those rooms,' he said, indicating the general direction by lifting his chin. 'They tried to clean it up, the coppers, but you can't get rid of a mess like that. You'd have to burn it down.'

'I don't think Harry Witherburn killed your mother,' Arthur

said, 'and I'm not as sure as Will obviously is that he killed your sister either. At least, I don't think he did it himself. He's a rich and powerful man. I don't think he'd get his hands dirty.'

'He might pay somebody else to do his dirty work for him, though. Is that what you mean?' Joe asked.

'If he's involved, then yes, that's how he'd do it.'

I saw Arthur's point, but I knew, too, that Harry Witherburn enjoyed beating up women. I could imagine a scenario where he went too far with Polly and killed her accidentally. Equally I could imagine him losing his temper and simply snuffing out her life in order to remove an inconvenience, permanently.

'I still think he killed Polly, but I can't see him disposing of her body. I think he would have had to get somebody to do that for him. And I agree with Arthur that Harry Witherburn would not have risked exposure by murdering your mother in that way. And why would he need to?'

'Maybe Polly told mum she was pregnant and that Witherburn was the father. Maybe mum let Witherburn know that, and threatened to tell his wife.'

I shook my head.

'Charlotte already knew.'

Joe's eyebrows came together.

'You know Charlotte Witherburn?'

'Slightly,' I said. 'We're doing a show for her at her fund-raiser. She's told me a few things.'

'Why?' he asked.

'Perhaps it's my open and trusting face.'

'You're fucking her, aren't you?'

I could not disguise my discomfort at the appalling accuracy of his intuition and so I hurried on, revealing more perhaps than I'd intended to.

'Fred tried to blackmail Witherburn. He just laughed at Fred.

Polly told Char … Mrs Witherburn, about her pregnancy, but she didn't want anything from her. Charlotte wasn't surprised. I think, more than anything else, she was surprised that anybody who wasn't obliged to would have sex with Harry. He's a truly horrible man, and he's violent. Capable of murder, certainly, but he'd pay someone to clean up after him.'

'And what about Fred?' asked Joe.

'I'll be frank, Joe. Your brother was mad as a cut snake. Psychotic, I suspect. On the night that Polly disappeared, the night I took her to the pictures, he had a fight with her. A physical fight. They were rolling around on the floor. Then he attacked me a few days later.'

Joe Drummond stood up and walked the few steps to where framed photographs sat on a table. He put his hands on his hips and stared down at them. The candle threw light on his back so the pictures must have been almost impossible to see in the shadow he cast over them.

'I didn't know Fred,' he said. 'Not really. We didn't spend much time together when we were growing up.'

He picked up a photograph and examined it closely.

'I never liked him much,' he said. 'The coppers think the plane crash was an accident, but Peter Topaz asked me if I knew any reason why Fred might want to kill himself.'

He turned to face us, and the feeble light made dark hollows of his eyes.

'Would he do that? Would he kill himself?'

'Well, if he did,' said Arthur, 'he didn't just kill himself, did he, he killed his flying instructor as well.'

'He owed a man named Mal Flint a lot of money,' I said. 'Do you know Mal Flint?'

'I went to school with Flint. He was a moron.'

'Yeah, well, he grew into a full-sized moron, and Fred got

mixed up with him. Flint was anxious to get his money and beat Fred up, just to remind him. Actually, I owe Flint a favour. Fred was attacking me at the time and Flint took him from behind.'

'Why was Fred attacking you?'

'He thought I'd kidnapped Polly. I told you he was nuts. He admitted a couple of days later that he was wrong. I saw him, just before the accident and he said he knew who'd killed Polly. He said "they", like he thought there was more than one person.'

'Why is it,' asked Joe, 'that at every turn, you're there? You're there the night Polly goes missing. You're there when Fred dies. Where were you when mum was murdered?'

This was clearly not the moment to reveal that I'd been right here, in this very room. I ignored the question.

'The person who actually pops up at every turn,' I said, 'is ...'

'Mal Flint,' said Arthur.

'Why would Mal Flint want to kill my family?'

'Maybe he doesn't,' Arthur continued. 'Maybe Fred was the only person he had a grudge against, but maybe he was paid to get Polly and your mother out of the way.'

Joe returned to his chair.

'Flint is not a nice bloke, I grant you,' he said. 'But I wouldn't have picked him as a cold-blooded gun for hire.'

'Maybe you haven't had the pleasure of meeting Flint recently,' I said. 'I met him in a toilet just the other day and ...'

'Is Flint queer, too?' Joe asked.

'What do you mean, "too"? I have no idea what his proclivities are, although quadrupeds seem possible. I was in the toilet urinating. I was not there hoping to score oral sex from Mal Flint. Now I've lost my train of thought. What was I saying?'

'Flint,' said Arthur. 'You were about to say that you met him and that he was extremely unpleasant.'

'That's right. He would have no qualms about killing for a fee.'

'Well, then,' said Joe. 'Flint sounds like a good place to start. We need to find something that connects him directly to Harry Witherburn.'

'We?' I said. 'That's the coppers' job.'

'So far they're not doing a very good one, are they? And we can do things they can't.'

'Such as?'

'Such as breaking into Flint's house and poking around a bit.'

My immediate reaction to this suggestion was to feel sick. I'm not ashamed to admit that the idea of being on the wrong side of Mal Flint scared me. I had hoped that Arthur would baulk at the idea and speak strongly against it. When he jumped in and agreed that searching Flint's house was a good strategy, it brought home to me that I didn't know him as well as I thought.

'Tomorrow's Friday,' Arthur said. 'Flint works at Walkers.'

'Hang on,' I said. 'We know nothing about him. We don't even know where he lives.'

'I know where he lives,' said Joe. 'The Flints lived at Granville, up at the end of Walkers Point Road. He stayed there when his parents died, and he's an only child. They probably took one look at him when he popped out and never had sex again. We won't run into anybody. It's practically the bush up there.'

'Somebody might be there. Is he married?'

'Who'd marry that arsehole?'

So that settled it. We agreed to meet the following morning at the Granville Bridge at eleven o'clock. I would plead a sore shoulder in order to avoid tomorrow's rehearsal. Arthur would stick to his room and get Augie Kelly to tell the others he was ill. He should also, I suggested, let Augie know where we were going, but not what we were doing in any detail. I didn't like the idea of heading off to Flint's house without having someone to look for us if anything went wrong.

On the way back to the George from the Drummond house, Arthur could barely contain his excitement about the next day's burglary — and what we were proposing to do amounted to burglary. I was feeling something closer to trepidation. Our last uninvited entry into someone else's house had not ended happily.

The Granville Bridge wasn't far from the George. We overestimated how long it would take us to walk there, and arrived fifteen minutes early. The gates at either end were closed, and the bascule was beginning to open slowly to allow the passage of a timber barge beneath it.

'What's Flint look like?' Arthur asked.

'You've seen him. He was the bloke who stopped and spoke to Polly that day, about the money Fred owed him.'

'I don't remember what he looked like.'

'He looks like he was bashed about the head as a kid. Pug ugly. Peter Lorre, only taller and built like a brick shithouse. He's like a wild animal. His eyes are as disconnected from compassion as a shark's.'

Joe Drummond arrived not long after we had. He looked like he hadn't slept at all. He'd shaved, but carelessly, and he'd cut himself in several places. He'd left home very early, he said, and taken a roundabout route in order to lose the copper who'd been assigned to watch him.

We crossed the Mary River into Odessa Street and walked

its length until it became Walkers Point Road. The houses in this part of Maryborough were squalid. The crying of a child and the barking of a dog were the only indications that these meanly constructed residences were occupied. Front yards were piled with the detritus of scrounged livelihoods, and the air was tainted with the unmistakable odour of poverty. This did not seem like a part of Maryborough at all. Even small towns harbour an underclass. The houses gave way quickly to unmanaged land.

'It floods here,' Joe said. 'It's not so bad this far up, but down on the flats it goes under regularly.'

'I don't suppose Flint lives on the flats,' I said. 'A decent flood is probably the only time he has a decent bath.'

'That's his place there,' he said, and indicated a structure that was more humpy than house. It looked as if it had been built before the turn of the century. It might have been quaint with its high, pitched roof and awkwardly proportioned verandah, if it hadn't been allowed to head towards its entropic destiny unimpeded by repairs. A lemon-scented gum rose elegantly on one side. The dead trunks of ring-barked trees studded the yard, and whatever greenery there was grew in chaotic, opportunistic clumps. The earth around the house was bare. Rain would turn Flint's yard into a quagmire.

The house was built close to the ground, although the left side was closer than the right, having subsided gradually in response to water swirling about its stumps. There were no front steps, although there must once have been. Arthur and I stepped up onto the verandah, and Joe went round the back. Several floorboards were missing, and it was bereft of furniture. A pile of rags sat in one corner. They had become the murmurous haunt of flies, to use Mr Keats' phrase, and I was not in the least curious to discover what lay beneath them. The windows on either side of the door were so filthy that peering into them revealed nothing.

Arthur tried the door. It wasn't locked. When it was opened fully, the house let out a long-held breath of stale, putrid air. How could anyone live and breathe in this cesspit of a house? We entered and felt immediately in need of a bath. The foetid atmosphere clung to us with the physicality of rancid animal fat. The two front rooms were dark, but it was obvious that one of them was a bedroom. A mattress thrown on the tilting floorboards was proof of this. There was only one other room, which opened out from the short corridor. A door separated it from the front of the house. When I pushed opened this door, the sawmill buzz of blowflies was remarkable in its intensity. The back door was closed, but several missing planks allowed bands of light in and gave free access to the rich variety of local insect life. In the gloom I discerned what they were interested in. A pig's carcass had been upended and was hanging from a rafter, its head just reaching the edge of the claw-foot bath over which it was suspended. The bath sat opposite a wood stove of primitive design. Flies danced around the stovetop, but it was the dead pig that was the main attraction. Its throat had been cut, and its blood puddled, black and congealed, on the floor of the bath.

'He must have slaughtered it this morning,' Arthur said. 'He's draining the blood.'

'It's disgusting,' I said. 'It'll be crawling with maggots by the time he gets home.'

'You just pick them off. Maybe he eats them, too. Good protein.'

'That sounds like the voice of experience,' I said.

'Hilarious. What are we looking for, anyway?'

'I have no idea. A note. A piece of clothing. Something to tie him to Witherburn.'

Looking around this frightful room, I realised the futility of our visit.

'You hunt about here,' I said. 'I'll check the front rooms. Maybe he stuffed £100 notes under his mattress.'

Flint's mattress was damp and smelled of stale beer, sweat, and urine. It also smelled strongly of dog. It struck me as I inhaled the odour that no dogs were barking. I knew that Flint ran dog fights and he almost certainly had dogs of his own. The discovery of a wet turd near the door confirmed this, and yet there was silence. This caused my stomach to tauten and a vein in my neck to pulse weirdly. I went back into the kitchen where Arthur was standing in the doorway to the backyard, blocking the light.

'Where are the dogs?' I asked, and my voice quavered involuntarily, the way it does when I feel the first tinglings of rising panic. Arthur said nothing, then almost fell through the door into the yard. I was blinded by the sudden burst of light, but I saw his silhouette hurry towards the back of the property. I followed him.

'Joe!' I called. 'Joe!'

'He's not here,' said Arthur, 'and the dogs are dead.'

I caught up with him in a corner of the yard. In a rough enclosure, three canine corpses lay, their eyes open and swarming with ants and flies.

'They've been dead a couple of hours,' Arthur said. 'Poisoned, I'd say. Someone got here ahead of us and didn't want the dogs carrying on.'

'Where's Joe?'

Arthur's calm in the face of what I was certain was an approaching firestorm of trouble was infuriating and unsettling

'I don't know,' he said, but we both had a fair idea that he wasn't playing hide and seek.

'How can you be so calm?' I said, annoyed that he wasn't suffering an alarm at least the equal of mine.

'I'm not calm,' he said. 'I'm terrified.'

Behind the makeshift kennel the thick scrub crouched, drawn in upon itself — enclosed protectively, it seemed, against any further encroachment by slashing and burning settlers. Whoever had been here was probably watching us from its shelter, his presence occluded by ti-tree and wattle, but his menace drifting towards us on aromatic wafts of eucalypt and sweetly scented leaf litter.

'Maybe he went back around the front,' I said.

'Maybe,' Arthur said, but he stood staring into the bush.

'I'll check,' I said and withdrew to the house. There was no sign of Joe.

When I returned to the yard, Arthur had barely moved. I stood again beside him and, for want of a better idea, began calling into the bush.

'Joe! Joe Drummond! Joe Drummond!'

'You're wasting your breath,' Arthur said. 'He's dead, and dead people have poor hearing.'

'We should look for him,' I said, hoping that Arthur would dissuade me from doing so. I didn't want to move any closer to whoever was lurking in the scrub.

'Yes,' he said, and as soon as he'd said it he became resolute. 'We should stick together. If this prick can take Joe by surprise and overpower him, I don't like either of our chances on our own. We've only got two useful arms between us if we have to defend ourselves.'

We pushed our way through a prickly tangle of under-storey, and were relieved to discover that it thinned a short way in. The air was still, and the hum of insects was the only insistent sound. Occasionally a bird called, and eucalypt leaves clattered together high above us. At any other time this would have seemed a pleasant place. Now, our observations warped by fear, its silence and the sense that it went on forever made it seem sinister and alive with the possibility of sudden and horrifying violence. I began to feel again that profound disturbance of equilibrium I had felt at Teddington Weir.

'We should leave here,' I said.

'There!' said Arthur, and pointed ahead and to our right. I saw what had caught his eye, or thought I did. There was an impression of a figure moving quickly through the trees. It was no more than a glimpse, followed by the unmistakeable crack of feet treading on dry twigs. Arthur began running towards the place where the figure had been. With every fibre of my being telling me to stay where I was, it took a considerable effort of will to take off after him. I could see Arthur well ahead, barrelling carelessly forward. He was fast. I fancied, too, that through the rattle of my breathing and the combined racket of our pursuit I could hear the fleeing footfalls of the figure we were chasing. I was gaining on Arthur when he tripped suddenly and fell heavily to the left. With no arm to put out to break his fall, he crashed sickeningly to the ground. I was upon him in seconds. He was lying with his face turned awkwardly, one cheek imbedded in the dirt. He was unconscious, and my first thought was that his neck had been broken.

I was aware of the sound of running up ahead; but as quickly as I noted it, it stopped. Perhaps the sound of Arthur falling had just reached him, and perhaps the silence that followed told him that he was no longer being pursued. Perhaps, I thought, with a dread that numbed me, perhaps he would now come back. With one hand on the back of Arthur's neck, as if my touch were enough to heal him, I scanned the trees around us. A snapping twig to my right brought my eyes round quickly to that point. Another to my left jerked my eyes there. He couldn't be in two places at once. My common sense told me this, but I had never before journeyed this far into the wilderness of fear, and I was beyond rational thought. With awful clarity I remembered that Fred Drummond had said 'they'. He knew who 'they' were.

As I was assimilating the hideous possibility of a posse of psychopaths falling upon us, a heavy crunch of leaves behind me and a shadow that swallowed us with the swift and callous certainty of a predator poised for the kill almost stopped my heart completely. Arthur stirred under my hands. He was not dead after all, although I was now certain he soon would be. I don't know why the realisation that I was about to die released a great calm within me. Perhaps I had exhausted my body's reserves of adrenalin. Arthur opened his eyes and looked over my shoulder. He would see my murderer — and his — in the few remaining seconds of his life. I simply waited for the blow to be struck, almost impatiently.

'Who killed my fucking dogs?'

This question, uttered in Mal Flint's unmistakably plebeian tones, was so bizarre in the context of impending death that it had an hallucinatory quality. It made me think that somehow I had not felt that final blow, but had slipped beyond the veil painlessly and had entered a purgatory where expiation involved eternal conversation with Mal Flint. The sensation was fleeting. Flint put his foot in the small of my back and sent me sprawling across Arthur's semi-conscious body. I felt the wound in my shoulder open and the sticky flow of blood soaking into my shirt.

'Who killed my fucking dogs?' he repeated, with a snarl of which his fucking dogs would have been proud.

I turned my head and saw his trouser bottoms and filthy work boots. It was a struggle to get to my feet, having the use of only one arm. (How did Arthur get through life so permanently discommoded?) Arthur had lapsed back into unconsciousness, so I was left to confront Flint alone. When I faced him he was standing with his arms hanging by his sides with the pendulous muscularity of his obviously recent simian ancestors. He was breathing noisily through his mouth, his already ugly features contorted so severely that he was more gargoyle than man.

'It wasn't me,' I said, but I knew I sounded defensive, frightened, cornered and, frankly, guilty. The tensing of his body and a further deterioration in his looks indicated that I had not won his confidence. I took a few steps backwards. He took a few steps forward. I thought he would simply stomp on Arthur's body, but he lifted his feet and stepped over him without taking his eyes from my face. I had never been looked at before with such unalloyed hatred. Mal Flint was a man with whom negotiation would not be possible. He had the crude, inflexible psychology of a wild animal.

'We didn't kill your dogs.' It was only at this point that I noticed the iron bar clutched in his right hand. He began to raise it slowly, and his features assumed the feverish concentration of a beast energised by the inevitable and unstoppable juggernaut that is instinct. I was frozen in fascination. I noticed tiny things: the spittle that had gathered in small, frothy mounds at the corners of his mouth; the fact that his left eye seemed to be set slightly lower in his face than his right eye; and the small and astonishing vanity of eyebrows that had been clipped to restrain their unruliness. He cocked his head slightly, worried that my failure to move might be a strategy rather than a physiological impossibility. When his arm reached the top of its arc, I think I may even have smiled.

What happened next remains a blur of movement and sound. I was watching Flint's face, so Arthur's initial action registered only peripherally. Using his legs with great force and dexterity, he seemed at once to collapse one of Flint's legs at the knee joint while kicking the other sideways and off the ground. Flint had no time to arrest his fall, and he fell with the graceless, bovine drop of a toppled buffalo. His head struck the ground with the sickening thump of a plummeting watermelon, and he did not stir.

'Help me get up,' Arthur said.

I was staring at Flint's prone form, and Arthur had to repeat the request.

'I just saved your life. The least you could do is help me stand up.'

Brought back suddenly from the calm acceptance of my impending death, my body reacted in the unfortunate way it tends to when greatly stressed. I threw up. Arthur waited patiently for me to finish and then, sweating and weak, I assisted him to his feet.

'I thought you were dead,' I said.

'I saw Flint when I came to. I thought it might be better to play possum.'

'Are you all right?'

'My head hurts like hell and so does my shoulder, but I'm not dead, so I'm ahead. You know, Will, we're in the middle of a big, big mess.'

Flint moaned and his leg twitched.

'At least I didn't kill him,' Arthur said. 'He's going to be pretty pissed off when he comes round.'

'We have to talk to him,' I said. 'Find out what he knows. Convince him that we didn't kill his dogs.'

Arthur gave me a look that was half pitying and half incredulous.

'Do you seriously think that this creature, half man, half ape, is going to sit down with you and have a little chat?'

'Short of shutting him up permanently, we have to try something.'

Arthur indicated Flint's body dismissively and said, 'All right, but we need to get him back to the house and tie him down. I'm not going to attempt any discussion unless he is immobilised.'

I nodded. I was uncertain about the legality of tying someone up, but this was no time to be restrained by such niceties. Flint uttered a small, helpless groan of semi-conscious protest as we each took a leg and began to haul him towards his house. The going was awkward. Because each of us had only his right arm with which to manoeuvre Flint's body, one of us had to face him and the other have his back to him as we dragged him, stumbling as we went. There was nothing we could do to protect Flint's head from the uneven ground over which we were pulling him. Occasionally it bounced with alarming vigour over a rock or a tree root.

'Fortunately,' Arthur said, 'there's not much brain to damage.'

I was incapable, at the time, of considering all the consequences of that morning's occurrences. Thoughts and feelings flew through my mind with the disordered and numbing violence of a blizzard. It was as much as I could do to help Arthur truss Flint securely to the heavy stove in his kitchen. There were no chairs. His head lolled forward onto his chest, revealing that his pate was thinning at the crown. This small exposure lent him a kind of humanity which the rest of him resisted. We stood looking down at him, hideously conscious of the Babel of Beelzebub's minions behind us.

'We are now in shit right up to our eyeballs,' Arthur said. 'This arsehole is not going to want to cooperate. Christ, it will be like trying to reason with a wounded boar.'

'Well, we can't just let him go. Not now. And we can't kill him.'

With stunning blandness, Arthur asked, 'Why not?'

'I believe it's against the law,' I said.

'I hope you're not expecting that same law to protect you from him.'

He gave Flint a vicious little nudge with his boot.

With a rush of moral rectitude I suggested that just at the moment it was Flint who needed protection from us, not the other way around. I didn't underestimate the danger he represented, but I had become slightly discombobulated by the topsy-turvy nature of the moral universe I seemed to have been dragged into. Charlotte and Arthur were two people whose characters I thought I understood, and both of them, within twenty-four hours of each other, had advocated the worst of crimes as a solution to an inconvenient problem. And they had both done so with unsettling ease. I couldn't blame the war for this. Whatever individual and collective suspensions of civilised behaviour were taking place in the Solomon Islands or at Stalingrad, they surely didn't apply here in Maryborough, where war was felt most profoundly in the unavailability of ice-cream and butter.

Flint began to come round. He gurgled, and lifted his head and shook it from side to side. He could not, initially, understand why he was unable to move his arms or legs. He flailed pointlessly because he couldn't budge the heavy stove, or loosen the knots Arthur had expertly, if monodextrously, tied. His breath was pushed noisily out through clenched, discoloured teeth, and sounded like air escaping from a small, punctured bellows. When he had gained sufficient consciousness to utter the word, 'Cunts!', Arthur took a handful of his greasy hair, yanked his head back, and told him calmly that, as he had only a few more minutes to live, he might want his last words to be a little more substantial. I was mesmerised by a quality in

Arthur's voice that I had never heard before. There was no hint of deference or sympathy. It was calm and steely, and the words slid from his palate with the unctuous certainty of the practised sadist. He was playing the role of his life. Flint, however, did not betray any fear. He looked furious and ill. I don't see how he could have been anything other than severely concussed given the number of heavy knocks his head had sustained. Flint's eyes followed Arthur groggily as he picked up a brutal-looking knife from a filthy sill.

'Is this what you use to butcher the pigs?'

Without waiting for a reply, Arthur moved to the carcass suspended over the bath. With a deft and sure stroke he opened its belly with the knife. The viscera tumbled forth, slick, obscene, and somehow animated in their coiling, glistening release.

'It's sharp,' Arthur said.

Flint looked from Arthur to me, and I didn't miss the inchoate presence now of fear in his eyes. Arthur came across to where Flint sat propped and restrained. He brought the knife, foul with pig's blood, up to Flint's throat.

'This is what it feel likes to die,' he said, and drew the knife savagely across Flint's throat. I let out a cry of disbelief, and Arthur stepped back to admire the effect. For a moment that seemed an eternity, both Flint and I thought that his throat had been cut — but Arthur had used the blunt, back of the knife, not its edge. Arthur laughed.

'Whoops,' he said. 'Wrong side. I'll have to try that again.'

Flint uttered an involuntary whimper, and the spreading patch at his groin indicated that he had lost control of his bladder. I began to feel sorry for him. Arthur was merciless in his harrying. He leaned down again, but this time he slashed the buttons from Flint's shirt and gingerly pushed the sides apart to expose his unexpectedly white, hairless chest and belly. He pushed the point of the knife into the soft V of the throat, and drew blood. He then drew the knife down over the sternum, and didn't stop until he reached the belt of Flint's trousers. He produced a thin line of blood as he went. At the belt he scratched a line from hip bone to hip bone so that an inverted, red T formed on Flint's torso.

'I could open you up like that pig,' he said, 'and your guts would fall into your lap and you wouldn't be dead. You'd see your own intestines. Would you like that?'

Arthur's voice was caressing. Flint shook his head, his lips quivering and tears, and snot running down his face.

'I'll start here,' Arthur said and dug the point of the knife into Flint's skin just below the navel. Flint began yowling in a way that was both pathetic and terrifying.

'What? What? What?' he said. 'What do you want?'

Arthur withdrew the knife and straightened up.

'Who paid you to kill Polly Drummond and her mother?'

It took a moment for the question to sink in. Flint was still shaking and blubbering, but I saw the bewilderment in his eyes when he finally understood Arthur's words. It was a reaction impossible to fake. Arthur saw it, too. His features sagged for the briefest of moments with the appalled realisation that he had wounded and humiliated an innocent man. Whatever unpleasant things Flint had done in his miserable life, killing Polly and her mother were not among them.

'I didn't kill anybody. I swear I didn't.'

Flint had not detected any change in Arthur's face and still believed that he was only a few seconds away from being disembowelled.

'Please,' he said. 'Please. I didn't kill anybody.'

'Where's Joe Drummond,' Arthur snapped.

'Joe?' he sniffled. He was thrown by the question. 'Joe left Maryborough years ago. I don't know where he went. Honest.'

The way he said 'honest' was almost heartbreaking in its transparent attempt to indicate that, although he did not grasp any of what was happening to him, he was prepared to answer any question, even if it made no sense to him, and he was prepared to answer it truthfully, because a truthful answer to an absurd question was all he had left. Arthur knew, and I knew, that he not seen Joe, let alone disposed of him. As I took in the scene before me, its ghastliness made my knees tremble. We had entered a world that was almost apocalyptic in its awfulness: the flies buzzed with renewed frenzy over the malodorous gralloch of the pig; Flint sat, bleeding and broken, and beginning to be plagued by flies as well; and Arthur stood, knife in hand, agog, I thought, at what he had wrought, and wondering what to do next.

'Suppose I believe you,' he said. 'Suppose I let you go. What's in it for me?'

I could see where Arthur was heading. Flint was too dazed and too naturally stupid to comprehend the fact that a deal was being offered, but it was a deal designed to protect us from him, not him from us. It was critical that Flint thought the latter. Arthur went on.

'Let's get one thing straight. We didn't kill your dogs. They were already dead when we got here.'

Flint looked blank. His terror was receding, and he was beginning to experience the mortifying awareness of the extent of his abasement.

'Do you understand that? We did not kill your dogs.'

Flint nodded.

'All right. Now, maybe you can help us. Do you want to help us?'

Flint nodded again.

'Because if you're not willing to help us, you're no use to us. And if you're no use to us, you're no use to anybody. And if you're no use to anybody, you might as well be dead.'

Flint flinched.

'I'll help,' he croaked. 'How? What do you want me to do?'

'We want you to help us find the lunatic who killed Polly and her mother, and now Joe.'

'I don't know anything,' he said, his voice tremulous.

'We want you to help us when we need it, that's all. You do a couple of small things for us, you get to keep your guts on the inside. Fair enough? And what happened here goes no further. The fact that Mal Flint pissed his pants can be our little secret.'

My knees were still trembling, and I did not trust myself to speak. My voice would reveal that Flint had nothing to fear from me. It was apparent, though, in the relaxation of his body, that he had accepted Arthur as a kind of pack leader. I didn't think that he would attempt to exact revenge when he was untied. He was in no physical condition to do so anyway. Arthur cut through Flint's restraints with the bloodied knife, threw it into a corner, and offered him a hand up. Flint barely moved, then slowly drew his knees up and wrapped his arms around his legs. It was a curious thing to do. I suspected that he didn't want to stand up and expose the shame of his micturition.

'What do you want me to do?' he asked, and looked first at Arthur and then at me. There was no defiance in his eyes; all that they revealed was total submission. Incredible as it seemed, Mal Flint had become our creature.

'Nothing for the moment. Absolutely nothing. We'll contact you when we need something done. In the meantime, just do whatever it is you normally do.'

He indicated the pig with his thumb.

'Enjoy your pork.'

I thought he was going to give Flint one final kick, but he turned and walked down the corridor and out of the house. I was left for a moment with Flint. When he looked at me this time, I thought that unless I moved quickly he would leap at me and wring my neck.

Once outside, I hurried to catch up with Arthur, who was already at Walkers Point Road.

'Jesus Christ!' I said. 'What happened in there? What got into you? You scared the shit out of me.'

'The idea was to scare the shit out of Flint.'

'Yeah, well, mission accomplished, I'd say. I've never seen you like that. What would you have done if Flint hadn't broken?'

'He's a bully, and bullies always break. But if he hadn't broken, I would have killed him.'

We were now in Odessa Street, heading back towards the Granville Bridge. I let Arthur's words sink in.

'Could you really do that? Could you kill someone?'

Arthur stopped and placed his hand on my chest.

'Could I kill someone? Yes, yes. I could do that. I wasn't acting in there, Will. You should know I'm not that good an actor.'

He gave my chest the slightest of shoves as he removed his hand. It was a small, telling gesture.

'Did you enjoy doing that to Flint?' I asked quietly.

'Oh, yes,' he said. 'I enjoyed it very much.'

I must have looked nonplussed. He went on. 'Listen, Will. You think you know me because you know that I've only got one ball, but what else do you know about me? Nothing.'

I shrugged.

'I respect your privacy. I'm not the kind of person to pry.'

He released a rather mean little laugh.

'No, Will. It's got nothing to do with respecting privacy. It's because you're simply not interested.'

He was becoming agitated — probably, I thought, as a consequence of the fierce encounter he had just had with Flint. I decided not to press him further. I had caught a glimpse of an Arthur Rank who was a stranger to me. A rather frightening stranger.

'Don't worry, Will,' he said. 'When we get back to the George I'll be the damaged, compliant Arthur you think you know.' He laughed again, and this time I could hardly fail to miss the hint of nastiness in it.

We didn't speak after that. The bridge was down, so we were spared the awkwardness of waiting. I wanted to speak, but felt constrained by Arthur's distance. I wanted my mind put at ease. How could we be sure that Flint wouldn't come after us? What were we going to say about Joe? The police were bound to think that I had had something to do with his disappearance. The closer we came to the hotel, the more urgent was my need to talk. There was something closed about Arthur now, and talking was out of the question. So when we entered the George and found Topaz waiting there for us, I experienced something close to internal hysteria. I may even have done a double-take the comic equal of Oliver Hardy. It did not go unnoticed.

'Surprise!' he said.

'I think we can match your surprise and raise you,' Arthur said.

My eyes must have widened significantly, and I think I may even have uttered a little gasp of shock, reminiscent of the first contact of testicles with cold water. This also did not go unnoticed.

'Will would rather you didn't know what happened this morning, but we have nothing to hide.'

Topaz looked at me as if to confirm this judgement. I

stared back, bewildered, struck dumb by Arthur's impending confession.

'Let's go into the bar,' Arthur said. 'Will and I could use a drink.'

'You could both use some iodine, too,' Topaz said. 'I'm beginning to think you should carry some with you at all times,' he said to me. I couldn't produce even the weakest of smiles. In a few minutes he was going to arrest us both for attempted murder.

There was no one in the bar, and Arthur helped himself to two whiskeys.

'We think Joe Drummond might be dead,' he said. 'He's certainly missing.'

It was hard to read Topaz's face. This news must have struck him as singular, but he gave nothing away. He scratched at his chest behind the second-top button of his shirt.

'Go on,' he said, and Arthur went on and told him everything. He admitted that what he had done to Mal Flint constituted serious battery. Just in case Topaz was thinking of offering self-defence as a justification, Arthur said, 'And there is no way my actions could be interpreted as self-defence. At least, not beyond the point where he was tied up. Unless it could be argued that I was defending myself against something he might do in the future, and I don't think the law works like that.'

Topaz leaned back in his chair and put his hands behind his head. The silence was like the silence before the detonation of a doodle-bug.

'It's amazing,' he said. 'The full resources of the Maryborough police couldn't protect Joe Drummond against two interfering actors.'

'Hey,' I said indignantly. 'We didn't twist Joe's arm. He had a personal interest, and wanted to see Flint as much as we did.'

'You just don't get it, do you?' he said. 'You shouldn't have been going anywhere near Flint. That's police business. How many more people have to die before it occurs to you that your investigating skills are not up to scratch?'

'I could ask the same question of you.'

This elicited the slightest of smiles.

'The most astonishing thing about you, Will, is your inability to take responsibility for anything you do.' He leaned forward. 'But I want you to know that if Joe is dead, I will hold you responsible. You may not have killed him, but you're still responsible.'

My mouth dropped open in a caricature of indignation.

'We almost got killed this morning,' I said, 'doing your job!'

'No, Will,' he said, his face flushing as his temper flared. I had never seen Topaz angry, and I was alarmed at the prospect. 'No. The two of you almost committed murder. That's what actually happened this morning — and, for all I know, maybe you did.'

'Flint's alive,' I said dismissively.

'I wasn't actually talking about Flint.'

'All right, all right,' Arthur said. 'Let's all calm down. I see your point, even if Will doesn't. We could be providing each other with an alibi to cover murdering Joe. But we're not. Obviously, it might look like that, but I think you know that that's not what happened.'

'I've got enough to arrest the two of you on suspicion. And yes, that's a threat. Conroy is not going to be a happy man when he hears about this, and believe me, Will, nothing would give him greater pleasure than to see you locked up. I'm beginning to come round to his point of view on that one.'

He stood up.

'I'm going to see Flint. He'll say nothing, probably. He doesn't like coppers. Unfortunately for the two of you, this is the type of thing he likes to take care of himself.'

'I think you'll find Flint a changed man,' I said.

'Flint's a mad dog. If you think you've nobbled him, you're kidding yourselves. I don't care if you've cut his balls off and made him eat them. He'll come back at you and beat you to a pulp. That's what he does. Nothing subtle, nothing planned. He'll just turn up and smash every bone in your face. I warned you to stay away from him. Take a good look in the mirror, Will. When he's finished with you, you'll never look the same again.'

With those comforting words, he left.

'Is he right, do you think?' I asked Arthur, who had, annoyingly, listened to Topaz without rancour.

'Yes, I think he's right,' he said flatly and then, to my horror, he added, 'But he won't come after me. He'll come after you. You're a softer target.'

Chapter Nine

SOUPE DU JOUR

ON SATURDAY MORNING it began to rain heavily. For a brief period it was so heavy I could barely see across the street to the river. I was sitting in the empty bar, staring out a window into the rain, trying to recall my speech from *Coriolanus*. I didn't see how I could retrieve my copy of the play from Charlotte before the performance on Monday, so I was going to have to paper over any cracks with my own inventions. The locals would never pick it, so I wasn't particularly concerned. My ruminations were interrupted by Augie Kelly.

'I don't like this rain,' he said.

'Worried about the river?'

He nodded.

'It'll be all right if it doesn't go on like this all day. It doesn't take much to make the Mary slip her banks.'

'It smells damp in here,' I said.

'Rain always does that. We've been flooded before, and rain draws out the smell somehow.'

Just as he said this the downpour eased off. The Mary River looked unchanged to me, now that I could see it again, but its latent power was apparent even as it moved ponderously beneath the dimpling spatter of more gentle rain.

'It's a full house tonight,' Augie said.

'Good. You must be glad you took a chance on us, Augie.'

'Oh, yes,' he said, and sat down opposite me. His pale green eyes, flecked with yellow, were watching me intently. They made me uncomfortable.

'Did something happen yesterday?' he asked.

'No. What do you mean?'

'I just thought something happened, that's all. You and Arthur weren't yourselves last night.'

'Well, I can't speak for Arthur, Augie, but apart from some pain, yesterday was a normal day.'

He didn't believe this and was waiting for some small intimacy from me. I was wary of his insinuations into my private life. He ran one hand over the hair on his sinewy forearm and plucked at something at his wrist.

'You should trust me,' he said quietly.

'It's not that I distrust you, Augie,' I said clumsily, 'it's just that I don't have anything to trust you with. No secrets.'

His lips were tight, and it was clear he was restraining feelings hurt by my apparent failure to honour the conditions of an established friendship. The fact that this friendship was a figment of his imagination was neither here nor there. There was some quality about him that I found depressing and creepy. I cannot explain why, but he had about him the air of a chronic masturbator, given to bouts of onanism remarkable for their frequency and for the perverse nature of the fantasies that fuelled them. As he was leaving the bar, he said with a viperish little sneer, 'By the way, Harry Witherburn and his wife are booked to eat here tonight.'

If he had wanted to agitate me beyond my already fairly comprehensive level of agitation, he succeeded in spades. I retreated to my room, anxious to avoid meeting Annie, or any of the troupe. Augie would have told them that Maryborough's richest and ugliest man was coming to dinner, and that he was bringing his beautiful, bruised wife. Speculation about how well I knew her would be rife. I didn't suppose that Augie had failed to pass on the fact that I had driven away with her in her car, despite his assurance that he would say nothing. I didn't even wish to speak to Arthur. Something had changed between us.

As I lay on my bed, wrestling with *Coriolanus*, there began to seep into my consciousness an awful, poisonous suspicion. An insistent Iago in my mind urged me to consider the horrifying possibility that Arthur was not just capable of murder, but that he was guilty of it. I resisted this traitorous flirtation as strongly as I could; but once admitted, it grew like Topsy, and as I examined each of the Drummond deaths I could not provide Arthur with an alibi that would definitively exclude him from suspicion. Polly? He knew her movements because I had told him everything. He could easily have followed us that night and waited for an opportunity. A one-armed man managing to get her up the water tower presented some problems, but Arthur was strong and resourceful, and so I did not wonder *that* he did it, only *how* he did it. Mrs Drummond? Arthur waited outside. Or did he? I didn't see the figure who emerged from Mrs Drummond's bedroom, but I sensed strongly that he knew I was there, in the darkness. And Joe? There was a period — brief, it's true — when Arthur was in the kitchen and I was in the bedroom. He could have done it then. I couldn't explain the dogs or the fleeing footsteps ahead of us. Nevertheless, the seeds of doubt had been sown, and I didn't think I could look at Arthur ever again without a damaging reservation.

Keeping to my room that afternoon, consumed by worry over what Harry Witherburn could possibly mean by bringing Charlotte to the George, and with suspicions running rampant through my mind about Arthur, I even began to wonder whether I was safe from Arthur's murderous impulses. I had worked myself into a highly nervous state, which is why I jumped comically when there was a rap on my door.

'Who is it?'

'Peter Topaz.' As he said this he opened the door, indifferent as always to the basic rules of etiquette. I must have looked wan about the gills, because the first thing he said was, 'Alone, I see, and palely loitering.'

'I am in a great deal of pain,' I said, hoping that might explain my unnatural pallor.

'If I had Mal Flint after me, I'd look like that, too.'

'I'm not afraid of that ape. What did he say?'

'I didn't see him. When I got there yesterday he'd gone, but he hadn't gone back to work. I checked. I imagine he's off licking his wounds somewhere. Getting his strength back.'

'What do you want?'

'Well, more and more I want to lock you up and throw away the key. Frankly, the better I get to know you, the less I like you.'

'The antipathy is mutual, I assure you.'

'I haven't come here to exchange pleasantries. You have no idea how anxious Conroy is to arrest you. When I told him about your little excursion out to Flint's place, he was apoplectic. The only reason he didn't turn up here with a warrant is that he thinks, if he holds out long enough, he'll get to end my career as well as nail you.'

'Why would he want to end your career?'

'Because he doesn't like me, Will. I'm sure you understand how he feels.'

'Oh, yes indeed, and his reasons are probably similar to mine.'

'I imagine they are. He doesn't like me because he knows I'm smarter than he is.'

I'd walked right into that one. In my defence, I had a lot on my mind and was not in the mood for verbal sparring.

'Why don't you just tell me why you're here?' I said, attempting to sound impatient with his tiresome point-scoring.

'You were seen driving towards Teddington with Mrs Charlotte Witherburn on Thursday morning.'

I said nothing.

'It's a small town, Will. Cars, especially expensive cars, are few and far between. You were bound to be seen.'

I still gave him nothing.

'Do you deny it?'

'No,' I said finally. 'So I was in a car with Ch ... Mrs Witherburn. So what?'

'So what were you doing?'

'Not that it's any of your business, but we were discussing the program for the Red Cross fund-raiser.'

'And it was necessary that you do this while mobile.'

'Is it illegal to discuss Shakespeare in an automobile in Maryborough? It wouldn't surprise me.'

'I would have thought you'd have had plenty of time to discuss him when you had lunch at Witherburn on, what day was it? Tuesday?'

'You're remarkably well informed about my social calendar. You must have quite a network of spies. Maybe you should consider using them to help solve these crimes instead of keeping track of my dining arrangements.'

'I think you must be unfamiliar with the way small towns work. You can't take a piss in this place without someone getting splashed. Your dining arrangements, as you call them, have attracted the attention of half the town, or did you think no one would notice? People are wondering if Charlotte Witherburn is thinking of running away and joining the circus.'

'That's just ill-informed, small-town gossip, and they can't even get my occupation right.'

'Your affair with Charlotte Witherburn is common knowledge because Charlotte Witherburn wants it to be common knowledge. The staff at Witherburn are discreet unless instructed otherwise.'

'Why would Charlotte put it about that she's committing adultery? She's terrified of her husband. Why would she want to antagonise him?'

Topaz looked perplexed.

'Can you really be so naïve?' he asked. 'I don't expect you to take my advice, Will, but you don't know what you're dealing with here. I'd end your little affair before you end up out too far to rescue. Harry Witherburn is Mal Flint with money. I don't think he cares particularly who his wife has sex with on the side, but he doesn't like the whole town knowing about it. He's happy enough to flaunt his own affairs, but I think hypocrisy is the least of his unattractive qualities. There's no point looking for any sort of morality here. The Witherburns don't worry too much about things like that. They're good Catholics, you see, and as long as there's a priest at the deathbed, they're all set. You can rely on two things about the Witherburns. They never miss Mass on Sunday, and if you cross Harry Witherburn, you'll wish you hadn't.'

The notion that Charlotte was as immoral as her husband

was insupportable to me.

'Are you suggesting that Charlotte is a strumpet?'

My choice of noun was unfortunate. As soon as I'd said it, I realised it sounded foolish.

'Strumpet? This isn't eighteenth-century London, Will. I'm suggesting that if you think your liaison with Charlotte is her first and only extra-marital affair, you're a damn fool.'

'Why don't you tell me why you're here and then skulk off?'

'All right, Will. I presume Charlotte has passed on to you, either directly or coyly, her suspicions about her husband.'

'I'm not going to betray her confidence by answering questions like that.'

'Very gallant. However, she has made no secret of her suspicions to me.'

'So why haven't you arrested Harry Witherburn?'

'Because the burden of evidence needs to be a bit heftier than the word of a jealous wife.'

'Harry has a motive.'

'Everyone has a motive. Charlotte's motive for dispatching Polly is as strong as her husband's.'

'That's ludicrous.'

'Is it? If all a jury had to go on was motive, I don't think they'd find the idea too ludicrous. But motive is the weakest proof in murder, Will. If it weren't, the jails would be stuffed with people waiting to be sentenced, and hanged in most states.'

'This is really too absurd. To suggest that Charlotte could murder anybody, let alone an entire family …'

'I'm not suggesting anything, Will. I'm just trying to put all this together, and I can't ignore possibilities because they are unpleasant or because they concern someone who, after the briefest of acquaintance, you consider above suspicion.'

'I'm not some love-struck youth, Topaz.'

'You're right about the youth part, but it seems to me you've lost perspective. All you know about Charlotte Witherburn is that she let you sleep with her.'

I stood up and made a fist of my free hand.

'Calm down, Sir Gawain. The last thing you need is to be charged with assaulting a police officer.'

'You have a grubby little mind, Topaz.'

'You're having sex with another man's wife. Grubby little mind sounds bloody hollow coming out of your mouth.'

He gave me a shove which caught me off guard and sent me sprawling on the bed.

'I am now officially out of patience,' he said. 'I came here to advise you to stay well away from the dining room tonight. I know the Witherburns are coming here, and it's a safe bet they're not coming because they've heard the food is good. I don't know what they've got planned, but I'm fairly sure it involves a public place, lots of witnesses, and you. Stay away.'

'What do you mean "they"? This has got nothing to do with Charlotte. Witherburn is bringing her here against her will. No doubt he wants to humiliate her. Do you really think I have any intention of giving him a helping hand?'

'Charlotte Witherburn will let you down, Will and, frankly, it couldn't happen to a nicer bloke.'

With that, he left.

I couldn't absent myself from the kitchen during the preparation for that night's dinner. Tibald was in a state of high excitement. Cooking for Maryborough's richest man might, after all, lead to better things. The rest of the troupe were strangely silent about the Witherburns. Maybe Arthur had had a word to them. Only

Bill Henty broke ranks and said, in a voice too low for anybody else to hear, that he was looking forward to seeing the kind of woman who would choose me over money. I told him that serving Mrs Witherburn her food was about as close as he was ever likely to get to a woman with real class, and that I trusted that he intended to keep his shirt on and refrain from doing press-ups while people were eating.

'Maybe,' I said, 'you could write a note to that effect on the back of your paw, just to remind yourself how civilised people behave.'

The kitchen was busy. Tibald was barking out instructions and working himself up into an haute cuisine rage. There were shortages of butter and flour, but this was no impediment to Tibald's genius. It was always a source of wonder to me how he could take the most unpromising of raw ingredients and turn them into sublime symphonies of taste.

Walter Sunder, who, since his retirement from performing, had learned how to trim vegetables and meat to Tibald's finicky standards, was removing the legs from a large number of fat, green, tree frogs. Tibald was not of the sentimental persuasion that credited animals with feelings, and he insisted that the legs be swiftly amputated from the live frog. The torso was then tossed into a bucket, where its life ebbed away among the quivering, shocked bodies of its fellows.

Limited to three courses by the austerity measures now firmly in place, Tibald had decided to take the daring step of having only two courses and not offering dessert for this meal. Despite his many local suppliers, he had been unable to acquire a decent amount of sugar, so he had no choice in the matter really. His suppliers had, however, provided him with snails (they could not believe that anybody would pay them to collect and purge these disgusting molluscs), yabbies, rabbits, pigeons, fish, eels (which Tibald also ordered to be skinned alive), and shellfish. There was also kangaroo meat, which Tibald turned into tiny, densely flavoured sausages and which he sent out of the kitchen disguised as *saucisses de campagne*. It was one of his most popular dishes.

Tonight, the patrons of the George could choose an entrée of *bisque d'homard*, with yabbies standing in for lobster (Tibald had begun work on this bisque early that morning); *escargots Bourguignonne*; or *cuisses de grenouille*. For mains, there were *lapins au saupiquet* (the rabbits had been marinating for almost two days in a rich stew of wine, vinegar, and herbs, with a pungent native berry replacing the juniper berries traditionally used); *coquelets sur canapés* — an elaborate and inspired version of roast pigeon, with a sauce that I would be prepared to consume as a beverage — and a simple *filets de poisson bercy aux champignons*, combined extraordinarily, but successfully, with the *saucisses de campagne*. All this at five shillings a head. Food like this had never been cooked in Maryborough before. Even a brute like Harry Witherburn would have to be impressed.

I knew that Topaz had been right when he had suggested that I make myself scarce that night. This was why I was not at all happy when Annie announced that she wouldn't be able to do table service, and that I would simply have to step in, one arm out of action or not.

'I have to record some advertisements tonight at 4MB,' she said. 'There's no other time it can be done. I can't get out of it.'

'I thought you said the radio work wouldn't interfere here,' I said.

'One night, Will. I know it's awkward, but look at the number of rehearsals you've missed. Don't start lecturing me about supporting the company. I can't help it if you've made things difficult by getting involved with that Witherburn woman. Just stay away from their table. Adrian or Bill can be responsible for them.'

'It was your mate Topaz who advised me against being around tonight.'

'Well, I'm sorry, Will, but these advertisements are for the War Office. I'm not being paid anything. Dealing with a jealous husband can be your little war effort.'

'Fine,' I said. 'Obviously we're not going to defeat Japan without your help, so off you go, but I won't be responsible if Harry Witherburn makes some kind of scene.'

'Of course you'll be responsible,' she said, and manufactured a little laugh. 'You're sleeping with his wife.'

The evening began quietly. I had decided to remain in the kitchen until the pressure on service made an appearance in the dining room unavoidable. The Witherburns arrived late. Most of the other diners were already onto their main course. Adrian reported that Charlotte was wearing a fascinator and perhaps a touch too much make-up. 'The kind,' he said, 'you wear to cover rather than to highlight.'

He had shown them to their table and had got close enough to Charlotte to identify her perfume.

'It's "Antelope" by Weil,' he said. 'They haven't said a word to each other. He is one ugly man. I don't care how rich he is, I still wouldn't want to wake up next to that. He should be told to stay indoors.'

When he returned from explaining the menu to them, he said that the mood in the dining room had changed. There was much whispering with heads cocked in the direction of the Witherburns. People seemed to be expecting something to happen. Harry Witherburn was not, they knew, above having a public row with his wife.

Adrian took their orders. Harry had chosen the bisque, and had ordered the snails for Charlotte. I assumed that he did this because he believed she would find them revolting. If this was the case, he would be disappointed. Tibald's snails would render the most squeamish of patrons unable to encounter the pest from that time on without the mouth watering. Harry ordered the rabbit for his main course, but had said that his wife's appetite was slight and that she would not be eating a main course. Charlotte hadn't said a word. It must have amused her husband to think that she would eat snails and nothing else. Doubtless, he intended to taunt her with this later. I was irrationally annoyed with Tibald for giving him this opportunity, despite the peerless flavour of his escargots.

The entrées had been sent out to the Witherburns when I was obliged to deliver a *filets de poisson* to a diner.

'Get it out now!' barked Tibald. 'It must arrive hot! Hot! Hot!'

The plate sat on the palm of my hand, scalding it, but I hurried into the dining room and delivered it without looking to where the Witherburns were seated. Had I done so, I would have seen Harry Witherburn rise from his seat and come towards me. I would also have seen that he was carrying his *bisque d'homard*, and I would have made a move to avoid what happened next. Having placed the fish before the patron who had ordered it, I straightened up and turned to find my way blocked. Without a word, Witherburn upended the bowl over my head, where it sat, like a porcelain Tommy helmet, its contents dripping about my ears and shoulders. Witherburn headed back to his table, loudly reordering the bisque as he went.

I was so stunned by his assault that I was rooted to the spot. It was not until the gasps around me had been replaced by sniggers, and the sniggers had swollen to laughter, that I reached up and took the bowl from my head. Let me assure you that it is not possible to stand in a room with bisque running down your face and with a bowl on your head and look dignified. I was, however, grateful for two things. First, that Tibald preferred to serve his bisque warm rather than piping hot, and second, that Annie was not there to witness my becoming an object of ridicule.

In a misguided attempt to retrieve some dignity I said very loudly, 'Harry Witherburn, you will regret this.' I then went into the kitchen. Needless to say, the people who should have been outraged on my behalf were in fact grinning with ill-disguised mirth. Even Arthur could not suppress a smile — although, given my suspicions about him, I was not entirely surprised by this. The only person who was not amused was Augie. His face was an angry mask. It was typical of him that he would not appreciate my distress, but be concerned only about the reputation of his establishment. He said nothing to me when I entered the kitchen, but his whole body had become rigid with fury. Perhaps one good thing would come out of this. If he disapproved so strongly of his dining room being turned into a vaudeville sideshow, he might decide that I was no friend of his and cease his clumsy attempts at mateship.

I went upstairs, having first complimented Tibald on the flavour of his bisque, and I ran a bath.

I couldn't hide from the troupe on Sunday. This was the day before Charlotte's Red Cross fund-raiser, and final rehearsals were essential. Wright's Hall was unavailable, of course, so we met for the run-through in the dining room. I'm not sure which was worse, Kevin Skakel's charitable query about my welfare or Bill Henty's snide 'I wouldn't have missed that for the world. I can't wait to see what he does to you tomorrow.'

'I'm not in the least bit concerned about that,' I said. 'What I am concerned about is the dreary nature of your reading. Perhaps you're holding fire until the performance, but I would like to see some indication that you actually understand the words you are saying. The last time I saw your piece you managed to convey the idea that Henry V was mildly retarded and a dullard. You seem to be using your own personality as the basis for your interpretation.'

Although there was no love lost between Annie and Bill Henty, she leapt to his defence.

'Don't take your embarrassment out on us, Will. We're all ready for tomorrow. How about you? No one has seen your piece yet.'

'All right,' I said. 'Let's stop arguing and run through our pieces like the professional actors we're supposed to be. I'm happy to begin.'

I took a deep breath, walked to the end of the dining room, turned and began:

All the contagion of the south light on you,
You shames of Rome! You herd of — boils and
Plagues
Plaster you o'er, that you may be abhorred
Farther than seen, and one infect another
Against the wind a mile! You souls of geese
That bear the shapes of men, how have you run
From slaves that apes would beat! Pluto and hell!
All hurt behind, backs red, and faces pale
With flight and agued fear! Mend and charge
Home,
Or by the fires of heaven, I'll leave the foe
And make my wars on you. Look to't. Come on;

If you'll stand fast, we'll beat them to their wives,
As they us to our trenches. Follow's

I spat the insults venomously, but moved smoothly to
the rallying cry at the end. It was Adrian who broke
the silence.

'You don't think the bit about the wives is a little provocative?'

'I didn't choose it with that in mind. But, after last night, it
will give me particular pleasure to say it.'

Tibald did his Falstaff next. He had blended bits from
various interchanges and ended, after a pause, with,

For we have heard the chimes at midnight
Master Shallow.

It made no sense in this context, but Tibald liked the
melancholy it provoked, and made his eyes dewy with the
emotion of it. When Bill Henty's turn came round, he took the
floor with an authority which surprised me, and delivered his
'Band of brothers' speech with a fire and passion that earned
a spontaneous round of applause. I have never been churlish
about acknowledging another actor's performance, and I added
to the appreciative clapping.

'That was splendid,' I said, 'but you won't be performing it
half-nude, will you. People will be eating their lunch.'

'If last night's anything to go by,' he said, 'you'll be wearing
yours.'

We rehearsed for four hours, and were exhausted by mid-
afternoon. It occurred to me, as I was resting in my room, that
Annie had said nothing about Joe Drummond's disappearance.
Given her inappropriate solicitude when he was in prison, I
could only surmise that Peter Topaz had not told her the bad

news. If he had, she would not have been able to refrain from laying the blame at my door, and relations between us would have seriously deteriorated.

I hardly slept at all on Sunday night. There was much that troubled my dreams. They were crowded with frightening images of both the living and the dead. I woke with a jolt when a piece of machinery, all flashing metal parts and leather belts, rose out of the huddle of images and tore Arthur's arm from his shoulder and dragged him screaming into its whirring, clunking centre. It was 4.00 am, and I was so uncomfortably sticky with sweat that I got up, put on a pair of shorts, and went downstairs to get a drink. I didn't want to use the bathroom because the noisy taps might wake someone. I was in the kitchen when I heard the scraping of a chair in the dining room. Someone had knocked against it in the darkness. Whoever it was, he was waiting to see if anybody had heard the noise, and only someone who shouldn't be in the George at four in the morning would be worried about that. Had Flint stepped out of my dreams — for he was one of the phantasms who harried me — and into the dining room?

Feeling slightly ridiculous — a condition I was becoming inured to — I crouched beneath the preparation table in the centre of the kitchen. The door opened and the figure, with carefully measured step, crossed to the sink. He moved with the certainty of someone who knew his way about. It wasn't Flint or a stranger after all, but I wasn't about to startle him by jumping out from where I had been hiding. He washed his hands as quietly as he could. He did not turn the taps on fully. He then bent and washed his face, at least that was what I assumed he was doing. From where I was crouching I could see only his lower body. As soon as he had left the kitchen, I followed him as he disappeared upstairs to the bedrooms. I couldn't tell who it was. His stealth seemed odd to me, and where had he come from at that hour? It might have been Adrian returning from a night's tomcatting, but he had never been too particular about disguising his nocturnal missions. I was used to him returning noisily at all hours. By the time I made it to the third floor, whoever it was had gone, and there were no lights showing under any door.

I slept fitfully for two more hours, gave up the struggle at 6.30, and rose, shaved, and dressed. But if I'd known how this day was going to end, I would have stayed in bed with the covers pulled up over my head.

Chapter Ten

BETRAYAL

THE DAY OF CHARLOTTE'S FUND-RAISER was overcast. It was warm and oppressively humid. After our final rehearsal we drove to Witherburn an hour before the event was due to start. We wanted to mark out the space in which we would be performing. As Annie turned into the driveway, Adrian let out a whistle of admiration.

'I'm beginning to see what you see in Charlotte Witherburn.'

I was never offended by things that Adrian said, and I didn't challenge the crassness of this remark. Bitchiness was as natural to him as breathing, and it didn't rankle in the way that Henty's surliness did.

Our performance space was a large army tent which had been set up on the side lawn. There were several staff, none of whom I recognised, hurrying to and fro. Perhaps they had been hired for the occasion. There were also several stalls, behind which people were busily adding final touches. As Annie cut the engine, Charlotte appeared on the verandah of the house. She was wearing the uniform of the Red Cross, and even from a distance her nervousness was obvious. I hurried up the steps to reassure her that Saturday evening's fiasco was of no consequence and that it would not affect our performance in any way. She smiled grimly at me and said, 'It was ghastly, wasn't it? I'm so sorry. I had no choice. Really, I had no choice. He said that if I didn't go with him, he'd ...' Her voice broke, and a shaking hand flew to her mouth.

'Of course you had no choice', I said. 'I don't blame you.'

I was aware that the troupe were watching us, and I took Charlotte's arm and led her into the house.

'Where is he?' I asked.

'He's not here. I don't think I could go through with this if he were here. He came in late last night. He tried my door, but I'd locked it. He was drunk, but not drunk enough to force himself in, not this time. He cursed at me and went to his room. This morning he was gone. He always said he wasn't going to waste his time coming to this.'

I kissed her. So agitated was she that her automatic response was to pull away. I did not press myself on her, but reached out and took her hand. She allowed this.

'It will all be fine,' I said. 'We're ready to perform, the garden looks lovely, Tibald has brought a few treats, and you ...' I moved closer. 'You're very beautiful.'

She smiled, but it was like the smile she had worn on the first day I had met her. There was nothing joyful in her eyes.

'I should check that everything's ready,' she said, and withdrew her hand.

A small, canvas cubicle had been set up at the back of the

tent. This was to be our changing room. Inside the tent, chairs had been placed in serried rows. It was already hot and stuffy under the canvas, with a strong smell of calico and grass. At the front of the tent a small dais had been erected. I began to feel the flutter of nerves I always feel before taking the stage.

We had decided to wear costumes for this performance. It took little extra effort and made a better impression than mufti. I was wearing a simple Roman tunic, gathered at the waist with a leather cincture, and Roman sandals, cross-laced around my calves. When we had all changed, we stayed in the dressing-room. We were to be the opening attraction at 11.00 am. After this, people were to circulate and purchase items from various stalls or have their fortune told by someone called Madam Anastasia.

As curtain time approached, the murmurs from the gathering audience grew louder. The tent was filling up. Perhaps I had been wrong about the people of Maryborough. They were obviously starved of culture, and this augured well for our production of *Titus Andronicus*. Bill Henty, who was wearing a brocaded robe (which I had worn in a memorable production of *King Lear*) and a paste crown, could not resist the opportunity to make one last, grubby remark before the curtain went up, as it were.

'They're here,' he said, 'for the same reason they'd gawk at a train crash. Don't kid yourself that they've suddenly developed a passion for Shakespeare. They want to get a good look at soup man.'

I didn't have time to reply. The crowd on the other side of the canvas had fallen silent. We could hear Charlotte's voice welcoming them and outlining the day's events. It was brave of her to face those gossipy matrons. She had more class than the lot of them combined. If she could stand unashamed before them, I would have no difficulty doing the same. Whatever their reasons for coming, I would give them a performance that would make them forget their tawdry voyeurism. They might begin by looking at William Power, but they would end by listening to *Coriolanus*. I took a deep breath and listened for Charlotte's cue.

'I would now like to welcome the Power Players.'

As soon as these words were spoken I thrust aside a flap of canvas and leapt nimbly onto the dais. I saw Charlotte leave the tent, but I didn't have time to wonder why she wasn't staying. Many in the audience were fanning themselves, and several were whispering behind their hands. I ran my eye over them, gathering the contempt I needed for the opening lines of my *Coriolanus* tirade. I raised my hand and described an arc over them, before curling my lips in readiness. I got no further than 'All the contagion of the south …' when a woman entered from the front of the tent, shouting hysterically and pointing behind her. She then did the most extraordinary thing. She stood stock still, rigid, with both hands clenched at her sides, and simply screamed and screamed. The effect was most disconcerting and seemed to be contagious. Almost immediately, another woman began screaming in sympathy. Fortunately, before the whole room erupted, a soldier appeared, placed his hands on the woman's shoulders, and span her round. The action subdued her, and her noisy sympathiser fell silent, too.

'In the toilet,' she stuttered, 'in the toilet.'

Her hysteria began to climb back to its initial pitch; but, instead of screaming now, she yelled, 'In the toilet! In the toilet! In the toilet!'

Many in the audience were shocked to hear the word 'toilet' used so publicly, and this delayed their understanding that she had seen a dreadful thing there.

The rest of the troupe came into the tent, anxious to see what the disturbance was, and we found ourselves carried along with a crowd of people heading off to the toilets in question. Witherburn was fully sewered (Augie had told me that the decision to sewer the town had been taken over the heads of the populace, who had voted against it when it had first been mooted); but, as Charlotte had not wanted hordes of people traipsing through the house, the ancient, backyard privy had been recommissioned and, beside it, two temporary toilets erected. They were unoccupied, as their open doors attested. The door of the permanent structure was slightly ajar, and onlookers formed a semi-circle around it. The soldier who had subdued the hysterical woman said, 'Stand back,' and approached the toilet cautiously. I pushed my way to the front so that I had a clear view when the soldier gave the door a gentle shove.

It opened to reveal Harry Witherburn, seated on the can, stark naked, pop-eyed, and very, very dead. His skin, and there was lots of it, was mottled and extravagantly befurred. His eyes were starting out of his head in an ugly parody of surprise. Perhaps the most extraordinary feature was his mouth, which was open and stuffed with paper rolled into balls and crammed between his teeth. Lying across one flabby flank was the open cover of a book. I recognised it immediately as my copy of *Coriolanus*. All of its pages were missing. I knew intuitively that at least some of them were in Harry Witherburn's mouth.

The sight of Harry, even more physically repellent — if that were possible — in death than in life, caused a few squeals and gasps, and one woman fell with a thud into a faint. My first thoughts were for Charlotte. I didn't for a second believe that she was in any way implicated in this. Although she had, in desperation, wished him dead, a woman of her sensibility would not have been capable of this brutal, squalid murder. I left the gawkers and went in search of her. She was her in her bedroom, sitting in the dark, in an armchair, her head resting in the splayed fingers of one hand.

'Charlotte,' I said quietly.

She looked up.

'I'm sorry,' she said. 'I have a dreadful headache. I get them sometimes.'

Her voice was strained, but calm.

'Why aren't you performing?' she asked. 'What's wrong?'

I had been the first to reach her.

'Something terrible has happened,' I said.

'What?' she asked quietly, so quietly I could hardly hear her.

'It's Harry.'

'What has he done?' she cried, and leapt to her feet. 'What has he done?'

I put my free arm around her.

'No. No, Charlotte. Listen to me. Harry hasn't done anything. Harry is dead.'

She pulled away, and now that my eyes had adjusted to the gloom I saw that one of the confusion of emotions that crossed her face was joy. It was fleeting, but she could not disguise it. She took my face in her hands and kissed me gently on the mouth.

'Thank you,' she said. 'Thank you.'

It took me a moment to register her meaning, but before I could disabuse her of this extraordinary error the door to the bedroom flew open, and Detective Sergeant Conroy, with two constables, entered. My wrist was grabbed and brought roughly down behind my back, where it was pinched into a handcuff, the other cuff being clipped around the leather cincture at my waist.

'William Power,' said Conroy, his eyes aquiver, 'I'm arresting you on suspicion of having murdered Harry Witherburn.'

As if this wasn't sufficiently surprising, he then slapped my face with his open hand, so sharply that my ears rang.

'It's all over, you prick,' he said.

Charlotte said nothing.

*

I had not been aware, until I was sitting in it, that the police had a vehicle. I had only seen them on foot, or on bicycle. It was a sort of Black Maria, and the back smelled like a lavatory into which an indeterminate number of drunks had vomited. Fortunately, the trip to the police station was a short one. On the way there I bristled at the memory of Conroy parading me through the crowd in Charlotte's garden. I didn't get the opportunity to speak to the troupe, who I saw in the distance, open-mouthed. I felt ridiculous in my Roman tunic.

At the station I was dealt with in a whirlwind of sudden efficiency. Very little was said, and I was dispatched to the cells with such speed that I thought several laws must have been broken in the process. I was in shock, I think, and I allowed myself to be carried along without protest, even though every fibre of my being was experiencing profound outrage. I was overwhelmed and helpless.

'I want a lawyer,' were the only words I squeezed out, and as soon as I'd said them I realised they sounded almost like a confession.

'You'll need more than a fucking lawyer,' said Conroy. 'You'll need a fucking miracle.'

When the door of the cell had been closed and locked, I discovered that I was shaking uncontrollably. I sat on the edge of one of the narrow beds — there were three in the small cell.

Joe Drummond must have sat in this very spot just a few days previously. It felt like it might have been a lifetime ago. As soon as this misunderstanding was cleared up I would do something about the blow that Conroy had struck. He had been foolish enough to hit me before witnesses, and I would press charges the minute I was set free. I would not accept a pusillanimous apology. The full satisfaction that the law allowed would be mine to enjoy.

In a remarkably short space of time I had calmed down. I was not in any danger, and it wasn't as if I would be required to stay in the cell overnight. I couldn't see myself using the malodorous can that was the cell's toilet. It was three hours before impatience got the better of me, and I began shouting through the cell door. Eventually my shouts attracted the attention of the slow-moving, slow-witted dolt who had been my escort in what was looking increasingly like a former life. It was, in fact, only two weeks before that I had been summoned from Wright's Hall to an interview with Conroy. Then, I had considered him — the dolt, not Conroy — pleasant, undemanding, and enviably content. As he lumbered towards the cells, I thought him wilfully stupid, almost to the point of being seriously retarded. He peered through the peephole and asked, 'What's up?'

'You can't keep me locked up like this,' I said. 'I haven't done anything. Where's Conroy? Where's Topaz?'

'My understanding,' he said slowly, 'is that Detective Sergeant Conroy has a reasonable suspicion that you've been on a bit of a killing spree. Now, I don't know what I think about that, and what I think doesn't matter anyhow. But if I were you, I'd shut up just at the minute, because if you don't, you'll find out what the inside of that dunny can looks like.'

He looked me up and down. 'So, if that's all, I'll get back to the desk. Nice skirt, by the way.' Here he inserted a dramatic little pause, before tipping his cap and saying, 'Ma'am.'

This brief, ugly exchange made me think that he was not as dull-witted as he appeared. Everyone around me was assuming a dangerous alter-ego. The world is a sorry place when you can no longer rely on the stupidity of others.

I waited two more hours before I was taken from the cell and placed in the interview room. Conroy entered a few moments later, accompanied by Peter Topaz, who did not meet my eye. A thin, pallid man, so bland in appearance that he almost merged with the wall behind him, sat off to one side, a notebook at the ready. Conroy sat opposite me, emanating self-satisfaction.

'Lovely outfit,' he said, and quickly indicated to the amanuensis that he was not to begin writing yet.

'I want a lawyer,' I said.

'You'll get one. This interview is just to formally charge you with the murder of Harry Witherburn.'

'On what evidence?'

'Well, now, it seems poor Harry was strangled with a cord, and then pages from a book were stuffed into his mouth and pushed down his throat — way down into the oesophagus. It must have taken quite some effort.'

I was suddenly aware that my bladder was very full, and I wished that I had used the can in the cell before the interview had begun. Conroy continued.

'Now, Harry wasn't a big reader, it turns out, and the book wasn't one of his. It was a play. Shakespeare.'

'I agree that narrows down the list of suspects in this town,' I said.

'Like I said, it was a play.'

He snapped his fingers, trying to recall its title, and turned to Topaz.

'*Coriolanus*,' Topaz said, and this time he met my eye.

'That's right,' said Conroy. '*Coriolanus*. Never heard of it. Worth reading, is it?'

'Might be a bit ambitious for you,' I said, and I felt quite pleased that my demeanour was not betraying my quaking insides.

'Maybe I could borrow your copy. You do own a copy?'

'Yes, of course I do.'

'Where is it?'

'In my room, I suppose, or maybe the truck. I haven't seen it for a while.'

He let that sit a moment.

'But it was a piece from *Coriolanus* that you were about to perform at the Witherburn's, wasn't it? Or have I got that wrong? Peter?'

Topaz said flatly, 'According to the other actors, it was a piece from *Coriolanus*, yes.'

'So,' said Conroy, 'I presume you used your copy to bone up on the part.'

'Naturally. So?'

'So what is your copy of *Coriolanus* doing down Harry Witherburn's throat and up his arse?'

He took great pleasure in delivering this little *coup de théâtre*.

'What are you talking about?'

'A preliminary autopsy has revealed that many of the pages of the play were rammed up Harry's rectum, probably with a broom handle. It's difficult to say whether this was done before or after he was dead. Perhaps you could clear that up for us?'

I then foolishly asked the question Conroy had been waiting for.

'What makes you think that copy has anything to do with me?'

He smiled.

'Right at the top of the rectum, like it was the very first page to go in, is a page with somebody's name in the right-hand corner. Guess whose?'

With an enormous act of control, I said, 'So somebody used my copy of the play to violate Harry Witherburn. So what? Is this your evidence? Why would I be so stupid as to use a page with my name on it, knowing full well that it would be discovered?'

'There are a couple of possible explanations,' he said. 'One of them is that you are in fact that stupid. Another is that it gave you a bit of a thrill to leave your calling card. I think a jury might buy either explanation, don't you?'

'You don't have enough evidence to hold me or charge me. I insist that you release me.'

'There is one other small piece of evidence,' Conroy said, and the smugness in his voice suggested that whatever it was, he knew it was going to shut me down.

'Charlotte Witherburn has told us that you told her you were going to kill her husband, and that you were going to do it last night. She didn't believe you, but when her husband didn't come home, she began to worry. She would have called us then, but it was late and she thought it was possible that Harry had got drunk somewhere, and she didn't want to make a scene. When the body was found, you went straight to her and said ...'

He stopped here and pulled a notebook from his pocket. He flipped a few pages and continued:

'... and said, "It's over, Charlotte. I've done it. We're free. I've got rid of Harry."'

He looked from his notebook to me. I couldn't grasp what was happening. Conroy said, 'Mrs Witherburn admitted that she had been having an affair with you, and that she had tried to break it off, but that you had become obsessed with the idea that, if Harry was out of the way, the two of you would live happily ever after, spending his money.'

Conroy's voice began to recede, and I felt suddenly very cold, despite the fact that the room was hot and close. Was he making this up, attempting to trap me into a confession? Were the police allowed to do this? I found my voice, although I barely recognised it when it emerged.

'I don't believe you. Charlotte would not say those things.'

'Oh, she said them, and lots more besides, and she signed a statement.'

He signalled to Topaz, who produced a typed sheet — the contents of which, when I ran my eye over it, were more or less identical to the words Conroy had spoken. At the bottom, with a confident flourish, was the signature of Charlotte Witherburn.

So far, Peter Topaz had been silent. Now he spoke. 'You'll need a lawyer. When you're returned to your cell, you'll find your clothes there.'

That was all he said, and his voice was carefully neutral.

'I didn't do this,' I said weakly.

'You might as well be hanged for a sheep as a lamb,' Conroy said. 'Figuratively speaking, of course. Why don't you save us all a lot of trouble and confess to the murders of Polly Drummond and her mother, and tell us what you've done with, and to, Joe Drummond's body?'

The matter-of-factness with which he said this drained the last vestiges of resistance from my body, and I began to sob. I sobbed like a broken and guilty man. I sobbed like a man betrayed.

On the short walk back to the cell I regained some of my composure. One thing was clear. I could not now afford to collapse or lose my grip. I had to suppress the overwhelming sense of abandonment that threatened to cripple me. Where was Arthur? Where was Annie? Where was anybody?

I had not until now allowed myself to ponder the implications of Charlotte's statement, except to assure myself that it must have been extracted under duress and amid the general trauma of Harry's death — or that it was a fiction, designed by Conroy to frighten a confession out of me. If I could speak to Charlotte, the hideous error could be corrected. The sight of me being taken away, handcuffed and humiliated, must have wrenched her heart. I could not, though, quite silence that unsettling 'Thank you' she had uttered.

When the door was closed behind me, I saw that a change of clothes had been put on one of the beds. A few minutes later I was taken from the cell by a constable I did not recognise, and told that I was to be driven to the courthouse, where I would appear before a magistrate named Murray. There was no one in the courtroom when the charge of murdering Harry Witherburn was read out, despite the fact that the George was only a short walk away. I could not believe that Topaz hadn't told them anything. They must all have decided that staying well away from me was the best policy. The police opposed bail, and the magistrate determined that I had a case to answer. All this was accomplished with expedition. I don't think I have ever felt so completely alone as when I walked from the courthouse to the police van and looked up at the upper verandah of the George Hotel. My despair was mirrored in the sky. Great banks of roiling clouds had gathered, and the light had assumed the blue-grey depth it acquires before a storm. There was a strong smell of rain on the still air, and the trees outside the courthouse seemed to have curled in upon themselves in an instinctive, protective gesture against impending violence. That is how it seemed to me, although my vision of the world had been warped by the collapse of all my certainties.

When we returned to the police station I was put into the interview room, rather than being taken directly to the cell. I was alone for a few minutes until Topaz entered. I had been standing, and he signalled that I should sit.

'Conroy's gone home,' he said. 'His wife's sick.'

'He has a wife?' Even through the haze of my desperation, the idea that that repellent, quivering-eyed robot was married struck me as extraordinary.

'Yes,' Topaz said. 'She's frail. Always ill.'

'I don't have the energy to talk to you,' I said.

'A lawyer has been organised for you. A good one. He's coming up from Brisbane tomorrow.'

'There's no money to pay for a good lawyer.'

'You do have friends.' He paused. 'And family.'

I felt ill.

'What do you mean?'

'It was Annie who suggested it. The troupe has put money in, but Annie said that your brothers and your mother would want to know, and that they'd probably want to help.'

'What do you mean "probably," and how does she know they even exist? I have never discussed my family with her or anybody else.'

Topaz had the grace to blush.

'Well, I'm afraid that's my fault. When I was checking up on you I found all that out, and Annie …'

'My family as pillow talk. Whatever gets you going, I guess.'

'Maybe it's me, Will. Maybe I bring out the worst in you. I know that your life has turned to garbage, and I know that you're terrified, but there you sit, still drawing on your bottomless reservoir of bullshit.'

I began to protest, but thought better of it.

'Look', I said, 'I am under a bit of pressure here.'

This was as close as I could get to contrition. To give Topaz credit, he had not yielded to what must have been a considerable temptation to gloat over my predicament.

'All right, Will', he said. 'I want you to listen to me without interrupting, and I'm asking you to trust that what I'm telling you is the truth. I shouldn't be talking to you at all. Conroy would spontaneously combust if he knew.'

I couldn't help myself.

'Just tell me one thing first. Conroy hates me. Why?'

'Conroy doesn't hate you, Will. Conroy hates me. But he does believe he's caught his killer. He really does. He isn't using you as a convenient stooge. He truly believes you're guilty.'

'He assaulted me.'

'He thinks you've murdered four people. If I thought that I might thump you, too.'

A great wave of relief washed over me.

'You still think I'm innocent?'

He leaned forward.

'I don't think you're innocent. I know you're innocent.'

'How?'

He considered that for a moment.

'I know you're innocent because I know who isn't. Now just listen, Will. I'm not going to give you any names. Not yet. Unless I get more evidence, you could still go down for Harry Witherburn's murder, on Charlotte's evidence alone.'

'But Conroy made that up.'

Topaz was genuinely startled, and looked at me as if he thought I might be mad.

'No, Will,' he said firmly. 'Conroy didn't make that up. Charlotte Witherburn couldn't wait to provide that information. I know this is hard for you to accept, but Charlotte Witherburn is as unpleasant in her way as Harry was in his. It's no coincidence that they were married. These people find each other.'

'She asked me to kill him.'

These words tumbled out of my mouth. There was no emotion in them. Some part of me had suddenly and finally surrendered any faith I had left that Charlotte would intervene and recant her testimony.

'She thinks you did kill him, and she's happy to let you pay for it.'

'She didn't kill Harry, then?'

'No. No. But she did interfere with his corpse. I can't prove it, but I'm pretty sure it was Charlotte who put your name up Harry's arse.'

'Why?'

'Will,' he said, with some exasperation, 'don't you get it? She wanted you safely out of the way. She thinks you did her dirty work for her, and she certainly doesn't want you under foot now. She's rich and she's free. She'll stand up in court, look you straight in the eye, and declare you guilty, and all she'll feel is relief.'

'OK', I said. 'I get it.' And, for the first time, I really did get it — fully, profoundly. I would wrestle with the consequences of this understanding later.

'What about the troupe? Do they know that you don't go along with Conroy?'

'Yes. I've told Annie, and she's let them know. They do want to help, Will.'

'No one's been to see me.'

'No one's been allowed to see you or to have any contact

with you whatsoever. Once your lawyer's here, that should change. I imagine you'll certainly be able to see your brother.'

'What?'

'Your brother is coming here as soon as he can organise leave from his teaching.'

'I don't want to see him. Things are bad enough without involving my family.'

'Too bad,' Topaz said with finality. 'You need all the help you can get, and your brother is willing to help. I don't give a rat's arse whether you want him here or not. He's coming, and that's that.'

With the interview over, I began to reflect on the impending arrival of my brother Brian. My relations with my brothers were perfectly civil. Both Brian and Fulton were younger than I was, and I didn't really have very much in common with either of them. The gap between Fulton and me was so large — he was just twenty — that I thought of him as a child. Brian was closer in age to me, but there was an edge of competitiveness between us that infected our interaction. I also didn't much care for his drab and silly wife, Darlene. I was aware of an unspoken, simmering resentment which he harbored because it had fallen to him to stay at home and look after our mother. He thought acting was a trivial profession, and in the course of one unpleasant fraternal stoush he had made the ludicrous suggestion that perhaps my ambition was greater than my talent.

'You might have noticed,' he had said, 'the dearth of Australian movie stars.'

'Errol Flynn. Merle Oberon,' I had replied.

'Hardly the last words in great acting,' he had said dismissively.

'Anyway, I'm not interested in the movies,' I had said. 'I am a stage actor.'

He'd snorted derisively. It had taken a great deal of self-discipline not to suggest that teaching adolescent boys in a dreary high school and curling up each night with an even drearier wife were not exactly the stuff dreams were made on. Not my dreams, anyway.

A roll of thunder made me jump as the constable took me back to the cell, and great pats of rain began to land with thuds in the dust and with slaps on the iron roof. Inside the cell a pale, low-voltage light, itself imprisoned in a protective cage, had been turned on. Its dimness seemed to accentuate the dark corners, rather than dispel them. An explosive crack of thunder sounded almost simultaneously with a fierce, blindingly white flash of lightning. It had the intensity of an x-ray. The thunder that followed began with a sound like the tearing of some unimaginably vast piece of fabric, and escalated into a boom that rattled the building and rattled me to boot. There was another split-second whiteout and another ear-shattering burst of thunder. The rain was machine-gunning on the roof with mounting ferocity, and I could hear through its rat-a-tat-tat that trees were being whipped about. Somewhere a door was slamming open and shut, and I thought I heard shouting, but I couldn't be sure amidst the general clamour.

I stretched out on the bed, conscious now of an ache in my arm, and I experienced a renewed annoyance about the unwanted involvement of my younger brother. The wind blew at a savage pitch for a full hour and then, incredibly, it seemed to surge to an even wilder level. The rain no longer fell noisily onto the roof. It must have been driven almost parallel to it. Then the dim light went out. It is astonishing how even the faintest of light can disguise the black reality of total darkness. I sat up and listened to the howling universe beyond my cell. There were new sounds in it. Iron roofs whined and groaned and clung to their beams, reluctant and complaining as the wind attempted to prise them loose and fling them into the night. A crash and scream of metal on metal told me that at least one piece of iron had surrendered and had been thrown against a building nearby.

The roof came off my cell with the swiftness of a sharply removed scab. One moment it was there; the next, rain was beating down upon me and the cyclone was with me inside the cell. Leaves and whole branches were tossed into the cramped space. I knew I had to get out of there and that the only way was up and over the wall. I turned one of the beds on its end and clambered to the bedhead, where I stood precariously, my good hand gripping the exposed wall-top above me. The bed moved under my weight, but it held and, with a manoeuvre worthy of the circus performer that half of Maryborough thought I was, I pulled down on my arm and swung my legs over the wall. It was unsightly and inelegant but, driven by pure adrenaline, it was successful, and I found myself sitting astride my prison wall. My wound, however, had been torn open, and the pain was excruciating. I waited for a moment to catch my breath, then dropped to the ground on the other side.

The extraordinary noise and the furious battering of wind and rain, and the realisation that I might be decapitated or cut in half at any moment by flying iron, made careful consideration of what I should do next very difficult.

I was in no danger of being discovered. No one was out in this weather. I could see nothing. The darkness was relieved only by momentary stilettos of lightning. The pelting rain fell so thickly it was as if Maryborough found itself at the bottom of the remorseless cascade of a mighty and pummelling waterfall. It was through this turbulent submarine world that I made my way towards Charlotte's house.

Chapter Eleven

WILD NIGHT

THERE WERE NO LIGHTS on at Witherburn. I could discern its shape dimly when I entered the drive, and then a white blast revealed it, vast and skeletal, like a giant carcass, gleaming, picked clean. Charlotte would, no doubt, be surprised to see me. A part of me was holding on to the absurd hope that there had been a ghastly misunderstanding between us, and that she was in no way implicated in the deliberate attempt to set in motion a series of actions that would lead to me being imprisoned for life.

I mounted the front steps. Lightning revealed that the furniture on the verandah had been tossed into heaps by the wind, much of it reduced to sticks. I knocked on the front door, but I could not hope that my knocks were audible above the competing hammering of the storm. I turned the handle and it opened. I thought it odd that no one had lit a candle or a hurricane lamp.

Somewhere in the house a door slammed and slammed again as the wind caught it.

'Charlotte?'

I called loudly.

'Charlotte?'

There was no reply. I took a few steps down the corridor and called again.

'Charlotte?'

I felt something then. Not a presence. An absence, and I breathed it in like swamp gas. I knew that someone had been here before me, and I knew what I would find behind one of those doors.

Not expecting the lights to work, I nevertheless found the switch in the hallway and depressed it. I narrowed my eyes against the sudden brightness, and made my way towards Charlotte's bedroom and knocked pointlessly. No amount of knocking will wake the dead, and I was certain that Charlotte lay dead on the other side of the door. I opened it slowly, allowing the light from the hallway to creep in ahead of me. The sweet, ferrous odour of warm blood reached me. I switched on the light and saw her sitting on the floor, her back against the side of the bed, her head lolled forward. Her nightdress was stained carmine, and a viscous pool of blood spread out around her. It was still flowing. Whatever had happened to her had happened only moments before. That she was dead I had no doubt, but I could not immediately bring myself to approach her body and examine her closely.

The sound of breaking glass in another room terminated any thoughts that I might have had of doing this. The murderer was still in the house. With me. My hand shot out and snapped off the light. Perhaps I believed that hiding behind night's skirts might protect me. I kept still for a moment, straining to hear a human sound through the storm's cacophony. He must know that he was not alone. Of course he knew this. I'd called out Charlotte's name and switched on a light. He was lying in wait. The glass had been deliberately broken to unnerve me. It had been successful. I was incapable of coherent thought and incapable, too, of action. I simply stood there and waited to be found.

I can't remember whether the darkness was so enveloping that not even the vaguest of outlines was visible, or whether I had closed my eyes in some childish belief that if you can't see anything, you can't be seen. It was a short, sharp sniff that told me he had entered Charlotte's bedroom. I reached for the light switch, suddenly determined to see him, whatever the consequences. My fingers found it just as his hand did the same. The sensation of his warm flesh was, oddly, chilling. Neither of us pulled away. For the briefest of moments we were frozen, skin on skin. Then, in one, startling movement, he flicked on the switch and closed his fingers tightly around my wrist.

I found myself staring into Arthur Rank's eyes.

He released his grip.

'What are you doing here?' he asked, as if we had met unexpectedly on a street somewhere. I turned my head to look at Charlotte's corpse, and his eyes followed mine. He did a passable impression of someone seeing her body for the first time, but I didn't allow him the luxury of playing out his charade. I slipped my arm out of its sling and brought the full weight of the plaster cast down onto the side of his head. A devastating pain suggested that I had re-broken the bone. Arthur dropped unconscious to the floor. Blood oozed extravagantly from behind his ear.

Although to some extent I had prepared myself for this ghastly revelation after our encounter with Flint, I nevertheless found it difficult to accept. What motive could Arthur have for murdering Polly, her mother, Joe, Harry Witherburn, and now Charlotte? Was there something in his strange and tragic past that linked him to all of them?

I nudged him gingerly with my foot. He didn't stir. When I felt his pulse it was strong, so I hadn't killed him, thank God. If I was to be cleared of suspicion I would have to deliver Arthur alive to the frightful Conroy. I allowed myself the momentary luxury of imagining his reaction to the news that he had been grossly wrong all along. I would not, I told myself, succumb to any bouts of euphoric forgiveness for his treatment of me, and I would pursue justice for the mortifying slap he had inflicted.

For now, though, I had no clear idea of what to do next. I tried the telephone in the corridor, but the line was dead. I had to get to Topaz. He suspected already that Arthur was the culprit; and now I had caught him, more or less, in murderous *flagrante delicto*. I couldn't afford to wait here at Witherburn for the storm to pass. That might take hours, and I couldn't face the prospect of speaking to Arthur when he regained consciousness. I didn't want to risk hearing his desperate lies, partly because I knew how easy it would be for me to believe them. Using a piece of curtain cord, I tied Arthur's arm to his ankle, and positioned him so that the first thing he saw when he woke was the body of his latest victim. When I stepped into the hallway I thought I saw at its far end a shadow, deeper than those around it, shift. I stared until I had reassured myself that there was nothing to stare at. I then opened the front door, crossed the verandah, and passed through its latticed door into the roiling fury of nature untethered.

The driveway was strewn with foliage and branches, and the debris leapt about as if animated by internal energies. The street outside Witherburn was alive with rolling, skittering, and flying detritus. And everywhere the wind, not contented with hurling objects willy-nilly, howled its presence with a terrifying voice. The rain fell in sheets still, but the lightning no longer cleaved the air with its hideous illumination. Heavy branches rolled languidly in response to the application of some unseen boot pushing them aside.

I decided that my best bet was to go to the George. There were people there who would be relieved to see me — people who, if Topaz had told the truth, believed in my innocence. I thought it likely that Topaz would be there, taking the opportunity to hold Annie close during the worst of the storm.

When I reached Queen's Park I saw people rushing about, oblivious to the danger posed by airborne missiles. They seemed to be mostly military people, and they were shouting, hurrying in the direction of the river. I followed, knowing what this meant, and I had not gone far when I realised I was ankle deep in water. The smell of the Mary River rose to my nostrils from where it swirled at my feet. Here, at the edges of its spill, I could feel the relentless tug of its current, and knew that the George must by now be within its grip. I knew, too, that Mal Flint's house would be washed by its waters, in some way temporarily cleansed, until the flood's withdrawal left behind its foul and stinking wrack.

No one paid any attention to me as I walked to higher ground up Adelaide Street. I thought I would come around behind the George and see how matters stood. When I reached the corner of Kent and March Street, I saw that the Mary River had engulfed the George to a point at least halfway up its lower windows. I imagined the furniture in the dining room and bar floating and crashing against masonry and glass as the river eddied and swished in the unfamiliar confinement of four walls. The sound of its rushing was unearthly to my ears, and triumphant, as if the river were declaring that its banks were a grace-and-favour confinement, and no impediment to the occasional demonstration of its true authority.

I couldn't get any nearer to the hotel without swimming, and the current was too swift to allow that. I wondered if the troupe had abandoned the premises. Surely they wouldn't have retreated upstairs, for they must have known that the very foundations might give way and bring the whole building crashing into the flow.

A hand placed solidly on my shoulder, with the proprietorial certainty of a walloper nabbing his man, made me jump. I turned, and was relieved to see that it belonged to Augie Kelly. His copper hair was plastered to his head, and his clothes were as saturated as my own.

'They've let you go?' he shouted.

I shook my head.

'I've let myself go!' I shouted back. I mimed the roof of the cell being blown off. He nodded.

'Where is everybody?' I asked.

'The Royal. They drove up hours ago when it looked like it was going to flood.'

I caught most of this. He then leaned towards my ear.

'I stayed as long as I could!'

I began to shout something about Topaz, but gave up as the wind roared with renewed vehemence. I made to move off, intending to find Topaz and the Power Players in the Royal Hotel. As I did so, Augie made a bizarre and disconcerting gesture. He reached out and brushed away a strand of wet hair that was lying across my forehead. I recoiled from his touch, a reaction he seemed to take personally. It was not so dark that I couldn't see the grimace of anger that crossed his face. He withdrew his hand abruptly, offended that I had misinterpreted his action, turned on his heel, and disappeared up March Street.

I followed, not in order to catch him up, but because it was the quickest way to the Royal. I needn't have worried. Augie had vanished. I couldn't gather my thoughts to interpret his action, not with the heavens bent on drowning the earth. Besides, nothing Augie did was without a whiff of creepiness.

I toiled my way to the Royal Hotel, terrified that at any moment something would be dislodged from its resting place and bring my life to a premature end. Somewhere, amid the crowded emotions jostling for position, the sense that my brother would only get the full story second-hand if I wasn't there to tell it, pushed its way out of the pack. If I died, it was entirely possible that Conroy's version — supported no doubt by Arthur, who would be free to declare that he had witnessed my killing Charlotte — would gain currency. I could almost hear my brother, even as he identified my body, telling himself, and my mother, that murder and a grisly death involving airborne roofing iron were a natural consequence of choosing acting instead of teaching as a career. I could also hear his pinch-spirited little wife clucking agreement and adding that, while it gave her no pleasure to say it, a person could not go about killing people and expect to die peacefully in his bed. Oh, no. It was of paramount importance that I lived to enjoy the haughty victory of the wrongfully accused.

The street outside the Royal Hotel was deserted. This was hardly a surprise. The only people not indoors were the volunteers who were pointlessly sandbagging the outer spill of the Mary River. Blackouts were in place, so I wasn't sure whether or not the power had been cut off.

I entered through the main door. The grand staircase, faintly illuminated by hurricane lamps burning in the dining room to its left, swept up into impenetrable blackness. There was a burble of conversation coming from the dining room. The timbre of the voices was familiar, but I could not distinguish individual words. Having arrived, I was not now certain what to do next. Should I just walk into the room and assume that people would be pleased to see me? It sounded as if there were more people in there than the players, though, and perhaps not all of them would be excited by my freedom. And what if Conroy was among them?

A figure emerged from the dining room and saw me before I could decide what to do.

'What are you doing here?'

It was Bill Henty. He would not have been my first choice as the person most likely to greet me sympathetically, and he didn't let me down.

'You're supposed to be safely locked up.'

'What do you mean "safely"? I thought Topaz made it clear that I wasn't their man.'

Henty grunted dismissively.

'How'd you get out?' he asked.

'Never mind. Is Topaz here?'

'No,' he said. 'He's out sandbagging.'

'Annie?'

'She's in there.'

He stood looking at me out of his different-coloured eyes, or out of the one that wasn't blind anyway, with that resolute sullenness that was his specialty.

'Well, would you get her for me?' I asked, and was displeased to hear the petulance in my own voice. Henty, more than anyone in the company, had a way of bringing out some of my very few less-admirable qualities.

He returned to the dining room, reluctant to tear himself away from the evidence of my discomposure. I must have presented a bedraggled spectacle. A great deal had happened since this morning, all of it calculated to put physical distance between me and my doppelganger, Tyrone Power.

A moment later, Annie came out and hurried to me. Wordlessly, she took me by the elbow and propelled me up the stairs to the point where the light died and where we could not be seen by anybody below.

'My God, Will,' she said. 'Are you mad?'

'I didn't have any choice,' I said defensively. 'The roof blew off.'

'And you were sucked out of the room like Dorothy,' she said sharply.

'Why are you so angry?' I asked, dismayed by her failure to show any interest in my welfare.

'Peter is trying to help you. You've only been in the bloody jail for a few hours, and you've already escaped. He's going behind Conroy's back for you, and here you are giving Conroy more ammunition.'

'You mean more ammunition to fire at your boyfriend, don't you,' I snapped.

'You,' Annie said firmly and clearly, 'are sometimes a stupid, stupid man.'

'Really,' I said and prepared to disabuse her of this ridiculous assertion by revealing that I had discovered the identity of the murderer.

'I know …' I began, but got no further because the door below us opened and Peter Topaz came in out of the storm. Before I could stop her, Annie had called out to him.

'Peter! He's up here. Will's up here.'

Topaz took the steps two at a time, and was with us in seconds.

'The roof blew off,' Annie said, like a school marm rattling off my misdemeanours before the headmaster. Topaz, obviously fatigued by his labours that night, could, nevertheless, barely contain the rage he was feeling when he said, 'All right. All right. That was a very stupid thing to do, but let's not panic. There's no one at the station. They're all out sandbagging, so you have to go back, like a good little suspect, and climb back into your cell, and I don't care how wet and wild it is in there. You're to sit in the corner until someone comes for you. Understand? No one need ever know.'

I said evenly, 'No. I can't do that.'

Annie jabbed me viciously in the ribs.

'Yes you can,' she said through clenched teeth. 'Bill Henty won't say anything.'

I was ready to drop my bombshell.

'I'm not worried about Henty. I can't go back because I've caught your murderer for you. I've got him tied up at Charlotte's house.'

I could not eliminate the glee from my voice entirely. Topaz's reaction was not at all what I expected.

'You've been to Witherburn? Tonight?' he asked, and his voice trembled.

'Yes,' I said, disconcerted by what that tremble might herald. 'I found Charlotte's body.'

Annie squeaked in horror.

'And I found her killer. He's tied up there, waiting for some dim-witted copper to go and arrest him.'

Very, very slowly, Topaz asked, 'Who have you tied up?'

'You know who,' I said. 'Arthur. Our Arthur. Arthur Rank.'

I didn't see his fist coming, but I sure as hell felt it when it connected with my jaw. There was a momentary sense of having been hit in the face with a brick, and then the plunge into the familiar deep well of unconsciousness.

Chapter Twelve

ERRORS OF JUDGEMENT

I WOKE WITH THE TASTE of blood in my mouth and with a suite of pains emanating from various sites on my body: arm, shoulder, jaw, neck, head. Amid this distressing orchestration I detected a new instrument. Acting as a sort of percussive accompaniment a new pain shot up and down my leg. I could see nothing when I opened my eyes, so these sensations assailed me without distraction. For a moment I couldn't recall what had happened. Then the shape of Topaz's fist dislodged itself from memory, and I winced at the retrieved recollection. With a nauseating rush of understanding I remembered that he had hit me after I had told him that I had found Arthur out.

They were in this together.

The weight of this realisation kept me pinned to the floor. So breath-taking was it that I was unable, for the moment, to move a muscle. But why? What was the connection between

Peter Topaz and Arthur? Their faces swam before me and, in a brilliant, intuitive flourish, I overlaid one face on another in my imagination. Why had I never seen this before? Why had I never noticed that Peter Topaz and Arthur Rank were brothers?

This revelation energised my aching body sufficiently to pull me to my feet. I was in a cupboard of some sort, tall and narrow. Feeling about me, my fingers collided with broom handles and mops. The door, when I found it, wouldn't budge. A heavy object had been pushed in front of it. I banged on it, but my bangings brought no response. I assumed I was still in the Royal Hotel, secreted somewhere on the top floor, or perhaps in the cellar. The incipient rumblings of claustrophobia began to assert themselves. The last thing I needed was that irrational, but unstoppable, freight train of fear.

As it happened, it was the phobia that freed me. Almost as soon as I had identified its presence within me, it broke free of its restraints and roared through every nerve. I flung myself against the door in a frenzy, oblivious to pain and possible injury. Again and again I threw my weight at it, until it gave way with a crash. The dresser that had been pushed against it fell forward and I burst from the cupboard into a room palely lit by the grey and feeble light of an early, sodden dawn. I didn't recognise any of its features, beyond establishing that it was not a hotel room. I was in someone's house.

The noise of the falling dresser brought no one running, so I assumed I was alone — an assumption that was overturned when a voice spoke from a shadowy corner.

'I wondered who was bangin' about in there.'

I could only see his muddy shoes and the filthy bottoms of his trousers, but there was no mistaking Mal Flint's barely human voice. Feeling as if I had somehow slipped into one of Dante's circles of hell, all I could think of to say was a numbly expressed,

'Where am I?'

Flint laughed, or at any rate emitted a noise which I took to be laughter. It might equally have been a snarl.

'You're kiddin', right?'

Bereft of a plan, and feeling perilously close to collapsing, I simply sat on a nearby, upright chair. The slump of my body must have convinced Flint that I was not kidding.

'You're in Topaz's house,' he said, and added, 'and this is a real bonus. I thought I'd have to come lookin' for you. Wasn't expectin' to find you here, all ready to be dealt with.'

'Well,' I managed to say, 'I think I can honestly say that I wasn't expecting to find you here either.'

There it was again: his strange, ugly, other-species laugh.

'Me house has gone under,' he said.

Why would he think I would be interested in his living arrangements, particularly as he was about to beat me to a pulp? I had lost the advantage of surprise here and, where Flint was concerned, that was about the only advantage one could hope for. If Flint had any lingering concerns about my capacity to overpower him, my appearance and deflated demeanour would by now have dispelled them. I spoke to him simply because there was nothing else I could do, and I was alarmed that any silence between us might encourage him to attack me.

'What are you doing here?' I asked, and tried to inject something like menace into my voice.

'I told ya, me house went under.'

'And has Topaz offered you his spare room?'

He snorted.

'You're a fucking moron,' he said, obviously unfamiliar with facetiousness as a conversational tool. 'I've got a few things to settle with Topaz.'

'What sort of things?'

My dismay was subsiding, and as I became more comfortable with my position I began to consider possible ways out of it. Just within reach, on a table, sat a large, heavy glass bowl. Its decorative qualities were less important to me than its potential as a missile.

'None of your fuckin' business,' he said.

'Is he expecting you?'

'Nuh. It's a surprise.'

He stood up suddenly. His face bore the marks of Arthur's punishing torture three days earlier, and his shirt, with three buttons missing, exposed the narrow scab that had formed over the shallow slash down his sternum. There wasn't time to ponder choices. If I'd thought about what I was going to do, I wouldn't have done it — and after I'd done it, I wished I hadn't. I grabbed the bowl and threw it at Flint, the way one might throw a pie in a slapstick fight. The idea was to knock him to the ground. The idea was not for him to catch it. Which is what he did. He was a little surprised to find himself holding an ornament, but so confident was he of his ability to dispatch me bare-handed that he simply tossed it aside. It thudded against the wall, but did not shatter. There he was before me, poised for violence with an ursine heaviness and assurance.

'I want you to piss your pants,' he said.

'Now that,' said a voice behind him, 'is something you'll have to pay to see,' and Adrian Baden came into the room. Flint turned sideways to see who had interrupted his pleasure.

'Who the fuck are you?' he grunted.

Adrian put one hand on his hip and described Flint's silhouette in the air with the index finger of the other one.

'Have you sucked my cock?' he asked.

Flint's reaction to this extraordinary question was itself extraordinary. He was flummoxed by it and uttered a strangled

'Whaaaa…?'

Adrian, with astonishing courage, sashayed to within a few inches of Flint.

'You look familiar,' he said, 'but all you brutes look the same in the dark.'

The delicate touch of Adrian's finger on Flint's bare chest nailed him to the spot more securely than if he'd been skewered with a lance. This gave Adrian plenty of time to guide his knee into Flint's groin with all the force he could muster. Flint doubled over and I winced involuntarily. The blow was so solid that Flint's testicles may well have been driven back up inside his body.

'The fear of the queer,' Adrian said, 'is a weapon mightier than the sword. Help me lug the guts into the cupboard.'

'I got out of there,' I said. 'He will, too.'

Flint was in no position to resist as Adrian tied his hands behind his back and tied them in turn to his ankles. We pushed and pulled him into the cupboard, and put the dresser back in front of it.

'Now,' I said, 'what are you doing here and what is going on?'

'I'm supposed to be guarding you, but Peter's got an outside dunny and I just had to go. You weren't supposed to escape. Peter is not going to be happy.'

'You seem very pally with him all of a sudden.'

'I've always been pally with him.'

'My God, Adrian, do you have any idea what's happening here?'

He was suddenly serious.

'Will, the only person who's got no idea what's going on is you.'

'Really?' I said. 'So where's Topaz right now, and why do you think he wanted me out of the way?'

'He's gone to make sure Arthur is all right, and he wanted you out of the way, because when you're not out of the way, you're in the way.'

'He's gone to free Arthur? Oh, God. And how did I get here?'

'Annie drove Peter and me, and we dragged you inside. I think I might have banged your leg on something. Sorry.'

'Where's Annie now?'

'At the Royal, I suppose. Why?'

I began to walk about the room in a cliché of distraction.

'We have to stop them,' I said.

'Who? The Japanese? Who are you talking about?'

Adrian's flippancy angered me.

'We have to stop Topaz and Arthur.'

'Stop them from doing what, Will? You're not making any sense.' He chopped the air with his hand. 'At all!'

'Topaz and Arthur are brothers.'

His jaw dropped, as well it might have.

'No!' he said, with breathy disbelief.

'Oh, yes,' I said, in a voice that conveyed my certainty on this point. 'They're brothers all right, and they're in this together.'

'You've lost me. In what?'

'Arthur and Topaz are responsible for the murders that I've been accused of.'

I said this slowly, savouring, in a strange, detached way, the drama of the moment.

Adrian withdrew a few steps from me and narrowed his eyes.

'You are a lunatic,' he said.

'Adrian, I was there when Arthur killed Charlotte Witherburn last night. I was there. There's a lot you don't know about him.'

'I know he hasn't got a brother.'

'He hasn't got two balls either. He lost more than his arm in that accident.'

'So what? I know that. Everyone knows that. It was one of the first things he told us.'

This took the wind out of my sails, and I was inexplicably wounded by it. I felt cheated of a confidence. My whole relationship with Arthur had been built on a lie. I could see that now. Why should this small revelation about Arthur's injury niggle so much? I think it was because I realised that I had not been the first person with whom Arthur had shared his little secret. I had been the last.

'You have to suspend everything you think you know about both Arthur and Peter Topaz. I can't tell you why they are doing these terrible things. I don't even know whether Peter is covering for Arthur, or whether he's actively involved, but believe me Adrian, they're both in it. We don't have time to stand here debating the facts. If Topaz has freed Arthur, they're going to come looking for me and anyone else who might now know the truth.'

I could tell from the blank look on Adrian's face that he had not believed a word I had said. In one of those frightening flashes of intuition that I had been experiencing lately, it occurred to me that the blankness of his features might not be a measure of his disbelief, but might be indicative of something far more sinister — prior knowledge. Was he involved in this, too? My God, who else? The whole troupe?

Adrian suddenly threw his hands in the air and said, 'All right. That's it. I have now officially had enough. Peter asked me to guard you to keep you out of trouble. Fine. I failed. I kneed some Neanderthal in the balls. That was fun. Now you're standing there saying crazy things and, frankly, Will, I've done my bit and I've lost interest. I am very sorry that you have become mentally ill, but I'm going now, and if you try to stop me you'll be adding crushed testicles to your injury list.'

He left the room, and I made no attempt to detain him. I felt that I had entered a bizarre dream world where I alone was innocent of unspeakable crimes, and where everyone I knew was engaged in a conspiracy to pin those crimes on me.

Mal Flint had recovered sufficiently to have begun shouting abuse from the cupboard, and he made ineffectual thumps against the door. I had no doubt that he would get out eventually, and I did not want to be there when he did. I didn't linger to explore Topaz's house, although I was sure that I would have found a photograph or some other piece of evidence to support my hunch about his relationship to Arthur. I might also have found something to link the accident that had disfigured Arthur to the Drummond family. I could not begin to imagine what this link might be, or why it would prompt such brutal vengeance, but I knew that the answers lay in Arthur's and Topaz's shared past.

It had stopped raining and the wind had died completely. The street had an exhausted appearance, as if it were cowering after a flogging. I looked back at Topaz's house. It was not raised on disguised stilts like its neighbours, but sat on low stumps. Only a few steps led to the verandah. He was not interested in gardening. There were a few trees — a pawpaw and a bopple nut among them — and a few scruffy, battered shrubs. His red, iron roof, which had survived unscathed, could have done with a coat of paint.

I didn't know what part of Maryborough I was in. The disarray in the street would have made even the familiar look unfamiliar, but I was sure that I had not been in this street before. A few houses down, a boy of about ten came out to inspect the damage. There was no one else around, and I was glad of it — I could find out where I was, without arousing suspicion. He whistled his surprise at my appearance.

'What happened to you?' he asked.

'The storm,' I said. 'I was out helping.'

He seemed satisfied with that.

'I seem to have got lost. Which way is town?'

He didn't seem to think the question was in any way unusual. Perhaps he thought that people could be blown off course, like birds.

'This is Ariadne Street,' he said. 'You go down that way to Walker Street, turn left, and just keep walking.'

I thanked him and set off. It was a long walk, and more and more people along the way had begun to emerge to see what the storm had done to their property and their neighbours' properties. Here and there pieces of iron swung like loose teeth, or were peeled back as if the wind's fingers had picked at them. A few houses sat shocked and exposed, their roofs completely gone. In one front yard a pawpaw tree lay uprooted, while nearby a straggly rose bush had maintained its grip on the earth. Nature's awful logic did not extend to an equitable meting-out of destruction.

My appearance, my cuts, bruises, and filthy clothes, made a kind of sense among the scattered wreckage. I was no more remarkable than any other evidence of the wild and ruinous night. Indeed, men returning from the sandbagging of the Mary River looked worse than I did. They were muddied and exhausted, and took no interest in me at all.

I was in a terrible quandary. The person I most needed to talk to — Detective Sergeant Conroy — was also the person least likely to listen. My escape would have been discovered by now, and the entire Maryborough police force, most of whom would have been up all night, would be on full, if bleary, alert. I couldn't join the troupe at the Royal. The police would be watching for me there. I thought about Wright's Hall. Today was a Tuesday, so there would be no children there roller-skating. Given all that had happened since Charlotte's fund-raiser yesterday — my God, was it really only yesterday? — I didn't suppose that the troupe would go there for a rehearsal. They would have been questioned by now, though, and someone, Bill Henty probably, would have mentioned Wright's Hall as a possible bolthole for me. I decided that my need for dry clothes was greater than my need for caution, and so I decided to risk going to the George Hotel. As well, I wanted a place in which to assess the damage done to my body. The uninterrupted walk towards the town centre had provided each of my hurts with the luxury of expressing itself freely. The worst of these was now my arm. The deep, dull ache that emanated from it indicated that it would have to be reset. I would have to endure another lecture from the matron about the shortage of plaster.

When I reached Queen's Park it was obvious that the waters of the Mary River had receded quickly. Clearly, this had not been a major flood, but more like the river heaving its weight on to dry land to remind the people of Maryborough that if they thought the Japanese army was the most dangerous force around, they'd better think again. The smell of river mud hung in the air so thickly that it was as if each nostril had been plugged with it.

The George Hotel had not been swept away, but the river eddied about it still. It could be entered, though, as the water was now at knee level. There were no police that I could see, and I convinced myself that they would have taken one look at this partly submerged hotel and crossed it off their list of possible refuges. I went in through the front door, which had been pushed open by the force of the flood. It is a peculiar and disturbing sensation to walk into a flooded room. It creates an unsettling simmer of impotent outrage. Why should the river wish to poke about in every corner of every room and leave its putrid excreta behind it when it departs?

All the furniture in the bar and dining room had been overturned, and lay crowded against the walls. There was a strange and dismal silence, unrelieved by even a single drip. So much water, and not a sound. This, I thought, is what happens when a building drowns.

Before I could slip any further into the metaphysics of a flood, a crash of metal on metal in the kitchen brought me back to earth. There was someone in there. Cautiously, I made my way towards the door. The last time I had done this I had been covered in yabby bisque, with a roomful of people laughing at my back. Then I had been mortified. Now I was afraid. I listened for a moment, hoping to determine how many people were in there. There were further scrapings of metal and finally a voice, obviously speaking to itself, said, 'What a bloody mess.' It was Tibald Canty, come to inspect his precious kitchen. I pushed open the door in relief, forgetting in my haste that I had no reason to trust any of my troupe.

Tibald was standing by the Aga, a saucepan in one hand and a sauté dish in the other. The sound of the door swishing water before it as it opened made him turn.

'You nearly killed Arthur, you stupid bastard,' he said.

While I hadn't expected him to embrace me with his huge, leg-of-mutton arms, I hadn't expected this ill-informed invective either. No one seemed in the least bit interested in my welfare.

'How do you know about Arthur?' I asked.

'He's in the hospital. He's still unconscious. They don't know if he'll ever come round.'

'How do you know about Arthur?' I repeated.

'Peter Topaz took him to the hospital and came round to the Royal afterwards. He said you hit Arthur over the head.'

Tibald looked at me with ill-disguised loathing.

'He said you tried to kill Arthur.'

The hand holding the saucepan drew attention to itself by rising and falling slightly.

'And did he tell you why?' I asked calmly.

'Yes.'

'Well?'

'I'd give up the amateur detecting if I were you, and stick to acting. Better still, find something you're good at.'

'So Topaz has pulled the wool over your eyes.'

Tibald sniffed derisively and said, 'Why don't you just piss off, Will? You're your own and everyone else's worst enemy.' He shook his head. 'Poor bloody Arthur.'

'Yeah,' I said. 'Poor bloody Arthur — only not quite so poor as the people he killed.'

'The fact that you actually believe that is an indication of just how big a dickhead you are.'

'I suppose Topaz gave you his side of the story, did he?'

'His side? His side? He's a copper. He doesn't have a side. He investigates. He looks for evidence. He follows clues. You, on the other hand, are clueless.'

I nodded sagely, trying to create an impression of both condescension and patience. I would accept Tibald's apology gracefully when the time was right, along with all the other apologies due to me.

I left Tibald to grieve over his extinguished Aga, and splashed my way to the stairs, climbed them, and approached my bedroom door on the third floor. I opened it to find Peter Topaz seated on a chair in the corner of the room. He was holding a gun, and it was pointed at me.

'Gedday,' he said.

I sat on the bed and waited for Topaz to speak. He was shaking his head slowly, and the muscles in his face were tense.

'You think you've solved it, don't you?' he said. 'You think you've worked it all out.'

'I have worked it all out.'

'OK. Why don't you tell me all about it?'

He settled the gun into a comfortable firing position, indicating that he intended to pull the trigger whether I spoke or not. This was not the time for obfuscation.

'I don't know everything,' I said. 'I don't know the why, only the who.'

'Really?' he said, raising his eyebrows in mock surprise.

'I know that Arthur killed at least some of those people, maybe all. I also know that he's your brother.'

His eyes widened.

'Given,' he said, 'that Arthur might yet die as a result of your assault, it would be inappropriate to fall about laughing at this point. That, however, would be the natural response to what you have just said.'

'If you're planning to kill me anyway, why don't you just tell me the truth, Peter? What does it matter?'

He sighed.

'I'm not planning to kill you, Will. I'm planning to take you to the hospital to meet someone. If I have to shoot you somewhere painful to do it, I will. Otherwise you could just come quietly.'

'Why would I want to do that? I don't want to speak to Arthur.'

'Arthur's unconscious. It's not him I want you to meet.'

He stood up and indicated that I should do the same.

'There's a car up the hill a bit,' he said.

The car, the same one that had taken me to and from the courthouse, was driven by a constable whose face was familiar. Topaz and I sat in the back. I thought it a most extraordinary demonstration of gall that he would continue to use the resources of the police force even as his guilt stood in peril of exposure.

The car didn't pull up at the front door of the Maryborough Base Hospital, but drew up round the back. We entered the building through a narrow service door and passed through the kitchen with its stale, unhealthy smell of unpalatable, overcooked, and probably poisonous food. Tibald's kitchen most certainly did not smell like this. We passed through a ward, and I saw Arthur lying on a bed, his head bandaged, his scarred chest exposed above a sheet pulled only as high as his waist. We didn't pause, but entered a room which, by its size, was never intended to function as a place where a patient might be put. It was the matron's station. Her presence, seated behind a desk that had been relocated to a corner, attested to this. It had been moved to accommodate a bed. Lying on the bed, propped on pillows, and almost unrecognisable behind swollen eyes and facial bruising, was Joe Drummond. He seemed to be sleeping.

'Mr Power,' the matron said, 'the circus left town a week ago. What are you doing here?'

I looked at Topaz. He obviously hadn't told her that I was responsible for Arthur's injuries. I had a sudden and sickening presentiment that my world was about to be turned upside down.

'I'm not with the circus,' I said dully.

'Mr Drummond is quite able to speak with you,' she said to

Topaz. 'But please, be brief.'

She left the room.

Joe's eyes opened, but they were little more than slits, with the pulpy red of the whites just visible.

'You're getting stronger,' Topaz said. 'You're going to be all right.'

'Can't believe I let him take me by surprise like that,' he croaked.

Topaz nodded.

'Insane people are much stronger than sane ones,' Topaz said.

In an effort that clearly pained him, Joe moved his head slightly so that he could see me.

'If you hadn't come out of Flint's house when you did, he would have finished me off,' he said.

Did he mean Arthur? I remembered there was that brief period when I was in Flint's bedroom and Arthur was, I thought, in the kitchen.

'Who?' I asked. 'Who was it?

Joe looked at Topaz, who nodded.

'You can tell him,' he said. 'He needs to know what a complete dickhead he's been.'

'It was that red-headed bloke from the hotel. Augie. Augie Kelly.'

This struck me as so ludicrous that, for a moment, my brain failed to put a face to the name.

Topaz was leaning against the police vehicle and I was standing with my free hand in the pocket of my trousers. My head was lowered, and I was trying to come to terms with what I had just heard.

'I don't understand,' I said. 'What is the connection between Augie and Arthur?'

Topaz pushed himself away from the car and grabbed my shirtfront.

'Both their names start with A,' he said, and pushed me backwards. I staggered, but kept my feet. He raised his hand to his face and rubbed at a spot between his eyebrows.

'This is like trying to explain something to an elderly, demented aunt,' he said. 'There is no connection between Arthur and Augie. None. Have you got that? None. Now, I'll try to keep this simple.'

I saw the constable in the driver's seat smirk.

'Arthur, your friend Arthur, who is lying in there unconscious, has got nothing to do with these crimes. He is *not* my brother. You are an idiot. Is there anything so far you don't understand? If there is, please tell me now, because if I have to go over this again, I think it would be simpler to shoot you.'

He paused. I said nothing, but was unpleasantly certain, with his real, rather than imagined, face before me, that he looked nothing at all like Arthur.

'Good,' he continued. 'Augie Kelly is the perpetrator of every single one of these deaths — not including Fred Drummond's, obviously.'

'How long have you known about Augie?' I ventured.

'I've suspected for a while, but he's a smart man and I couldn't catch him out. I've known for sure only since yesterday when Joe was able to speak. I can't guess at his motive. That's a mystery.'

'And Conroy?'

'He knows. There are people out looking for Kelly. Naturally he's disappointed, and not entirely convinced either. I need hardly remind you that escaping from custody is still a crime, so next time you see him I wouldn't piss him off any further. Bashing Arthur over the head is also a crime, so don't think for a minute that you're off the hook.'

'How did Joe get here? Why didn't we find him?'

'You were looking in the wrong place. Augie knew you were going to see Flint — I presume one of you told him, or he overheard you — and he got there ahead of you. He only had a few seconds to deal with Joe before you and Arthur went outside. He knocked him about and pushed him under the house at the side — there's a space there. I don't know whether he thought Joe was dead or not, but he took off into the bush before he could make sure. Maybe he was going to come back and finish the job.'

'Why didn't he?'

'Because Mal Flint found him first. After you two goons had finished torturing him — also a crime you could be charged with — he heard Joe moaning, and discovered where Kelly had stowed him. He could see that Joe was in a bad way, so he got him to hospital.'

'How?'

I was astonished to learn that Mal Flint was capable of Samaritan behaviour, and was even more astonished when Topaz said, 'He carried him as far as the Granville Bridge, and an army truck took him the rest of the way. Flint didn't go with him, but the driver recognised him and told me. Flint hasn't been around since then, but I left him a note asking him to call on me. He saved Joe's life, so without Flint it would have taken much longer to nail Kelly. In fact, you might have been given a life sentence before then, and the investigation might have been closed.'

'I saw Flint this morning,' I said. 'He was at your place.' I could not prevent a sheepish expression from crossing my face.

'Where is he now?' Topaz asked.

'He's tied up in that cupboard,' I said, and added quickly. 'It was self-defence. He was about to attack me when Adrian kneed him in the nuts, and then we ... well, we were obliged to restrain him. For safety reasons.'

Topaz spoke even more slowly than he usually did.

'So the man responsible for saving your bacon is trussed up in a broom cupboard. Is that about the size of it?'

'Well, to be fair, he didn't know he was helping me, and he would have killed me, I'm sure of it, if he'd been given the chance.'

'Get in,' he said suddenly, his voice edgy with exasperation.

'Where are we going?'

'I'm dropping you at the Royal, where the rest of the troupe is, and you're not going to move from there until I tell you to. Understand?'

I wanted to say that my arm needed attention and that, as we were here at the hospital, it might be a good idea to have it looked at. Somehow, though, my instincts told me that it might seem tasteless to request medical attention while Arthur lay unconscious nearby. Besides, I was feeling rather vulnerable to disapproval, and could not face the matron's hectoring. Facing the troupe was going to be bad enough, if Tibald's reaction to me was any guide.

Topaz deposited me at the front door of the Royal Hotel. I took a deep breath and went into the foyer. It was empty. When I went into the dining room there were only half-a-dozen people there. Two of them noticed my entrance but, after a desultory glance in my direction, returned to their conversation. One of the six, seated with his back to me, was Kevin Skakel. The sudden rush of affection I experienced for this church-going, club-footed, McGonagall-admiring, journey-man actor indicated to me how desperate I had become to experience sympathy rather than the more familiar enmity. Skakel, of all people, Skakel, who'd perversely chosen to love the God who had so afflicted him, would appreciate the awful circumstances which had forced upon me the choices I had made. When I tapped him on the shoulder, however, the look on his face fell somewhat short of Christian charity.

'How's Arthur?' he asked coldly.

'I'm fine,' I said. 'Thanks for asking.'

'I can see you're fine,' he snapped, 'and I don't really care whether you are or not anyway. How is Arthur?'

'He's still unconscious,' I said, and felt keenly how this dismal fact put me at a disadvantage. Why couldn't people understand that I had attacked Arthur in good faith?

'Thinking that Arthur was ... well, it wasn't an unreasonable conclusion to jump to,' I said peevishly. 'I mean, it did look like ... Arthur was there and ... I mean, what was he doing there in the first place?'

Kevin Skakel had the nerve to sound impatient.

'I don't know, Will. But he didn't break out of prison to get there, and he didn't bash you over the head, so he hasn't actually broken any laws. You, on the other hand ...'

Annie Hudson's voice broke in before Kevin could leap to his good foot.

'You've got a nerve, coming here.'

She called this out from the other side of the dining room, and the vitriol that dripped from every syllable ensured that the five previously uninterested occupants were now very interested indeed. Having no wish to become part of a public spectacle yet again, I hurried — an unkind observer might have said scurried — across the room and brushed past Annie into the foyer. Deserted a few moments ago, there were now several people there — wives attended by their air force officer husbands. Annie was not above launching into a tirade against me whether there were people about or not, so it was imperative that I ignore Topaz's instruction and leave the Royal, at least temporarily. Annie was at my shoulder before I could determine which exit to take.

'Peter should have whacked you a lot harder last night,' she said.

I looked at her and noted that a sneer disfigured her Greer Garson face unpleasantly.

'You shouldn't do that to your face,' I said. 'It doesn't do you any favours.'

The slap of her palm against my cheek was sharp. The sound rang out in the foyer with the clarity of a gunshot, and all eyes turned to us. It wasn't particularly painful, but blood rushed to my face so furiously that I thought it might break through the pores of my skin. I suppressed a powerful impulse to strike her back, which is why the second slap took me completely unawares. I should have known that it was not in Annie's nature to stop at one.

Because I was standing close to the staircase it provided me with the most convenient egress from this ghastly slap-dance. I mounted them quickly. To my dismay, Annie followed. On the first floor I headed down a corridor, with Annie in hot pursuit. I thought I needed to bring this to an end, so I stopped abruptly and faced her.

'Don't hit me again,' I said firmly. 'I'm a little bit sick of people hitting me.'

'Not as sick as Arthur is,' she said.

That was when I lost my temper.

'Arthur! Arthur! Arthur! I'm sorry. I'm sorry he's hurt. I'm sorry I hit him. But what was I supposed to do? It looked like no one was helping me. I was going to go to jail for life for crimes I didn't commit, and the only person interested in doing something about it was me. And don't tell me your boyfriend was on my side. I was irrelevant. He wanted to solve the case for his own benefit. The fact that I would be released was nothing more than an unfortunate consequence of him winning his precious battle with Conroy.'

'You ungrateful bastard!' Annie dragged these words up from the pit of her stomach and threw them at me like darts.

'There's no point discussing this with you any further,' I said. 'Arthur was in the wrong place at the wrong time.' I don't know why, but I added for good measure, 'Unless, of course, he wasn't.'

It wasn't until I had spoken these words that it occurred to me that Joe's identification of Augie Kelly did not let Arthur completely off the hook. With Annie before me, her face mobile with disgust, it was impossible to consider a coalition between Augie and Arthur clearly. I had to get away.

At the end of the corridor a door opened onto a fire-escape, and I pushed through it without further conversation. Annie followed, obviously believing that although she had sunk her fangs into my conscience, she had not yet given it a good-enough shake. She was right. My conscience was well defended by my firm belief in the rightness of all that I had done, and I wanted to explore the comforting possibility that Arthur was not quite the victim my colleagues wanted him to be.

The exterior stairs led into an untidy, unpaved parking area at the rear of the Royal. There were a couple of military vehicles there, a few bicycles tossed carelessly against a wall, and the Power Players' truck. I headed for it, simply because it was familiar. With Annie yapping at my heels the truck's cabin seemed like the closest place of refuge. I wasn't paying particular attention to the sound of her footsteps, so I didn't notice that they had stopped halfway across the parking area. I reached up to open the truck's passenger door.

'Will?'

The sound of Annie's voice made me freeze. It was stretched taut with fear, and quivered with a panic that passed into me with electric suddenness. I turned and saw that Augie Kelly was holding Annie, one arm around her throat, his free hand clutching a hank of her hair.

'I'll break her neck,' he said calmly, and gave Annie's hair a little tug to indicate the ease with which this might be accomplished.

'Why would you do that?' I asked.

'Get in the truck,' he said, and began moving towards me, pushing Annie ahead of him. The look of unalloyed terror on her face made further discussion impossible.

'The driver's seat,' Augie said.

I climbed up, and Augie shoved Annie in at the passenger door and followed rapidly. There was only a moment when he didn't have both hands on her, but neither Annie nor I was able to take advantage of it. In a most peculiar and awkward way, he placed both hands around her throat and squeezed so that she choked. He then relaxed his grip. The ropey muscles on his hairy forearms jumped.

'Teddington,' he said. 'We're going to Teddington.'

'Teddington Weir? Why?'

'Because,' he said tightly, and pressed his fingers into Annie's neck, 'I want to.'

The Power Players' Bedford truck was not unobtrusive, and on any normal day its progress through Maryborough would have drawn stares. Today, in the aftermath of the storm, there were more vehicles than usual on the roads as the army and air force pitched in to help with the clean-up. We drove all the way to Tinana without exciting a single glance. When I turned on to the Teddington Road, Augie seemed to relax. He took his hands from around Annie's throat and put one arm around her shoulders instead.

'What's all this about, Augie?' I asked.

'Gratitude. It's all about gratitude.'

With her throat freed from immediate danger, Annie began to regain her customary *savoir combattre*, if there is such a thing. Out of the corner of my eye I saw her turn her head to face Augie.

'How dare you touch me,' she said. 'Peter will hear about this.'

The slightly sulky tone Annie was prone to adopt when arguing was not affected by her proximity to a multiple murderer. Topaz must not have told her about Augie. That would be just like him — a policeman to his boot-heels. He wouldn't identify his suspect until he had him charged and jailed. He would consider this a virtue. Annie might not agree with him at this point. Telling me about Augie was a special case, and I suppose it rankled with him that he had been obliged to do so.

'Peter can go fuck himself,' Augie said, and withdrew his arm. 'And if you say another word I'll rearrange your face so that you look like Judith Anderson.'

He laughed at his joke. In other circumstances I might have laughed, too. Annie stared straight ahead, and a slight tremble in her fingers indicated that she knew suddenly that Augie Kelly was a dangerous man. I was afraid to say anything. Augie was so tense I could smell him. The wrong word might trip some wire in his head and unleash the dogs of his psychopathy.

There were no vehicles and no bicycles at Teddington Weir. I turned the engine off, and we sat in silence for a moment. Augie looked around him and, when he was satisfied that there was no one else about, he said, 'Get out of the truck.' As he did so, once again he closed his large hands around Annie's throat. She was now beyond resistance, and passively accepted this necklace of flesh and bone.

Augie pulled Annie down from the passenger seat so roughly that I suspected he no longer had a sense of her as a person. She had become, for him, as insensate as a rag doll or a burlap sack of meat. Her neck was red from where his fingers had gripped her. She choked and bent double when he let her go.

'There's no need to hurt Annie,' I said.

'No,' he said, 'There's no need at all.'

He turned to her and shoved her to the ground.

'No *need* at all,' and he stressed the 'need' with the subtlety of a pantomime dame. Annie's face twisted in pain as her elbows took the brunt of her fall. I raised my one hand in a mollifying gesture, and felt keenly our species' preference for two in such situations.

'I don't understand, Augie. I don't understand any of this.'

I thought if I was sufficiently insistent about my incomprehension, Augie might take some pleasure in setting me right. 'I am completely bewildered,' I added.

'You messed up last night. You shouldn't have done that to Arthur. He's done nothing to you.'

Without thinking, I said, 'How do you know about Arthur?' It sounded horribly like I was goading him, but it did not agitate him.

'I was there. I saw you,' he said simply.

I remembered the movement of a deeper shadow within the general shadows at Witherburn, an impression that I had dismissed as fancy.

'Were you,' I said matter-of-factly, with no hint of it being a question.

'She had to be punished,' he said. 'I knew you'd want that. You got the blame for killing her husband. She shouldn't have done that.'

'She shouldn't have blamed me, or shouldn't have killed her husband? What do you mean?'

He furrowed his brow and shook his head, as though he thought I was being deliberately obtuse.

'She didn't kill him. I did,' he said. 'You know that. He embarrassed you in front of all those people. He deserved to die. But she should have left his body alone.'

He came close to me and leaned towards my ear. I wanted to shrink from him, but I was afraid to upset him. He whispered, 'She didn't love you, Will. She might have let you fuck her down there in the trees, but she didn't love you.'

While he was saying this, my eyes were locked on Annie's. If she was afraid, it was no longer showing in her face. She was gathering her forces, regrouping in order to give Augie a run for his money. I didn't like her chances. But there was something in her eyes that disturbed me. From her point of view it must have looked almost as if Augie and I were embracing. His words, 'I knew you'd want that' and 'You know that', struck me now as they must have struck her when she heard them. Her mouth moved slightly. Augie could not have seen this, but he must have glimpsed peripherally that Annie's face was not immobile, and he swung round on her.

'Get up!' he said savagely.

Annie got to her feet and assumed a pose that left no doubt that this time Augie would meet resistance if he attempted to grab her. The contest was as uneven as that between a wren and a hawk. Augie laughed, and Annie flew at him. This small miscalculation — his assumption that Annie would attempt defence rather than offence — allowed her to reach his face. She grabbed his ears and brought his face down to meet her rising knee. The ensuing contact wasn't particularly solid, and Augie was more stunned at having been caught off-balance than by the blow. He fell into her, and the two of them began to grapple on the ground. In only a few seconds Annie would be overpowered. I hurried round to the back of the truck and clambered in. There, among the props and costumes of our craft, I found a solid, wooden, stage sword, painted silver to simulate metal. When I jumped down from the truck I saw that Augie had Annie pinned to the ground, her arms outstretched, with him sitting astraddle her, circling each of her wrists with his large, violent hands. He was breathing heavily and staring at her. Fear had reasserted itself in her features.

The prop sword was sufficiently heavy to make wielding it with one hand difficult. I chose instead to drive its blunt point into Augie's kidneys. He let out a yowl of pain, released Annie's hands, and fell sideways. Annie was now livid with indignation, and she wriggled out from under him, leapt to her feet, and began kicking him ineffectually in the buttocks. She bent down, pulled off one of his heavy shoes, and began striking him about the head with it. He tolerated this only briefly before rolling away from her and standing up, uttering deep, guttural obscenities as he did so. Neither Annie nor I moved and, as Augie's voice spent itself, there settled between us a strange, ponderous silence into which only birdsong intruded. The sword in my right hand felt suddenly ridiculous, and the shoe which Annie held seemed incongruous and almost comic. I hoped that my action had dispelled any misconceptions Annie might have been forming about my relationship with Augie Kelly.

Augie spoke while looking directly at me.

'This is a fine mess, and after all I've done for you.'

Implicit in the injured tone of his voice was the notion that I knew what he meant when he spoke of all that he had done for me. This did not seem like the right time to go exploring the surreal and blasted landscape of his mind, so I let his statement go unchallenged. Instead I asked a more practical question.

'Why have you brought us here?'

'It's romantic,' he said. 'Didn't you think it was romantic when you fucked Charlotte Witherburn down there?'

'Were you watching us, Augie?' I kept my voice calm.

'I wasn't watching you. I was watching over you.'

'My God,' Annie said. 'You killed all those people. It was you.' She dropped Augie's shoe, as if this realisation had paralysed her muscles.

'They chose to die. They all hurt Will. We needed to punish them.'

Annie looked at me, her face rigid with shock.

'The two of you,' she said in numb wonder.

'No, no, no,' I said. 'No. Augie and me? No. We're not … I'm not … No.'

'My God,' she said again, and her mouth stayed open. I let the prop sword fall to the ground and put my hand out towards Annie. She waved it away.

'The two of you,' she repeated.

Augie walked towards her, and with the casual fluidity of the physically powerful he put his arm around her neck and began dragging her down towards the bank of the weir. I followed because there was nothing else I could have done. My mind had gone blank in its refusal to consider the implications of what Augie had said. We stopped at the place where Charlotte and I had made love.

'This is where he fucked her,' Augie said, and roughly released Annie. 'She used him.'

'How long have you two been lovers?' Annie asked.

'That's filthy talk,' Augie said. 'We don't do that. It's unnatural.'

'We!' I said, unable to keep the outrage out of my voice. 'We don't do anything. There is no we!'

Augie looked at me in disappointment.

'Polly Drummond was using you,' he said. 'I had to stop that. You were so naïve. She was putting it about. That bloke she was flirting with at the first dinner. Smelt. And that Lutteral boy. And Harry Witherburn. She was dirty, but she wasn't going to get her claws into you. I saw to that. And her mother was a mad old bitch. I saw the way she looked at you at the funeral, like she was accusing you. It was a real pleasure snuffing her. I knew you approved of that one. We almost spoke. It amounted to that, didn't it? You there in the dark, come to watch, come to see me let the old bitch know who's boss.'

'That was you in that room that night?'

'You knew it was me, Will. I could practically hear your thoughts. I was happy that night, I can tell you. I'd done what you wanted me to do.'

I shook my head in bewilderment.

'No. I didn't want that. I didn't …'

'And then you got rid of Fred Drummond, so I didn't have to. That was brilliant. I don't know how you did it. That was when I was absolutely certain that I hadn't been wrong about you, that we were in this together. Nothing mattered more than our friendship. Fred Drummond falling out of the sky was the greatest gift anyone has ever given me. Right then, I knew our friendship was a sacred trust.'

'I was never your friend, Augie.'

'Of course, you couldn't let anyone else see it. I understand that. You wanted my protection, though. We looked out for each other. You always let me know somehow where you were going and what you were doing.'

'I didn't tell you anything.'

'Yes you did, Will, and sometimes you let me overhear things, or got Arthur to tell me. I always knew. You always let me know.'

Augie seemed to have slipped into an unbordered realm of madness, but his eyes did not glaze over and he was acutely aware of our presence. Annie inclined her head at one stage, and Augie's weird eyes snapped to her with the concentration and focus of a chameleon stalking a fly. Then they swivelled back to me.

'I messed up with Joe Drummond. I wanted to do something as soon as he shot you, but I didn't get the chance. Then you gave me the chance when you took him to Flint's place. That was clever, but Arthur came out of the house too quickly. I know Drummond's not dead. I've been watching out for you ever since you came to me last night at the George.'

'I didn't come to you. You happened to be there, that's all.'

He ignored this.

'I saw them carry you into Topaz's house. I knew you'd get out. I knew you'd want to find me. I followed you and Topaz to the hospital, and that's when I guessed that Joe Drummond was still alive and that he'd told Topaz about me. About us.'

'There's no us, Augie. There's just you, and you're crazy.'

Augie laughed unexpectedly.

'We're both crazy, Will. That's why we get along so well.'

Annie sat down suddenly on the ground. This simple action seemed to ignite something in Augie and, enraged, he threw himself at her. Before I could intervene, he had tossed her bodily into the weir. He followed her but, before he had taken more than a few steps into the shallows, Annie had struck out for deeper water.

'We didn't want to hurt you, Annie,' he called. 'We like you, Will and I. Will masterbates over you, but you see it's impossible now, don't you.'

Annie was waist deep. She stopped, and looked behind her. In a voice of heart-breaking acceptance she said, 'I can't swim,' and waited for Augie to come to her. I had by now entered the water and was gaining on Augie.

'We're coming,' he said. My need to silence him, to put an end to this grotesque melding of us into that single, vile 'we', was overwhelming. I was concentrating on the back of his copper head and the red neck above the collar when he turned to face me. He smiled as if he believed that I was running to embrace him.

'I did it all for you, Will. All for us.'

There was a moment when he was smiling at me, and in almost the same moment his smile vanished and was replaced with an expression of puzzlement. His lips were drawn back over his teeth in a grimace that could have been produced only by great pain. Something had happened to him and he was in agony. His hands flew about, and he shuddered and swayed and emitted a cry like a dog caught in a steel-jaw trap. Annie and I watched him in astonishment. His body began to convulse and then he vomited into the water in front of him. Again he cried, held in the tenacious thrall of blinding pain.

I reached him and he clawed at me, gasping and choking and

incoherent. His skin was alabaster and his lips were blue. On his face there was a look of such helpless terror that I almost felt sorry for him. Frothy spittle gathered at his lips as whatever cataclysmic physical event raged within him. He pitched forward, and I caught at his shirt with my hand. Annie had reached us by this stage, and it was she who dragged Augie's helplessly compliant body to the bank of the weir.

'What is it?' I asked as Augie continued to shudder and convulse. 'Is it a stroke? A heart attack? What?'

Annie walked around Augie's juddering form, her face a mixture of distaste and nervousness. When she reached his feet, she stopped. The shoeless foot was bleeding through the sock. She pointed at it.

'Pull his sock off,' she said. 'I don't want to touch him. Obviously you're quite used to it.'

'You didn't believe any of that crap, did you? Oh, come on. You must know that it's all in his head.'

'Just take his sock off, will you,' she said and, because it was evident she was in no mood for listening, I gingerly peeled Augie's filthy, bloodied sock from his strangely swollen foot. Annie peered at his instep and then looked back at the water of the weir.

'I think he stood on a stonefish,' she said.

'Is that bad?'

'Yes, Will, that's bad, or in this case, good. It's got spines on its back, and it's just about the most painful venom there is. It couldn't have happened to a nicer guy unless, of course, you'd stepped on it.'

In a way I was relieved to hear this insult. If Annie truly believed that I was Augie's accomplice, she wouldn't have taken the chance.

'So what do we do? How do we help him?' I asked.

'I'll drive back into town. Very slowly. I wouldn't want him to miss a minute of pain. I'll get Peter and medical help.'

'So I'm supposed to wait here with him?'

'That's right.'

'But what if he recovers?'

Annie produced a withering look from her extensive repertoire of such looks, and said, 'You can enjoy a bit of private time together.'

Augie was still convulsing as the Bedford drove away. Odd, burbling sounds came out of his mouth. There was nothing I could do for him; nothing I wanted to do for him. I stood in silence, watching him, unwilling to say even a few soothing words. He was unworthy of sympathy. It was beyond my knowledge of human behaviour to understand why someone would offer murder as a token of friendship. As I looked at him I decided that I didn't want to know the psychiatric cause of his obsession — that, in explaining it, it might somehow be explained away. He was Caliban, gnarled and pinched by poison, and I had no wish to accommodate his sickness by comprehending it.

I turned my back on him and emptied my bladder. When I had finished, I turned around again and Augie Kelly had died. He was still, with his eyes open. I walked up to where the truck had been parked and waited for Annie to return. I didn't feel relief but instead a terrible despair, because I knew that Annie would always suspect that I had hastened Augie's death somehow. A part of her would always wonder whether I had protected myself against any more of Augie's revelations by silencing him forever.

Chapter Thirteen

JUDGEMENT OF ERRORS

IT WAS FRIDAY, 18 September 1942. Ten days had passed since Augie Kelly's death. The papers were full of the news that things weren't going well with our troops in Papua New Guinea.

I was sitting in King's Cafeteria, nursing a lime milkshake and trying to avoid the serious conversation my younger brother Brian had been attempting to have with me ever since his arrival four days previously. At my feet was a suitcase, packed and ready to accompany me on the train back to Melbourne. My tail wasn't exactly between my legs, but there was nothing left for me in Maryborough. I had been cleared of all suspicion in the murders committed by Augie Kelly. There were no other charges pending. Arthur did not wish to press them, and neither did Mal Flint. Flint still posed a serious threat, in my opinion, although Peter Topaz had assured me that if I kept out of his way there would be no trouble. I had also been cleared of any suspicion arising from the death of Augie Kelly. An autopsy had revealed that he was susceptible to the toxin injected by the stonefish, and that he had sustained such a large amount of it that his heart had given out.

Arthur and Joe Drummond were not yet out of hospital. Arthur had regained consciousness and was expected to make a full recovery. I had spoken to him on the day that I had gone in to have my plaster reset yet again. He would suffer no ill-effects, but the same could not be said for our friendship. He had revealed an unexpected tendency to bear a grudge, and he made it clear that it wasn't the blow that bothered him; it was my willingness to believe that he was the murderer. I thought, when he pointed out that he had never for a moment entertained that thought about me, that he was adopting an unpleasant moral tone.

I attempted to explain myself by insisting that his presence at Witherburn that night would have tested the faith of St Thomas himself. He said, rather coolly, that St Thomas was the doubter, and that he had gone to Witherburn because he had had a suspicion about Augie and had followed him there. He added, unnecessarily, that he had risked his life in the storm to do so, and that he had been motivated by a desire to prove my innocence. I suppose being knocked into a coma by the very person you were trying to help would be something of a disappointment.

The George was now under Tibald's direction. Its ownership was uncertain, at least to me. I was excluded from any discussions. From what Brian had told me, I gathered that Tibald and old Walter Sunder had formed a partnership to buy it, with small investments from the rest of the troupe. Of course, I was not invited to join this consortium. I learned later that Brian had been approached, but that he had declined.

Annie had been even more unforgiving of me than Arthur. She remained convinced that there was some substance to Augie Kelly's insane infatuation.

'Why would anybody become obsessed by you?' she had asked.

'Because he was a madman,' I replied, and saw that the implications of that ill-considered remark were not lost on her. There was a distance between us now that my sincerest expressions of regret couldn't bridge — and I had tried. I didn't want to leave Maryborough with the sour taste of broken friendship in my mouth, yet such a sad conclusion had become inevitable.

The other members of the Power Players followed her lead, and were stand-offish and uncooperative. Working with them had become impossible. They were now, as the Bedford proclaimed, 'The Annie Hudson Players'. They had ditched *Titus Andronicus* and were close to opening at the Town Hall with a production of *The Philadelphia Story*. Unsurprisingly, ticket sales for this lowbrow fare were brisk, and it was expected to return a tidy profit.

❦

'The train leaves in half an hour,' Brian said. 'Mother will be glad to see you. And Darlene.'

'Your wife won't be pleased to see me, Brian. She's no fan of mine.'

'She never thought you'd done those things, Will. She always said she couldn't believe you had it in you.'

'That's because she's drab and thinks everyone else is, too, not because she's loyal.'

This was cruel, and did not need to be said, but I was in no mood to express gratitude for Brian's presence. I knew that, despite his concern, he was happy to survey the wreckage of my career, and pleased to be escorting me home.

'I won't be staying in Melbourne long,' I said.

'Darlene and I are happy to look after Mother. No-one's asking you to take over.'

This was a timely reminder that it was inadvisable to assume a lack of astuteness in my younger brother. I was not looking forward to travelling with him. He had heard a great deal from Peter Topaz, and had spoken at length with Annie and the rest of the troupe. They had been wary of him at first, as if being related to me was some kind of disadvantage. Annoyingly, they were soon quite taken with him. Several times over the past few days I had gone into the dining room at the George to find him laughing with Bill Henty, of all people, or Kevin Skakel, or Adrian Baden (God knows what he found to talk to him about). The conversation stopped when I entered. The estrangement from my troupe was irremediable.

There was no one to farewell us at the station. I half-thought that Mal Flint might turn up to have one last go at me. As the train left Maryborough I could not quite suppress a nagging and dull sensation of failure. Brian sat opposite me, reading that day's *Chronicle*. He looked up.

'How's your arm?' he asked.

'Better.'

'Darlene's pregnant,' he said.

'Who's the father?' I asked.

He didn't bite. I thought to myself that the chances of Darlene giving birth to a child were slim. Whatever emerged from her womb was more likely to require veterinary than paediatric care.

'I like that Annie Hudson,' he said. 'She looks a lot like Greer Garson, don't you think?'

I said nothing. He smiled at me and added, 'She reckons I look a lot like Tyrone Power. What do you reckon about that, Will?'